CLIVE WRIGHT

COLD GHOST

CW

All characters & places in this book are figments of the author's imagination. Any resemblance to persons living, dead, or yet to be conceived are purely coincidental.

9 8 7 6 5 4 3 2 1

ISBN 0 9547485 0 6

Published by Clive Wright.
Printed and bound in the UK by Halstan & Co. Ltd., Amersham, Bucks.

www.clivewright.com

For Gonzo

Prologue

February, Democratic Republic of Congo.
The year after next.

Of the three men grouped in the shade of the porch, the only one not visibly shuddering was the colonel. Sweat poured from the faces and necks of Sylvester and Carl, who shared the second of the four concrete steps, and the cords in Carl's neck stood out as though he was suffering cold-turkey, coming down with a tremendous crash from some terrible hallucinogenic experience. His arms were crossed over his belly, but that didn't seem to stifle the shaking very much. Sweat stains from his arms had joined with those from his chest, turning his khaki shirt a yellow the colour of English mustard. He was a large man, but at that moment he resembled nothing more than a lost and regretful teenager, back several hours early from his first alcohol binge at the older kid's all-nighter.

Sylvester was coping surprisingly better, for he was a much smaller man - all wiry and packed close - a package wrapped too tightly, straining at the seams. He too was drenched and shivering, but appeared to be in a lot less pain, at least as far as the man with the rifle could ascertain, and he intended to get no closer. He could feel his hands trembling on the stock of the rifle, and he had to will himself to hold it level. Will himself unafraid.

The colonel's shirt was dry. There was no trace of sweat on him whatsoever, which should have been impossible in the suffocating heat. They had all suffered in the heat of the last five months - the sun never letting up - bullying the moisture from their bodies. It had made them tense and irritable at times, but none of them had succumbed to sunstroke, or been driven crazy with the heat. No, that had been something else. Something else entirely.

'Stay still, Andrew.'

It had been the rifleman's voice, though he himself hardly recognised it as such. The colonel did as he was told, after standing and making himself more comfortable by leaning against the doorframe. The rifleman didn't know whether he was simply fidgeting or planning something a little more desperate. He suspected the latter, because he believed the colonel could have stayed in one position for hours on end, perhaps days - the man had the patience of a rock.

They'd been there for a little under two hours. The rifleman had the advantage of the shade from the acacia tree that looked as though it had erupted from the patchy scrub of ground that made up the front yard, and to which Carl had hooked one end of his hammock in those optimistic early days. The hammock was still there, its other end tied to the back of one of the Landrovers. It swayed softly over his head, though there was barely a breath of wind. He was sitting, pondering and simultaneously fighting down his growing dread, his back against solid, stone-like roots. He knew he was going to run.

He was going to run because he couldn't kill them. He suspected that they knew this. No, he was certain that they did. At least the colonel must - the rifle belonged to him, and he was looking too relaxed. Relaxed was not the man's usual demeanour. Quite the opposite, in fact. He couldn't kill them for any number of reasons. First, and most practically, there was only one bullet in the rifle. He supposed he could have asked them to stand in a neat row for him, allowing him to pass the bullet through each of their yielding skulls in turn, but even if they took his request seriously, which he doubted, how could he rely on the bullet travelling cleanly through, without being deflected by bone or gristle. He could hardly rely on his compatriots' co-operation, and he wouldn't have blamed them. He'd have hardly co-operated with something so outlandish either. He'd never killed anyone before, and really didn't think he had it in him: that was reason number two. Lastly, these people were his friends, even now. They'd been together for too long. So he was going to run. But if he couldn't kill them, then at the very least he could slow them down a little.

The rifleman eyed the colonel. There was no malice in his stare, not as such. It was a look made more from a questioning fear. The look asked too many unanswerable questions at once. Why did you do it? Why did you deceive us all? What were you thinking? Who did you think you were trying to help? Why did you have to fuck up everything? Why did you need to fuck up the whole world? And, moreover, how in hell am I supposed to stop you?

He was sweating too much - it wasn't just the heat. The stock of the rifle felt slippery in his grip as he raised himself to his feet. The time for action had arrived. Any action. His head was swimming. He shook it and his vision blurred momentarily before clearing. There was sudden movement in the doorway, and he swung the rifle up once more, his nausea forgotten.

Just Carl, leaning over, looking ready to vomit. The rifleman moved cautiously around the front of the nearest Landrover, tethered to the trunk of the tree, as though it might have grown restless and wandered off to find more luscious grazing elsewhere. Both the Landrovers were old Series Three models, discontinued long since, yet common enough to pick up for next to nothing anywhere on this boiling continent. They were inconspicuous, reliable, and easy to maintain. Easy to disable, too. He unsnapped one of the bonnet catches and then, moving crab-like around the front of the vehicle, facing the door of the Nissen Hut all the while, he fumbled the second catch open. Holding the rifle with one hand was tricky enough, but there was worse to come. He raised the lid of the bonnet high enough for the stay to snap into position, and glanced inside, locating the distributor cap on the side of the engine easily enough. It was fastened in place by two metal clips, which he unsnapped, all the while watching the colonel's unmoving, unnerving features. He was working blind, but the work was simple enough. He twisted off the cap, dropped it, and then grasped hold of the rotor arm housed beneath, which fell into his hand after a little tugging and levering. He dropped it into his trouser pocket, where it jangled against his keys.

He paced to the other Landrover, not hurrying for fear of overlooking anything in his haste, but not dawdling either. He shoved the large briefcase from the driving seat over to the passenger side, and climbed in. It was a moment of vulnerability, and he fully expected the colonel to launch whatever surprise he had been cooking up, so he was relieved when no such thing happened. He lowered the rifle into the passenger footwell. Still no movement from the three men. What were they waiting for? He felt sure that they knew he had no intention of shooting them. They *must* know that, surely? You don't spend eight intimate months with someone without getting to know them inside out. Perhaps the two on the steps were still coming through, but that needn't have stopped the colonel. If anyone could prevent him driving away right now, it would be him. But the colonel didn't move: simply regarded him coolly, a tiny smile threatening to crack the thin straight line marking his lips, although it did not manifest itself fully. The rifleman started the engine, dropped the Landrover into first, and swung the wheel hard around. As he began to move, so did they.

He accelerated in a sweeping arc, first toward

them and then pulling away, bouncing over the ruts and scrub of the courtyard and out onto what passed for a road. If he expected the group to move quickly, he was disappointed. The colonel turned slowly on his heels and disappeared into the relative cool of the Nissen hut. The remaining two followed equally slowly, though their movements were less sure and their eyes seemed fixed on something distant and unknowable. Watching their movements, the rifleman was reminded somehow of marionettes. He turned his eyes from the wing-mirror and concentrated on the road ahead.

It was twilight when he stopped driving. He'd covered seventy miles in a little over three hours, which was exceptional going considering the terrain over which the majority of his journey had taken place had been far worse than any dirt-track he'd ever known. He didn't feel that seventy miles was nearly enough. However, it would have to suffice for now.

His bladder was ready to burst, and he relieved himself in the open. When he'd finished, he heaved out the heavy briefcase from the passenger seat. He placed it reverently on the cooling bonnet, unsnapped the latches, and opened it up. From the briefcase he extracted and set up a satellite phone, unfurled the receiving dish, joined the two with a thick wire. He dialled in, punching in the requisite codes while adjusting the dish. After what seemed an age he could hear the line ringing at the other end, and then the answerphone cut in. He left a brief message, then opened his laptop and dialled into another number, a short wait before the "message sent" alert appeared on his screen, and then he unplugged and repacked the equipment carefully. Then he climbed back into the driver's seat and resumed his journey. Dusk was slowly shifting into dark, and fatigue was beginning to gnaw at him. He couldn't recall his last meal either, come to that. He'd gained a little time over the three men he'd left behind but not, of course, enough. There is never enough time, he thought. Never enough time for any of us. And there was the final reason he found himself incapable of murder: that even death would not have been an end, would not have been enough. Even dead, the threat lingered. It lingered in their blood. Their busy, roiling, cursed blood.

He'd been back on the road for quite some time before he even noticed the tears he'd shed.

PART ONE

WARNING

One

The television was still glowing, and it took Kathy a moment to focus on the screen and bring the picture to life. An underfed woman in a leotard was jumping up and down and breathlessly encouraging the watching nation to join her. Kathy groped for the remote control at the side of the sofa on which she had slept and, scrabbling over the buttons with her fingertips, managed to switch the thing off.

She yawned briefly, swallowed it, and swung her legs off the sofa, rubbing at her right arm as she did so, which was suffering from pins and needles where she had slept on it. Her jeans had become uncomfortable and the black sweatshirt she was wearing was wrinkled and stretched. Her underwear had twisted and ridden up, and she felt like a badly-packed suitcase. As soon as her faculties returned, she would get up and run a bath. Or perhaps put the kettle on first. Or maybe whip up a little breakfast. She reached for the remote and switched the television back on. The woman in the leotard, presumably too tired to continue, had been replaced by a short man in a snug suit who stood in front of a map of Great Britain which was largely obscured by cloud-shaped symbols.

Kathy fell back into the cushions, trying mentally to shake off some of the feelings of sloth that had somehow come to dominate her life over the past few months. She felt lacklustre and drained, tired almost continually. Her doctor had diagnosed a mild depression, and subsequently prescribed anti-depressants; he being a practitioner of the old school: if you're remotely unsure, chuck a pill at it. Each morning, religiously, she would pop one of the little purple and green capsules out of its casing and drop it delicately into the wastebasket by her bedside cabinet. Some mornings she would intone 'Say aah' in the manner of a dentist as she dropped the tiny messenger of joy into the waiting maw of the by-now deliriously happy wastebasket. Let the quacks believe as they chose: a chemically induced happiness was no happiness at all in her opinion.

Her ailing moods were one of the reasons she had taken the week off. The other reason was less substantial. The past few weeks and months had seen her moods slip away from loneliness and depression and into a more forbidding anxiety. Forbidding in that it was essentially groundless. The ever increasing lucidity of her dreams confounded her. She'd been waking lately from nightmares in which she had placed Ian in yet another hopeless, desperate death-trap, only to slip into sleep once again to repeat the exercise in even more gruesome, unwarranted detail. She dreamed as though she wished him harm. As the frequency of his calls diminished, so her dreams became more persistent. They had spoken every other day at first, and then it had been once a week, then twice a month. It had been three weeks since the last call. As soon as he had mentioned a small delay her heart had dropped into the pit of her stomach, and the rest of the conversation, for all the notice she took of it, needn't have happened at all. She had caught the excitement in his tone, and it had told her all she felt she needed to know. Work came first, Kathy McCleane came second. As though he had been reading her thoughts, Ian had said,

'I will keep my promise, Kathy, I swear it. When this is over we'll get married and do all the things rich, retired couples do...'

'Whatever they may be.' She had been intentionally curt with him.

It washed straight over him. 'Yes, whatever

they may be. Trust me, I'll be back before you know it. Won't be much more than a couple of weeks now.'

'Promise me.'

'I'll do my best, that I can promise.'

And then nothing for three weeks. The previous Monday she had spent her birthday alone. He hadn't sent a card. She had been too miserable to bother going out, even though she considered visiting her mother, where she knew she'd have been more than welcome, or going out with Paul, whom she'd known since college, and who counted as the brother she'd never had. But she'd been in no mood for their sympathy and the company she chose that evening – the insipidly glowing box in the corner of the living-room – was in no condition to provide it either.

She relinquished the sofa finally, deserting the pitiful companionship of the television, and made her way to the kitchen. Tea and buttered toast, that would have to do. She had neither the energy nor the inclination to prepare anything more complicated. While the kettle boiled, she shrugged out of her sleep-bedraggled clothes and dumped them unceremoniously into the linen-basket in the bathroom. Turning to the sink, she splashed cold water onto her face and then picked up her toothbrush. The toothpaste's heavily-manufactured mint flavour proved a sharper introduction to the morning than either the leotard-woman or the man in the bad suit. 'Congratulations Kath,' she muttered through a mouthful of foam. 'When brushing your teeth becomes the highlight of the day, you know you're in trouble.'

When she looked at herself in the mirror, her mouth distorted by the toothbrush, and with white paste-spittle on her cheeks and on her chin, she appeared rabid. The effect was enhanced by the wildness of her hair, which was sticking up and out at every angle after its restless battle with the cushions throughout the night. Its usual serene waves had been replaced by far choppier waters: had become rapids before the storm of the waterfall. Her pale blue eyes stared bloodshot back at her. She spat, rinsed, spat again. She grinned broadly at the mess grinning back at her.

'When you get to the bottom, girl, there's only one way to go – and that's sideways.'

It had been one of Paul's favourite expressions at college, but she'd have bet that he'd lifted it from one of his comedy videos. He had a seemingly inexhaustible supply of the things, and on more than one occasion she'd had to shut him up, and warn him that if he carried on in this vein he'd be in danger of turning into a walking cliché, forever repeating stolen remarks and phrases.

In the hallway, near the front door, on the low table which stood next to the palm, the tiny red light on the telephone flashed on and off, repeating its signal over and over, as faithful and ignorant as a retriever.

Dressed once more: clean blue jeans, denim shirt, trainers; Kath took up her post in the living-room, munching toast and gazing at the screen in the corner, ignoring the mug of tea cooling at her feet. Her chewing slowed and she struggled to swallow as the image on the screen blurred, and the newscaster became at first a shadow, and then less than a shadow. Something rippled, but she couldn't tell if it was the screen flickering or her eyes watering. She'd been prone to the odd unexpected outbreak of tears lately. She dropped the remains of her toast when Ian's ghost shimmered momentarily into the shadow-space where the newscaster had been. She could see his features clearly enough, but it seemed she was able to see through him at the same time, as if he were transparent, or close to. His eyes were staring out at her: wide, accusatory.

With a start, she snapped her head back, and her right foot sent the mug cartwheeling away, brown liquid spraying out over the cream-coloured carpet.

Kathy let out a low groan, no more than a guttural hissing breath, as she rolled herself quickly forward off the sofa, and tried to snatch the mug up before any more damage was done. Quick as she was, it was too late. The mug was empty and the tea was already soaking its way into the carpet.

'Shit.' Kathy swore under her breath. She glanced back at the television and was only half relieved to see the newscaster back in his familiar place. Now that she'd been forced into action, her mood seemed to lift of its own volition. On her way back from the kitchen, a cold, damp cloth in her hand, she noticed the message-light, and had to force herself on into the living-room, to take care of the stain first.

As she scrubbed briskly, and for the most part ineffectively, at the stain, she tried to imaginc who might have called her. Even though a call from Ian was long overdue, she scarcely believed it could be him. Ian was a stickler – no, scratch that – had used to be a stickler for routine. Until recently, that is. He'd always been aware of the hour or two time difference, and besides had made a point of only calling her in the evening, her time. Mind you, she'd no idea how long she'd slept last night. It seemed to be a longer period with each day that passed. When did she hit the sack last night? Good question. She couldn't remember much of the evening, so it must have been pretty early, even by her standards. He wouldn't have called before she'd woken, would he? No, what would have been the point of that?

It must have been Paul. At this thought, she smiled – even though Paul lived in the same country, no more than twenty minutes from her, in fact, he was possibly less aware of the time than her fiancé in Africa. Apart from Ian or Paul, she could think of no-one else who would likely choose the middle of the night to call her. Her circle of acquaintances was not a large one, and she was happy to keep it that way. Her mother certainly wouldn't have called anytime before the afternoon, and it was extremely unlikely to be Daniel Johannsen, her Danish employer (probably soon to be ex-employer if she continued to take so much unwarranted time off). No, it had to have been Paul, and she suddenly began to dread just listening to the message.

She'd been seeing an awful lot of Paul since Ian had been away, and occasionally she'd felt a tiny twinge of guilt. She knew this was a ridiculous feeling to have, especially as they'd seen no less of each other, probably more of each other in fact, when Ian himself had been around. She mused on the two men. As boys they'd grown up on the same street, been to the same schools, and shared almost everything. Kathy had met them both at college, where she had at first been amused, and then charmed, by their inseparability. The three of them gelled quickly, not least because of her shared interest with Paul in the Arts. Ian had more concrete interests, though his love of numbers came as much from the heart as did Paul's love of Art. It was the boys differences as much as their common interests, Kathy quickly came to realise, that bound them so closely together. At times she felt envious of their intimacy – envious of the obvious yet invisible bond between them that she could never either fully understand or be privy to. If Ian or Paul had the slightest idea of the way Kathy felt she stood outside looking in at certain times, they were at least generous enough not to show it, and the trio inevitably grew close in a short period of time. When, in their second year, Ian had started dating an overly-pretty first-year blonde, Paul and Kathy had at first welcomed the transition from trio to quartet, even though the newcomer – Christina 'Call me Chris, I hate Tina' had been unjustly wary of Kathy's relationship with Ian. The situation resolved itself nicely three months later at the Christmas party where, the morning after, Kathy woke in a familiar room, though not her own. The alien lumps in the duvet next to her had proven to be Paul, but then she had deduced that much already from the Gauguin print on the back of the door and from the interestingly messy desk and overflowing wastebasket in the corner.

Lunch that day had been at first mildly uncomfortable. Paul and Kathy finally enlightened Ian as to the new state of affairs between them, and he had been delighted, and behaved as though he had seen this coming for a very long time, and was only too happy to be proved correct. 'I hate Tina' mellowed significantly when she arrived some time later and Ian allowed the penny to drop ever so gently. For Chris' part, she was only too happy to be part of a 'proper' quartet now, and for once was wise enough to keep her opinion to herself.

Kathy had been rubbing the cloth across the carpet with more force than she realised. It suddenly rolled out from under her bunched fist, and she scraped her knuckles painfully against the carpet, friction burns turning three of her knuckles instantly red. She sat back on her haunches, licked her knuckles, and blew on them to cool them down. On her way to the phone, she tossed the cloth all the way from the kitchen doorway to the sink where, rather than landing with a neat little plop in the bowl, it chose to drape itself over the front of the cupboard doors, before dropping onto the floor. Kathy didn't even notice, intent as she was on the flashing message-light. She leaned over the little black plastic machine, and pressed the button marked PLAY.

And listened with growing horror as the world she knew dropped away from her like a stone.

Two

Paul Scaife woke to the sound of the insistently jangling phone. His sheets argued against the idea, tangling his arms and legs as he tried to roll out of bed. He was inclined to agree with the sheets actually, but the phone had gone on for far longer than the ten rings Paul normally allowed before answering, so he came to the reluctant decision that it was a reasonably important call. He struggled out of the sheets and emerged naked into the bright morning glare of his studio flat, pausing only to scrape the sole of his foot painfully on one of the protruding slats of the accursed futon and to mentally swear at Ana, before limping over to the corner table on which the telephone squatted. The chrome and glass monstrosity stood hideously out of place in the airy, pine and ash-wooded theme of his flat.

'Yeah?' Always just "yeah". He never answered

with his name or number. If someone called him, he liked to presume that they knew who they were calling and why.

'Paul?'

'Kath. Hi.' Her singular enquiry and the tiny wobble in her tone gave up a wealth of information that immediately disturbed him. She was worried about something. More than that. Something serious. Well, Paul could do serious when really pressed.

'Paul, it's...' Another pause.

'I'm listening Kath. Tell Uncle Paul what the problem is.' He mentally kicked himself. Serious. Yeah, right.

'Well, I... I don't really...' She trailed off again.

'Do you want me to come over? Talk face to face if it's easier?'

'No, it's... hold on a sec.'

Paul could picture her. In his mind's eye he could see her covering the mouthpiece with her palms and slowly drawing in two or three deep breaths. He knew her routine. She would compose herself, counting slowly with her eyes shut, and then allowing the strong part of Kathy to take the helm.

'Look Paul, can you get away for a few days?'

'Well, er...'

'I wouldn't ask if it wasn't important. You

know that.'

'Sure. I know that. I can. Of course I can. I don't have another assignment pinned down yet.'

'Assignment? That a new code word for your bimbos?'

'They're not... Jesus, forget it. When are we leaving and where are we going?'

'I'll be at your place in about an hour. Could you be ready by then?'

'Okay. But where...'

'Wales.'

'Wales? Wow, how glamorous. I'll not bother with my trunks then. How long are we going to be away?'

'Truthfully, I'm not a hundred per cent sure, but it shouldn't be any longer than a few days. A week at most.'

'Why, Kath? What's going on?'

'I'll tell you when I get there. It's kind of hard to explain, especially over the phone.'

'Sounds a little paranoid to me, girl. MI5 on your case again?'

'Funny boy. Just pack. I'll see you in an hour.'

'This table has *got* to go.'

'What?'

'Nothing. I'm packing. See ya.' He dropped the receiver back into its cradle, and then lifted the whole set off the table and placed it on the floor next to the lately-becoming-irritating table, which he picked up and then placed in the centre of the studio – a lonely right-angled triangle of chrome and glass – an island of low taste. Paul stood back and surveyed the offending article, his hands on his hips and his head slightly cocked.

'Right.' He spat the word out, but the resolve he'd hoped would appear along with the decision was nowhere in evidence. He'd simply have to act without it. Despite himself, he'd let Kathy climb beneath his skin with as much ease as though he were a comfortable old sweater she'd thrown aside only the day before. He had no resolve to steel. So resolution would have to wait. Hell, it had been waiting thirty years, so he could hardly expect it to show up at a single snap of his fingers. He trudged off to the bathroom, and the vigorous refreshment of his prized power-shower, with the thought in mind that where he was going he'd be lucky to get a tin bath and lukewarm, murky water for the best part of the coming week. Still, he'd known worse.

Three

'We may not have transport, but we still have communications.'

'We can hardly call for a taxi.'

'I was thinking more along the lines of a delivery of spares.'

The evening had cooled considerably, but the air in the cabin was still humid. The three men seemed not to notice either the humidity or the cold, however. Outside, the sun had finished with the day and a large moon hung low in the sky. The muted, distant cries of animals, though carried for miles in the still air, seemed to peter out and die at the doorstep of the cabin, as though it were surrounded by thicker, somehow sound-proof air. Animals and birds padded and flew through the forests surrounding the outpost, but in the enclosing courtyard not a living thing moved. The remaining Landrover squatted, tethered to its hammock-leash, reduced to redundancy. It was to this problem the three of them now addressed themselves.

'Why didn't we stop him when we had the chance?' asked Sylvester.

'He wouldn't have used the rifle,' added Carl. 'Not on us.'

'Agreed. He wouldn't have.' The colonel joined them at the table, depositing a glass of water in front of each of them as he sat. 'But we could no more take a life than could he.'

'It never had to come to that,' said Carl. 'We could have stopped him from leaving without any bloodshed. The very least we could have done was stop him disabling the Landrover.'

'True enough,' the colonel replied. 'But then neither of you were in a fit state for any action at the time.'

'Even so...'

'Even so, yes, I could have stopped him. As to why I didn't, well, I'm not one hundred per cent certain. Only that it goes a little deeper than Ian versus the rest of us. Remember who financed this project, after all. Without him, we'd have been exactly nowhere.'

'So you felt we owed him something?' Sylvester spoke bitterly. 'Even after his betrayal?'

'It was a choice, Sly, not a betrayal. Just an

ordinary, rational, human decision that he made.'

'An emotional decision.'

'He also decided not to kill *us*, remember?'

'Stranded here?' Sylvester choked. 'He may as well have pulled the trigger.'

'Where do you think he's gone?' Carl moved to lighten the subject, and Sylvester's darkening mood.

'Not to any of the authorities, if that's what you mean. There wouldn't be much point, would there?'

'All the evidence will have been destroyed by then. That what you mean?'

'That, and the very implausibility of anything he might say being taken seriously. No, he's only got one place he can go.'

'Home?'

'Home.'

Sylvester toyed with his glass. 'Bringing us back to our more immediate problem, what are we going to do now?'

'I can't speak for the two of you,' the colonel replied, 'but I would most certainly like to see Ian again. I feel he may come round to our way of thinking if only I could get the chance to sit down with him and work this through. And besides, I think this whole thing should be done properly. Ian was there at the beginning, and I should like to see him there at the end as well. It's only fitting.'

'So we go after him.'

'This isn't a gangster movie, Sly. Ian may be on the run, but I don't think he even knows what he's running from.'

'How could he?' asked Carl.

'Which is why I think it's important to catch up to him. By the time I do, perhaps he'll have had a chance to calm down and think things through.'

'There's another possibility,' Sylvester said in low, growling tones. Carl raised his eyebrows enquiringly, but the colonel looked at him squarely and asked,

'Such as?'

'We might simply be giving him time to find a way to fight back.'

'Ian?' The colonel lost himself in thought for a moment. 'Very doubtful. A longshot at best. We've been cosseted together too long. I could not for a second see Ian as either an enemy or a threat. I can't see him as anything other than the friend he has always been to us.'

'A friend who turned on us all at the last,' said Sylvester.

'You made your choice, Sly, and Ian made his. You feel this nonsensical betrayal only because you were the one so opposed to the final stage of this project. You feel betrayed because Ian argued the pros against your cons. Now he's up and run off, you yourself feel emotionally as well as physically stranded.' The colonel slowed his pace, trying to measure the depth of Sylvester's sense of betrayal from his stress-lined face. 'And I don't remotely blame you. But time cannot be undone, and we must go on, because there is no way back now. No, what I suggest is that we stick to our original itinerary from here on in. I'll get in touch with you when the time comes.'

Sylvester looked as close to tears as the colonel had seen any man, but he knew that he would not, could not, cry. That was behind him also.

The chill air that the African night brought to their attention through the open cabin-door raised no goose-bumps, nor produced any shivers. The temperature had dropped rapidly, and the cool stickiness of the air announced the storms that were undoubtedly on the way. The rainy season had only just started, but the colonel knew what was coming, and secretly welcomed it – it would at least remove from Sylvester's mind any problem other than the one at hand. From his past, the colonel dredged up the memory of a Texan colleague, who had once described the monsoons to him as "like a horse pissing on a flat rock," which he considered an eminently suitable description of the rains he could feel coming. It would be a hard trail out of here, he knew, but one which the three of them were more than well-equipped to deal with. He needed some space away from Sylvester and Carl – a little time to put his plans in some sort of order. The relative solitude of his quarters would have to suffice for the time being.

'I suggest we retire for the evening. We'll make a fresh start with clearer heads come the morning.'

'I'm not feeling remotely tired,' said Sylvester, 'and I know that you don't either. Why should we postpone any longer?'

'You'd like us to march straight off into the night?'

'What's stopping us, exactly?'

'How about we compromise?' the colonel felt a tiny vestige of frustration, but it disappeared quickly enough. 'I would like a little time alone to get one or two things straight in my mind, and to prepare for the trek. I'm assuming we're agreed that we're not going to call on any outside assistance, so we all have to prepare, if only mentally, for a couple of days slog before we reach any civilisation. We'll set off at first light – I trust that will be soon enough for the pair of you?'

The night passed swiftly for all of them. Only Carl appeared to manage any sleep, even though his mind was reluctant to join in the same dormancy as his body. Sylvester spent the night first pacing his room, and then walking around outside, as though practising for the walk to come. The colonel gave up any idea of sleep, and spent the time writing in his journal. This tome, which he'd kept regularly since his teenage years, was the colonel's only real treasure. His whole life, it seemed to him, could be found in these volumes. Here were his parents, his college education, his career and his ex-wife, the Texan beauty Jo-Beth, and her Texas-sized appetite for life, for love and, more desperately, for alcohol. Here were the plans and dreams of his teenage self – some of them realised and others still-born. Here was his transition to adulthood and maturity, and the army career it had brought. Here was the fast-track through the military ranks culminating in the posting at USAMRIID, where his specialist knowledge of level-four hot agents had placed him in one of the most revered, and feared, positions, along with a tiny handful of other scientists, both military and civilian. Here was the death of his father, who had struggled with Alzheimer's for nigh on ten years. That death hit the colonel harder than he could ever have imagined, and far harder for some reason than that of his mother's, who had passed away fourteen years previously. Here was the germination of his plan, and the lengths he'd gone to in order to secure the right people, not to mention the necessary capital. Here lived ream upon ream of copious notes and diagrams he'd spent year upon year outlining, and here lay the last seventeen months – painstakingly laid out – the discoveries, the setbacks, the many and varied experiments and their cause and effect upon the next. Here lay London, and the move to Africa. Here was M4, and Cecily, and their fates. And here also was his need to find a fitting ending to his own story. There was no future for his past; and his future, so far as he could divine, held no place for this catalogue of memories. This was, he believed, to be the last entry of his ongoing autobiography, and he wished to make something special of it. After tonight, he somehow felt, there would be no need for this written history. After tonight, the whole planet would hold his life in its collective memory.

Sylvester continued to pace around the outside of the huts, which had struck him as hideously barrack-like when he had first arrived, although he could see now a certain stark beauty in their simplicity. As he walked he lost himself in his recent memories. They flooded through him, for what he hoped would be the last time. He was impatient to be away from here. Away from the tragedies he'd gladly leave behind and off into the revelations of their tomorrows. He envied Carl his easy-going manner and acceptance of fate, and secretly knew that his anger with Ian had been rooted more in their similarities than in their differences. But he was cursed lifelong, it would seem, with impetuosity. He had made his decision that way, even with all due regard to the consequences, yet only the day before had been arguing against that very decision with Ian, who had proven more cautious, perhaps inevitably so, than had he.

He passed by the colonel's window for the umpteenth time that night, and glanced in. He could see the colonel hunched over his desk, lit by his little gas-powered lamp, scribbling furiously in his diary. Sylvester had never kept a diary himself, even when, as a child, it had seemed that every Christmas would bring him a new book of blank sheaves that were destined to remain that way for the forthcoming year. He'd never been much for writing anything down – the complete opposite of the colonel, who couldn't pass water without logging it down immediately afterwards. There was no chance at all that the colonel could have heard his silent, inward chuckle, yet he had stiffened slightly and stopped writing, so that Sylvester knew the colonel was somehow aware of him. He broke his gaze from the mans back and continued his patrol.

Carl watched the shadowy figure of Sylvester pass by his window. For all that he feigned sleep, he was no more capable of it than were the others. His mind raced agitatedly along paths he had trodden well in the last few months. Sylvester's thin apparition disappeared from view, and Carl sank back further into his pillows, though he knew no real reward lay there. He folded his massive arms behind his head and craned his neck to look at the ceiling. He'd been cramped in these tiny quarters for five months now, and it had taken him very little time to outgrow the restraining metrics of them. But then Carl outgrew everything he encountered, whether it be a room, a career, or yet another failed relationship. Carl was simply bigger than life, and far bigger than his own life. His surroundings had always struggled to contain him. The air itself changed density when his presence invaded a room. In his contemplative torpor he could feel the colonel hard at work on his beloved diary, and could hear Sylvester retreading his over-trodden path around the barracks. He felt a kinship with Sylvester but would have been hard pushed to say why. Only that, as Sylvester was the very antithesis of him – white, moneyed, spoilt, and given to rashness – so he felt they had an invisible bond of brotherhood, obviously more so now, since the decision. But even before then, there had been that spark of something unspoken between them: of something that would fit where only chalk could fit cheese. Carl knew Sylvester pretty much inside-out, and was not remotely surprised at the younger man's inclination to go walkabout on the eve of their departure. He knew also what the colonel would undoubtedly be doing – writing in that accursed journal of his – trying to make sense of something which essentially had no sense. But let the colonel have his folly – he had been the one to instigate the decision – had forced it upon them all – and if he was now suffering from any doubt then let him try futilely to work through it in his own way. The colonel had his journal, Sylvester his agitated pacing; but Carl would come to acceptance of the decision in his own manner – his usual manner – which was to let all of life's many decisions wash up against him and break their foamy outlines against the solid rock of his being.

He was looking forward to the following day's journey. It would give them all a chance to settle into their new roles and to plan the future with some precision. He knew that Sylvester had not really considered future events much beyond finding Ian and settling whatever score he so obviously felt, but the colonel must have analysed the time ahead in far greater detail, as was his natural wont. For Carl's part, he would be happy to go with whatever flow proved agreeable for the time being. There was plenty of time to work out an agenda of his own at a later date. These thoughts should have settled his mind and allowed him the sleep he felt he deserved, but his mind was having none of it. He was not used to over-analysing any given situation, but he could not stop his incredibly active mind from spinning off into the more obscure dimensions of their collective predicament. And the more he analysed, the less clear their position became. He tried desperately to force his old way of thinking to the forefront of his mind, but it proved fruitless: the old ways were more than gone – they were relics of a past that could now never be recaptured.

The morning caught none of them by surprise. Each man had been awake most of the night, yet seemed to suffer little or no ill effects from the loss of sleep. They had gathered before dawn in the kitchen, and sipped coffee together in silence.

During the night, Sylvester had spent some time carting several large cans of petrol into the huts. The colonel now waved his hands in their direction and peered enquiringly at him.

'I presumed we'd be leaving nothing behind.' Sylvester spoke without raising his voice above a whisper. He dragged his eyes from the colonel, returning them to the mug in his hands.

'Yes. Exactly so,' the colonel replied distractedly. 'Was that simply a lucky guess on your part? A leap of intuition?'

Sylvester gazed up at the colonel from his chair. 'I hope so,' he said.

The colonel made a humph sound, snorted out through his nose and throat, but refrained from any further comment. Carl drained the rest of his coffee and grimaced slightly. 'Must be losing my taste for it.' He stared at the other two men for a moment. 'Well?'

'No time like the present,' said Sylvester.

The colonel said nothing, but finished his coffee quickly and then threw the mug into the sink. It wouldn't be needed again. Carl stood, grabbed up one of the jerry-cans as though it weighed no more than a milk-bottle, and heaved himself through the rear door. The colonel heard the slam of the trap-door followed by the thudding rings of Carl's boots on the metal ladder.

'That's downstairs taken care of, then. Where do you want to start, Sly?'

Sylvester struggled another of the cans up into a two-handed grip and waddled awkwardly after Carl. He side-stepped the yawning square gap in the floor and made his way through to the private quarters at the rear of the building. The colonel had an uneasy feeling that Sylvester would be paying special attention to Ian's lately-deserted rooms. With a grunt, he lifted another of the jerry-cans and made his way out of the front door and into the yard. He unscrewed the cap and slowly made his way around the large hut, splashing petrol against the walls and walkways as he did so, until he had come full circle, arriving once more at the front door as Sylvester emerged. Carl joined them less than a minute later.

In the yard, no more than twenty feet from the door, lay each man's rucksack, containing only those very few treasures that none of them could bear to part with. 'Would you care to do the honours?' Carl tossed a box of matches to the colonel, who caught them adeptly, before striking one and flicking it through the open door.

The petrol-soaked floor caught quickly, the flames exploding in a greedy frenzy, desperate to devour. The fire raced through the ground floor of the building, leaping the gap to the basement level and entering each of the men's quarters simultaneously. The thin layers of paint on each door bubbled in the heat, before catching and turning to runny soot. The colonel's collection of books first curled, and then turned themselves inside-out, finally bursting into instantly-crumbling flame. Ian's wooden trunk, carefully stored beneath his desk against the wall until very recently, when it had been dragged out into the centre of the room and had its lock kicked into pieces, was set upon by the flames like a predator finding an easy kill. His photograph album, the pictorial history of Paul and Kathy and himself, was first pawed at, and then mauled, and then finally torn apart by the merciless, ravenously hungry flames.

The rooms of Sylvester and Carl fared no better. The wood-slatted beds made easy targets, the mattresses melting through their own springs. Shelving crumbled, the desk-lamps toppled as the desks upon which they rested keeled to the floor, legs breaking into ebony ash. Windows exploded outward into the yard and surrounding scrub. The light-bulbs hanging overhead popped and their plastic-coated wires dripped and fizzed.

Long before the fire had made it through the floor-hatch into the lower level, the three men had turned their back on the camp and struck eastward. By the time the outer walls collapsed in on themselves they had covered three miles. Forty minutes in real-time, but a fraction of that in fire-time. As the flames finally found their way to the basement, and the source of fresh nourishment, the men had reached the crest of the nearest hill. They started down the far side without a backward glance, while behind them the orange glow grew briefly brighter, before fading along with all things past.

Four

He'd been walking on the edge of exhaustion for the last hour. The temptation to stop and curl up in sleep was overwhelming, but even though the road seemed to stretch endlessly ahead of him there was enough light in the moon and stars to see by, and the knowledge of civilisation, or semi-civilisation at some point along this journey drove him onward. The comforting weight of the rifle in his hand warmed him against the unknowable out of sight: of animals or bandits or whatever other monsters that sprang forth in his imagination. The water-satchel over his shoulder was no longer heavy, and he guarded what remained with jealous little sips.

Perhaps he should have stopped driving when night had fallen, but he could not shake off the urgency he had felt. Fear had fogged his concentration, and he had been lucky to survive the plunge into the ditch that had forced him out on foot. The Landrover fared well enough, and still ran, but without either winch or anchor to tie it to, it may as well have been parked on the moon.

His imagination played havoc with his senses, and the surrounding darkness proved fertile ground for his fears. Everywhere he looked he saw the colonel, or Carl or Sylvester, tracking him at the periphery of his vision. His former friends had taken on a far more sinister countenance in the gloom, and with each step his spirits sagged into the welcoming embrace of his dark and surely inevitable fate. He entertained thoughts of laying a trap for them at some point along the road or in the town he knew to be not that much further ahead. At least he hoped he knew. He could not be wholly sure of the distance left to travel, nor even of the distance he had covered thus far. It would be beyond his sense of irony to die this close to either the danger behind or the salvation that surely lay ahead.

His confused scheming plagued him, but it had at least the positive effect of pushing to the back of his mind all thoughts of rest, and he ploughed doggedly onward. He forced himself to think of Kathy, the light at the end of this dark journey, but he found it impossible to focus on her. He knew her every feature intimately, her frowns and smiles, her hair and the smell of her, yet for the first time since distance had separated them he could not feel her as a tangible presence. She had been at his side every waking moment as inspiration and muse, as comforter and tormentor, and yet now he felt her invisible presence slipping away from him, as insubstantial as the darkness surrounding him, and as impossible to picture. His loss was immeasurable and irreplaceable, and filled him with both desperation and new courage. A fresh strength revived his flagging limbs, and though his gait changed but little, it seemed to him to be relentless and unstoppable. He was going to make it all the way home. No microscopic forgotten death awaited him on this road. Nothing could touch him save the glowing reward at the end of this journey. Her image swam away from him still, but the ideal of her remained firm in his mind. He coursed and sailed blindly through every conceivable aspect of their now-inevitable reunion, playing each scene in his head like a story already done and simply waiting to be told. The taking up of her hand, her welcoming embrace and warm kisses, the smile at her lips when she answered his proposal. Futures mapped themselves at his dust-stirring feet, and they were none of them unattractive or unattainable.

And then his thoughts simply stopped.

Blankly. Wiped clean. His mind now a white space where even a mote of dust would have felt unwelcome. The firelight he saw ahead filled his mind like the sun. No star had ever shone brighter. The unattainable was within his reach, and his stumbling footsteps redoubled their speed, so that when he broke into the circle of the camp he was practically running. He came to an abrupt halt in the centre of the circle and stared wildly around him, scaring the handful of nebulous, gauzy faces surrounding him, his mind was white with a relief approaching ecstasy. And when he passed out in a dead faint it was with a longing to fall, and to keep falling; into a warm, embracing, rescuing depth.

Five

Paul hadn't needed to peer through the security spy-hole in his door when the bell rang. He'd known it would be Kathy, and he'd peered anyway. Except the hallway was empty. Puzzled, he snapped the catch back and swung the door wide.

'What *are* you doing?' He addressed the back pockets of Kathy's jeans.

She was bent double, rummaging around in an oversize handbag. It was more of a hold-all really, but then Prada-style impracticality had never impressed Kathy. She straightened up with a telephone in her hands.

'I don't get it.'

'Message from Ian. Are you going to let me in? Hmm?'

He stood aside as Kathy swept past him, straight to the chrome monstrosity in the centre of the room, on which she unceremoniously plonked the phone.

'Plug socket?'

With an inward sigh, Paul swept up the hold-all Kathy had left in the hallway and let the door swing back into its frame.

'Under the window. There,' he pointed.

'Nice table. New?'

'You like it?'

'Well...'

'You want it?'

'Er... no.'

'Me neither.'

'Ah. That's what you meant on the phone earlier. You're easily distracted, Paul. Anyone ever tell you that?'

'I seem to recall it being one of your favourite topics. Right up there along with my idleness and potential infidelity. Coffee?'

'That would be nice.'

While Paul busied himself in the kitchen, Kathy plugged in the phone and then settled herself on the wide windowsill. From where she sat, the River Thames was just visible through the light morning rain. She swept her eyes around the interior of the flat. It looked comfortable, if a little Spartan, and too obviously furnished around the needs of a single man. The masculine feel was evident in almost everything – from the imitation open fireplace to the overly-elaborate entertainment centre. Two of the walls were almost entirely covered with black-and-white photographs, which she recognised as Paul's favourite examples of his own work. Amongst the close-ups of intricate architecture and portraits of many ethnic, mostly elderly, characters, his portrait of Kathy, taken in a Soho coffee shop – her head bent forward over a cappuccino which she cupped with both hands, steam obscuring her features – seemed at the same time distinctly out of place and yet right at home there. "Comfortably incongruous" seemed to sum up both Paul and his surroundings. Then he arrived with the coffee, and Kathy slid gently back into the present.

To Paul, Kathy seemed distant somehow, even melancholy. Seeing her in his window stirred memories he was certain he did not want activated once more. The rain outside softened her edges, and paled the red in her hair. She appeared horribly fragile all of a sudden, and he couldn't reconcile that with the storm of the girl he'd known for so many years. Her slender, pale hands reached up for the mug he was proffering, and a smile broke across her face when she lifted it and inhaled the aroma.

'The message?' he prompted.

'Yeah. Okay. Coffee first.'

She seemed altogether too hesitant, but Paul

was in no hurry, and he did not want to rush her. He changed tack. 'He's still in Africa, I take it?'

'Still there, yes. For the time being at least.'

'When did you last hear from him?'

'A little over three weeks ago.'

'Doesn't sound like him at all.' And it really wasn't like Ian. Mister Reliable. Captain Steadfast. Even in their university days, when four years of hedonism was traditionally only interrupted by brief bursts of all-night study and all-day examinations, you could have set your watch by Ian Ashbury.

'He even missed my birthday.'

'Whoa.' Paul took a step back. 'Is he ever gonna pay for that. He'd better bring something special back with him.' He grinned widely. 'Like your very own dictatorship.'

Kathy smiled up at him. Paul's particular brand of irreverence was working to cheer her up, whether she liked it or not.

'Go on, play it,' she said finally.

Paul strode over to the answer-phone and blinked down at it for a few moments. He was nervous suddenly, and had no idea why. 'Isn't this supposed to have a little cassette in it, or something?'

'It's digital, doesn't need a cassette. Just press the play button.'

He did so, and the voice of Ian Ashbury immediately filled the room.

'Kathy. I...' A pause. 'I haven't got too much time to try to explain this and... and anyway, I'm not sure I can over the phone. Something went wrong. Something important.' Another pause. 'Shit. I'm not making much sense. Look, I need you to get away from London. Go to Aunt Edie's. The air's good. I'll meet you there in a few days.' More dead air. 'Take the laptop. I'll mail you my diary. You might... it might explain a little. I'll come as fast as I can. I love you. Now do as you're told.'

That was all. The silence that followed pressed down on them both like a physical weight. Kathy was staring into her coffee, and Paul got the impression she was struggling to hold back her tears. The machine gave a little click, which Paul presumed indicated that it had finished its task.

'Brief. To the point. Much more like the Ian I know.' Paul grinned his best grin, but Kathy seemed to be having none of it. She continued to gaze blankly out at the rain. Paul pressed on, regardless. 'I didn't know you had an Aunt Edie. Is she the one we're going to Wales to see?'

'Yeah. Kind of,' she answered.

Paul felt it was time to stop pressing.

'Are you ready?' She looked up at him expectantly, failing to hide what Paul at first took to be impatience, and then realised was frustration, mixed with more than a little fear. The look on her face made him want to hold her: to comfort her and assure her that everything was going to be just fine, but that would mean a confrontation that he was certain he was not ready for, let alone Kathy.

'Nearly. Just got to grab a couple of bits. Two minutes.'

Kathy packed her answerphone back into her bag and took the now empty coffee mugs back into the kitchen while Paul fussed and busied himself in the bathroom, emerging only when he was good and ready. In his subconscious, Paul knew that he was trying to slow the pace down significantly. He'd never been wholly comfortable living at Kathy's speed. It was far too frenetic for him. For her part, he knew, she believed Paul's existence trundled along at a snail's pace. A very old, asthmatic snail at that.

'Ready,' he finally announced.

'Possibly a new record for you. Not quite half an hour.'

'Okay, okay. Point taken.' He hefted two large hold-alls and followed her out of the flat.

Six

He handled the coffee carefully, as though it might wriggle, snake-like, away out of his grasp. The petite woman studied him warily. She sat splay-footed on a large rock, forking bacon and beans into her mouth from a metallic plate. He forced out a tired smile, to show how harmless he was, but he might as well have smiled at the rock on which she perched. He unlocked his eyes from hers and finished his coffee in uneasy silence.

'Coffee okay?' The voice came from behind him, and he twisted around in time to see two men emerge from the roadside brush. They were both tall, lean men, and could have been cast from the same physical mould, but their poise and garb gave lie to any relation. Tom introduced himself, and Ian found himself liking the man immediately. He was South African, his accent diluted by an English education. A great wide smile broke out over his entire face as he extended a hand out to Ian. His blonde mop shook as he nodded his head in the direction of his companion. 'And that there's Jex. J.E.X. Crazy name for a crazy fella.'

Jex gave him a little half-smile and nod, which seemed to be all he could manage for the time being. Where Tom was fair, Jex was dark, and that appeared to hold for his clothes and demeanour also. Tom struck him as the epitome of the Marlboro Man, dressed head to foot in khaki and looking very much the part of the safari guide, which Ian presumed him to be. But with this presumption he could make neither head nor tail of the roles of the other two. Jex looked younger than his years, and paid no deference to the heat by covering himself in a black Iron Maiden Tee-shirt, black jeans and black boots. Gail, on the other hand, could have stepped straight from a holiday resort. Shorts, bikini-top, and a sarong slung round her tanned waist. The only jarring note were the immaculate trainers. How any material, least of all footwear, could stay un-dusted in this country was a mystery to him.

'And you got Gail here. Our merciless leader and tyrant of the trails.'

Ian smiled at the practised introductions, before palming them off with one of only a few lies he had ever told. 'I'm Ian, first-rate anthropologist and second-rate Landrover driver. I lost mine in a ditch last night God only knows how many miles back.'

'You're lucky to be alive, then. Night-driving? On *these* so-called roads?'

'Uh-huh. Stupid, I know, but I've got a very important appointment to keep.' Not really a lie either, that one, he thought.

'We've got a winch, we could get you going again.' Jex showed his human side.

'Not in the state I left it in, I'm afraid.' Another lie.

'There's a mechanic in Kundasa,' said Tom.

'Exactly where I'm headed. If you can get me there, I'll gladly make it worth your while.'

'Don't worry about that mate, this is a sponsored venture. Forty miles out of our way isn't going to hurt anyone.'

'It'll lose us a day's walk,' said Gail, who then turned instantly sheepish under a glare from both Tom and Jex. While the two men clattered their equipment back into the vehicle, she rummaged about and appeared with a tin of white emulsion paint. She prised the lid off with a screwdriver and then painted a great X on the rock where she had been sitting. She looked at Ian, and finally donned a smile for him. 'Gail woz 'ere.'

Forty minutes later they were on their way to

Kundasa. Tom handled the wheel of the enormous Discovery with an adroitness that left Ian envious, and as Tom threw the four-wheel drive into corners and tiny rutted tracks he filled Ian in on the details of their venture.

Gail was a walker, as simple as that. At seventeen, she had walked from Land's End to John O'Groats, and raised more than seven thousand pounds for the Multiple Sclerosis Society in the process. Two years later she had taken a year out of college and crossed the United States from East coast to West. This feat had not gone unnoticed, and the moment she popped out the other end of college, the venture through Africa had begun in earnest. Many months of preparation in England, attending corporate lunches and presenting new and interesting ways to write off taxes to her favourite charity, had paid off in this extended sponsored walk. She was to cross the continent North to South, wearing brand-name trainers, drinking brand-name water. The brands paid for the Discovery and a back-up team, of which Tom had been a member since day one, being joined in Yola, on the Nigerian border, by Jex, who replaced the unmissed and still-bitter original third party.

'And the graffiti back there?'

'So I know where to start from,' returned Gail. 'The emulsion will disappear after a few days rain, if that was what you were concerned about.'

Last thing on my mind right now, thought Ian, though this remained unvoiced. The remainder of the journey passed in relative silence, broken only occasionally by Gail, who probed Ian gently and unsuccessfully on his offered occupation. When they at last reached Kundasa, Tom dropped him outside the mechanic's garage, and they arranged to meet up in the only legal bar in town, which also happened to be in the only actual hotel. Ian waited and waved the Landrover out of sight round a corner, then walked quickly away from the mechanic's.

On the next street he quickly located the tiny surgery. The only clue to its purpose was the small, half-hidden plaque on the wall next to the door. He grabbed the handle and stepped through into the comparative coolness of the reception room.

'Mr. Ashbury.' The girl's eyes lit up on seeing him, and she came quickly around the edge of the counter, rushing up to him and grasping both his outstretched hands, planting kisses on either side of his face.

'It's good to see you too, Elise.' He dropped her hands and asked, 'Henry not here?'

'Not until the morning.' She looked up at him disappointedly. 'You didn't come to see me then?'

He returned her flirtatious smile. 'Of course I

came to see you. You know there's no-one else I dream about.'

'Except the girl who wears your ring.' She grinned broadly and made her way slowly back to the counter. 'So there's nothing I can do for you?'

'Not unless you have a plane.' He watched her jaw drop open, before she caught herself.

'You're leaving?'

He looked for words and failed. How could he possibly explain? Even he wasn't a hundred per cent sure of why he was running, or even from what. And there was no chance whatsoever of explaining it to Elise. She'd think him insane.

They'd met three months earlier, when Ian had come to them for a replenishment of some standard, non-prescription drugs for his team's occasional maladies: headaches and upset stomachs for the most part, and as there was no drugstore in Kundasa, the surgery doubled as a replacement. From the outset, there had been a strong mutual attraction between Ian and Elise, who was the only full-time employee of the clinic.

The clinic itself was run by Henry White, who serviced three other outlying townships, which he flitted between in his four-seater, twin-engine Cessna. He made it into Kundasa usually twice a week, using a makeshift strip of land on the outskirts, from which Elise usually collected him.

For Henry, she was the single most valuable asset at his little surgery. She was a local girl, brought up and educated in Kundasa itself and, although Henry's knowledge of the majority of local languages was reasonably polished, she proved an invaluable interpreter as well as a very able nurse. There was an obvious bonus also, as although Henry had been seeing to the township's ails for almost twenty years now, the local population could not yet bring themselves to trust him fully. Considering the past behaviour of his race, Henry didn't entirely blame them, but this was a ravine being patiently bridged by Elise. The only tiny drawback, it seemed to Henry, was that Elise was so damned attractive. Nowhere else on his travels had he had to treat so many grazed knees, skinned knuckles and phantom stomach-aches among the young male population of the town. She appeared to have eyes for no man, however, and Henry was therefore doubly surprised at the behaviour of his nurse when Ian had first arrived. Her usual grace had deserted her, and her heretofore latent clumsy-gene had suddenly gone into overdrive. Coffees were spilt on a variety of visitors, and previously easily-gripped items became transformed into grease-slicked, sentient, vengeful pieces of flying metal and crockery. Her actions around Ian had reduced her to the status of a fumbling, inept teenager, and it did not go unnoticed by Ian. He had done what he thought was best by pretending it did not exist, this thing between them, but the more he ignored it, the stronger the bond seemed to become, and over the ensuing months the situation had progressed to two-way traffic, and their flirting had intensified. There was no advance beyond flirting, however, as his memory of Kathy, and the image of her waving him off at Heathrow, was a vision he did not wish to relinquish.

'What kind of trouble are you in?' she asked from the safety of her counter.

Ian gazed at her, unable to form a straight thought, let alone an answer. Weariness seemed to overtake him once more, and he wanted nothing on earth more than to sink down into someone's welcoming arms and just let go. Just let it all go. But something held him back.

'I don't know, Elise. I really don't know.'

He seemed a different man, she thought. He was a broken thing suddenly, and Elise's every nursing instinct washed quickly into her, and she felt only the urgent need to protect him, to make his demons go away.

'What about the other guys?' She knew he'd been part of a team, though she knew little else.

'The other guys. Jesus.' He was suddenly anxious. He could be putting her in danger simply by association. His head-start had been a good one, but there was no measuring the resourcefulness of his new enemies – as he now regarded them. 'They just might *be* the problem.'

An hour later he was at the front desk of Siddi's – Kundasa's only hotel. No-one seemed to know quite how the hotel had got its name, but myths, as myths tend to do in smaller towns, abounded of an Afrikaaner or Englishman who had dragged the town into existence from its mud-hut roots. There was exactly no physical proof of their existence whatsoever, and the myth was perpetuated solely on the tongues of the few drink-sodden whites as were left in Kundasa. The hotel was run by John and Yasmin N'Gobo, who'd been there a mere four years and who were also, they held proudly, the first black owners of the establishment. Ian's transaction was completed swiftly, partly because every one of the rooms was not only identical, but also identically empty. Having bagged his stop for the night, he went in search of the bar, which proved an easy find. Remarkably, none of the cross-country trekkers were there, and finding himself the sole occupant of the bar, Ian swallowed his bottled beer quickly and went in search of Jan.

Jan De Voers was a true Boer. Descendant of

the original Dutch settlers and a bore by nature as well as name. It was his much-considered opinion that the blacks had been far better off before the demise of apartheid, and that there was a damn good reason Mandela had been locked up in the first place, his release being unfathomable to Jan. Ian had once been amazed that Jan had survived this long with the same attitude, which was rarely, if ever, kept to himself. But now he was long past being surprised by Jan, who was not only tolerated by the local community but actually welcomed by most, if only as an example to their children of what life could hold in store for them should they stray too far from the right path.

But there was one thing Jan was extremely useful for. He was a procurer. Even here, in a place God deemed too hot and dusty to visit that often, Jan could find you next to anything. And Ian found him at Stefan's. Stefan's bar did not officially exist, and its patronage grew only through word-of-mouth. A white-washed door set in a white-washed wall gave at Ian's easy touch, and he descended the few steps down into the cool interior. It was the coldest place in town, where temperatures rarely crept above twenty-eight or nine degrees. There were two working fridges, of which the owner was justly proud and even, set on a table toward the back, that miracle of the twentieth century, a television. How many of the hidden bar's accoutrements had been gleaned for Stefan by Jan, Ian would have found impossible to name, suffice it to say that here Jan's credit was always good. It was a narrow place and, being practically the basement of the house above, very low-ceilinged. Ian stooped his way along most of it, took two proffered bottles of beer from Stefan – cold bottled beer being the establishment's sole service – and crunched himself into a chair facing Jan, who greeted him without removing his gaze from the television set.

'Long time, Mr. Ashbury. What can I do for you?'

Ian hated him. Hated every detail of him. Twisted, lazy fucking bigot. Hated the sight of his overweight frame straining at the seams of his khaki short-sleeved shirt and matching shorts. Hated his receding mop of pale-ginger hair over jowls that threatened to melt into his chest at every word uttered. Hated the simple fact that this man was tolerated, let alone even liked by some. And hated the fact, above all else, that he had need of his services now.

He placed the sacrifice in front of the ugly Afrikaaner and sat back in his chair to take a pull on his own bottle. He wiped his mouth with the back of his hand and answered, 'I need one or two things.'

'Such as?' Jan's eyes never left the television. He was watching a particularly exciting re-run of "The A-Team."

'Shells. For a Ruger.'

'Not a problem. How many.'

'Twenty.' Ian stared intently at the Afrikaaner, whose face had not twitched so much as a single muscle. 'Fifty', he revised.

'Fine.'

'And a sidearm. A good one.'

The Afrikaaner's eyes broke contact with the television for the first time, and they met Ian's with the same suspicion one would a cobra.

'Nobody hunts with a handgun, Mr. Ashbury. Nothing *to* hunt.'

Ian's gaze remained impassive. He was not going to let this single-minded prick anywhere near his reasoning – the price might just treble.

'Well, you ain't hunting food.' Jan applied a little more pressure.

Ian remained silent. Of every argument he could think of to convince Jan to supply him with a handgun, there were none that would not simply arouse the man's curiosity further. He applied to the man's baser instincts, which Jan carried comfortably close to the surface.

'How much?'

'A thousand.' Jan's eyes remained locked on

his own. 'Forty for the shells.'

'A thousand.' Ian struggled to return the man's unwavering stare. 'You *are* joking, I assume?'

'I see a seller's market here, Mr. Ashbury. Correct me if I'm wrong.'

'That's still an awful lot of money.'

'Firstly,' Jan fixed him with a glare, 'I see a man who's in a hurry. I see he's got something to hide, and maybe an enemy or two. I also see a man with plenty of money and no-one else he can turn to. That about sum it up, *Mr.* fuckin' Ashbury?'

The feeling of hatred was all too apparently mutual, and there was nothing Ian could, or wanted, to do about it. The Boer was welcome to his money.

'A thousand and forty. I'll get you the money. When can you get me the items?'

'Items? Don't fart around with lawyer-speak, Ashbury. I'll bring the gun and the ammunition to your hotel room two hours from now. What's the room number?'

Ian told him, and then got up and left immediately, his beer unfinished, no further pleasantries exchanged. He felt sullied somehow simply being in close proximity to this nightmare Afrikaaner.

There was precious little to do in Kundasa, and he fled back to the hotel and straight to his room on the first floor. There he tried to force time to pass more quickly, but it moved with leaden steps. He broke down and cleaned the rifle, which had been wrapped, though not particularly well-concealed, in his jacket. Small, oily wads of hotel toilet-paper littered the floor around the waste-basket, where he had thrown them with only half-hearted attempts at accuracy. When he was satisfied, he reloaded his single shell and slid the rifle under the bed. He would have welcomed the chance of a nap, but sleep eluded him, and he stood instead at the window, his eyes rarely leaving the road into town from which he'd come that morning. He reckoned he had three days – two at worst guess – before they got here. That was more than enough. Come the morning, if he could not persuade Henry to fly him straight out of here, perhaps he could bribe him, or if the worst came to pass, and Henry proved incorruptible, hijack him. It was a grim thought, and one which Ian did not want to spend too much time trying to analyse. One way or another, he figured, by mid-morning tomorrow Kundasa would be nothing more than a receding memory.

A hammering on the door snapped Ian from his reverie. Time was finally moving at a speed which suited him. He opened the door to the Afrikaaner, who thudded his way into the room without a word. He approached the bed and dropped two boxes onto it.

'Shells,' He pointed at the first box. 'Fifty. Bullets, box of fifty,' indicating the second. From an inside pocket he pulled out about the smallest handgun Ian could ever recall seeing. It was bigger than a Derringer, though not by much. Dirty Harry wouldn't have been seen dead with it, he thought.

'Beretta point two-two. Good for stopping just about anyone close up. It ain't a sniper rifle, and it ain't a rhino-stopper, but anywhere around ten or fifteen feet away, your target will stop in its tracks. Best of all, it doesn't ruin the line of your suit. Just stick it in your pocket and Presto! Invisible.'

He held the gun up to Ian, but before letting the other man have it, he turned it over in the ham of his hand and pointed to the tiny lever on the side. 'Safety catch. Forward on, backward off. Never, never leave it off while it's in your pocket. Might sound obvious, but I've known smarter men than you lose their bollocks. Not pretty. Used one before?'

'No.'

'Point and squeeze very gently. Don't pull on the trigger 'cause you'll go high. Just squeeze, it's a hair-trigger, and there's no recoil to speak of. Try it.'

'Try it?'

'It's not loaded.'

Ian studied the tiny weapon. After the comforting weight and authority of the rifle, the pistol felt about as dangerous as a paperweight. Jan showed him how to thumb the safety on and off quickly, and Ian dry-fired it twice, the gun making happy little snap-noises each time. Ian was shown how to load it, and then he dropped it onto the bed among the boxes. Satisfied, he handed the Afrikaaner a roll of notes he'd separated out earlier, and waited patiently while Jan counted through them, occasionally holding a note up to the light. Ian thought the Boer might have a promising future behind a till. The money must have been hot in Jan's pocket, for Ian noticed the sweat he had broken into. The signs of his alcohol dependency were obvious to even the most untrained eye, and Ian knew that he would be off to Stefan's for a little celebratory drink or nine. He almost – not quite but almost – felt a little sympathy for the Afrikaaner, but this feeling fled at the thought of the insane profit the man had just made out of Ian's own plight.

Seven

'We'll never make it in that,' said Paul, as they descended the last steps to the underground garage and his eyes fell on her two-door Mini Mayfair. Two large suitcases took up the entirety of the back seat.

'I was hoping we could use that monster of yours. You still have the Range Rover?'

'Yeah. You'd better park in my space while we're gone. Don't want the resident's association up in arms.'

Less than ten minutes later both of Kathy's cases were loaded into the Range Rover along with Paul's luggage, her Mini luxuriated in the first covered parking space it had ever known, and they were easing their way through the perpetual London traffic, away from Docklands, heading into the city, seeking the start of the motorway and their journey west.

Along with her suitcases and hold-all, Kathy

had two further pieces of baggage. The first a fabric briefcase, which looked to Paul like it should contain a laptop computer and the second... Well, the contents of the second item he had no need to guess at. He could see the pair of white mice perfectly well through the bars of their cage.

Those parts of the journey through London not occupied by silence were filled with inconsequential chit-chat. Driving in the capital was a test of nerves and concentration at the best of times, and neither of them felt inclined to the slightest distraction until they had put the city firmly at their backs. Kathy had an open copy of the A-Z propped on her knee, although the journey to the head of the M4 was hardly a long one. They averaged somewhere around five to ten miles an hour, with each successive jam fuelling Paul's irritation, while Kathy struggled to navigate what conversation there was away from his frustrated ranting and into calmer waters. Eventually, they broke surface in the slowly swelling rush of the motorway. Paul visibly relaxed, and Kathy put the book back in the glove compartment.

'Still a country boy at heart, aren't you?' Kathy teased him gently.

'Oh, I don't know. I mean, I love the city, don't get me wrong. It's got all the excitement, and all the energy, but sometimes,' he paused, groping for the words. 'Sometimes it feels like too much energy, and all of it directionless.' He glanced quickly at her. 'Do you know what I mean?'

'Like something pent up and ready to explode?'

'Kind of. Life seems to get dragged away from you here. The faster you move, the further away everything seems to get.'

'You can get that anywhere. It's simply the days vanishing more quickly the older you get.'

'No, it's more than that. I always get a feeling of relief whenever I leave London. Like all the tension just slides away from me. I can actually feel my neck and shoulders unknotting.'

'So why do you stay?'

'The work, naturally. I couldn't get by anywhere else.'

'Seriously?'

'Seriously. Unless you happen to be in the top ten or twenty most wanted photographers, you've got to keep your name on the surface constantly. In Sticksville, I'd be forgotten in an second. Less than a second.'

Kathy found that difficult to believe, but held her silence. Paul, like many in his profession, had himself a good agent – one who'd do the remembering for him, who'd plug him at every opportunity. The real reason Paul still lived in

London was the imaginary kudos – the remnants of his boyhood yearning for the bright lights.

'Also,' he went on, 'London's gotta be the first port of call for any wannabe model. There's no better place to start.'

Kathy's tone changed. She allowed a sarcastic note in as she said, 'I knew it. There's the real reason. You'd be so lost without your regular supply of bimbos, wouldn't you? I wonder how you'd survive without the dress-dropping little dollies? I wonder *if* you'd survive?'

'It's not *all* like that. The majority of my shoots are fashion. You know, clothes and the like?'

'And that brings us to the lovely Ana, does it not?'

'Hardly, she's an interior designer, she's never modelled.'

'Not for want of trying on your part, I'm sure.'

'You're unbelievable.' Although horribly close to the truth, he had to admit. And that had always been the problem, hadn't it? The fact that she knew him as well as, perhaps even better than, he himself. Paul was a natural born liar. He believed it to be pathological – a knee-jerk reaction to any prying question, particularly when the questioner was female. But then Kathy had been the one to point this out to him all those years before. 'Partly right, okay?' he conceded.

She grinned, mentally tossed a coin and decided to let him off lightly. 'Was she responsible for the chrome thing?'

'Yeah.' It was Paul's turn to crack a smile. 'You'd never guess her occupation from a little clue like that, would you?'

No, she agreed silently. Interior decoration was about the last thing Kathy would have pegged her for. Ana was about five foot ten – a couple of inches taller than Kathy – skinny as a whip, and with looks typical of her native Sweden, all blonde locks and blue eyes. She was prime model material, and Kathy would have been extremely surprised had Paul not tried to tempt her in front of a lens. Still, if their tastes differed in the slightest, she did not see how Ana could survive much longer in their relationship. Kathy knew Paul's dim view of the table – not to mention the dim view he took of anyone who tried to impose their own tastes on his domestic realm – and she'd seen him cast them loose for lesser transgressions. Not that it was her business any longer, she reminded herself. It was still entertaining to wind him up now and again though, if only to watch him squirm.

They were ensconced snugly between two enormous lorries in the slow lane, and Kathy wondered if he had always been this cautious on the roads. It was verging on the dangerously boring.

Road-spray coated the windscreen with dirty water, the tarmac beneath their wheels whispered wetly by, and Kathy felt the urge to doze – to just nod off there and then, if her mind would only slow down to the same speed as her body. It was simply not going to happen, though. Her thoughts raced frantically, and it felt like a million things occurring at once, though there was really only one thing on her mind.

'Right,' said Paul. 'Wales is about three or four hours away. So now would be a very good time to get all forthcoming with the information, capice?'

Kathy was silent for a moment, pondering just how much she really knew before answering, 'I wish I knew even half as much as you suspect. The truth is I have absolutely no idea what we're supposed to be running from. I'm beginning to hope that I didn't know Ian as well as I thought I did, and that this turns out to be a completely unnecessary trip.'

'Something did occur to me, as a matter of fact.'

'Such as?'

'Well, I'm only speculating, you understand, but what if he simply wants to meet up with you and celebrate the end of whatever it is he's been up to?'

'Nobody, Paul, with the possible exception of your good self, is that cruel and twisted.'

'Well, a surprise trip, you know?' He was floundering.

'Trés romantic. Scare the crap out of me first? What a novel idea.'

'I'll admit it doesn't sound exactly like Ian's sense of humour.'

'That wasn't a sense of humour. That was exactly what it sounded like. It was a warning.' Kathy paused, and then seemed to collect herself. 'Besides, you know as well as I do that he never had a sense of humour.'

'Not for want of trying, Kath. He didn't exactly relish always being the last to cross the punchline.'

'He wasn't always last.'

Paul was momentarily lost, but then managed to dredge something up from memory. 'Oh yes. I'd nearly forgotten about our darling Chrissy.'

'How, exactly?'

'Not easy, I have to admit. The therapy helps.' They passed a signpost for Reading. 'Good job Betjemen never visited this place.' He threw the remark casually, but she failed to catch it, and continued to stare out of the side window. 'Slough might have come in for some competition,' he added under his breath.

'We're going to catch the A4 somewhere soon.'

'Change of plan? No more Wales? Say it ain't

so.'

'Only a slight change. We're going to stop and see Penny first.'

'Penny?'

'A real Aunt, unlike Edie,' Kathy began to explain. 'My Dad's sister. Proper old spinster type. Mad as a Custard Cream. You'll love her.'

'Should I have brought a camera?'

'She wouldn't look out of place on your wall of fame, it has to be said.'

'This is more than a social visit, is it not?'

'Yes. We've got to have access to a phone. There isn't one in the cottage.'

'It all sounds horribly primitive, if you don't mind my saying.'

'It's really not, don't worry,' Kathy managed a reassuring tone. 'All mod cons bar the communications.'

'Call me slow, but you might want to take this opportunity to tell me all about your non-existent Aunt Edie.'

'Oh, she existed all right. She just wasn't related to me, not by blood at any rate, but a very close friend of the family, and I always called her Auntie. I think she must have enjoyed that. When she died, she left me the cottage. I don't think she had any relations of her own.'

Paul looked disappointed. 'Well, that's taken

all the sinister out of it.'

'If it's adventure you're after, Scooby-Doo, I'm sorry to have to let you down like this.'

'Petrol.'

'Huh? Oh, sure.' Her responses slowed to match the speed of the car as they pulled off the main road.

'You hungry?' he asked, indicating the Happy Chef restaurant that lurked colourfully at the far end of the drab car park. There had been no let up in the rain for the entirety of their journey thus far, and the restaurant managed the enviable trick of appearing inviting against the noise and dirt of the main road. With the petrol tank once more replenished, they parked the Range Rover and then parked themselves in a corner booth as far away from the front door as was humanly possible.

Paul scrutinised her closely throughout the indifferent meal. It had been a number of years since they had shared a table – at least on their own, rather than with their respective partners. He liked to think that he was comfortable with their relationship, and for all their sakes he had put the majority of his memories a long, long way behind him. It didn't stop them crowding to the front of his mind now. Uninvited and less than welcome they clamoured for his attention. So naturally familiar to him - the way she held her cutlery, lifted the cup to her lips, crumpled the paper napkin at the end of the meal. Even the way she chewed. Tiny, insignificant things that meant so little individually but when taken as a whole seemed to capture the essence of her perfectly.

They had stayed together all the way through their University years and then, a few months after graduating, at the time of Paul's first foreign assignment, they had fallen apart with a speed that had shocked them both. They stayed in touch, naturally enough. In fact, it would have been next to impossible not to have done, what with Ian's constant presence in both their lives. He and Chris had gone their separate ways long before finishing University and, although he appeared to have a partner in tow most of the time, liked to proclaim himself happily single. If it had not been for Paul's constant pressuring, Kathy and Ian would likely never have discovered each other, as though their close proximity to each other had an inversely proportionate affect on the likelihood of their mutual attraction. The new arrangement seemed to suit everyone perfectly. Ian and Kathy found that the attraction they felt grew swiftly into love and respect for one another. Paul still had his two best friends, and seemed content to waltz from bimbo to bimbo, as Kathy would have it. Human relations, naturally enough, were hardly likely to be pigeonholed so simply. While Paul appeared content to treat Kathy as the kid sister he never had there was always, lurking hidden in the depths of his mind, the question: what if?

He hated his mind for its trickery at times like this. He felt like the worst kind of voyeur, as if his thoughts themselves regarded Kathy, or simply the image of her, as prey to be feasted upon, and picked over at their leisure. Perhaps there was something in the argument that men and women could never be simply friends, and that the sexual element was constantly present, lying just beneath the surface, ready to snare the unsuspecting. Well, perhaps. This was hardly the time nor the place for the question to be thrown up for discussion, however. This was neither the time nor place for anything other than putting some distance between themselves and…

And what exactly?

Eight

Gail and Jex were noisily sucking cool beers straight from the bottle when Ian joined them in Siddi's Bar. He brought his own to the table and sat with them.

'No Tom?'

'He's at the mechanic's,' Jex informed him.

'Trouble with the Landie?'

'None whatsoever. He just loves tinkering about with it. Found himself a kindred spirit up the road too, sounds like.'

'There's a slate here for all of you. All you can eat and all you can drink for as long as you want to stay. And I'd also like to pay for your rooms.'

At the mention of the rooms, Gail interjected, 'That's really very nice of you, Ian, but it's a bit much. Besides, we've already paid for our accommodation. And you have no idea the amount of beer these boys can pack away, particularly free beer.'

'I would've fried out there, Gail. If it hadn't been for you guys, well, I don't know. You literally saved my life. A few bob on booze and food won't even come close to repaying what I owe you.'

Jex said 'Lucky us. We rescued Rockefeller.'

Ian cracked a smile and began to relax for the first time in days.

'So where'd you get a name like Jex?'

'Short for Jeremy. Better than being called Jez. I hated that at school.'

They slipped into easy conversation and the afternoon slid quietly by, Jex destroying three or four bottles to each that Ian took. He was perhaps still not as wholly prepared to relax as he assumed, and this did not go unnoticed by Gail, who supped as infrequently as he did. Tom finally joined them around six, and when the news of free nourishment had sunk in, he applied himself to the bar with a relish that made Jex seem cautious. Ian made excuses and turned down their invite to join them for dinner. He'd already made that promise to someone else, he explained. Gail followed him out of the door and caught him on the hotel steps.

'I appreciate the free beer, Ian, but your debt isn't even halfway paid.'

He turned back to face her. She was not a tall woman, but three steps advantage gave her an air of dominance.

'What's going on? Really going on? You owe us that much.'

He stayed where he was for a moment, then climbed the steps to her. They deserved something, that was certainly true. But they couldn't have the whole truth. That much was unthinkable.

'I want you and your team to leave here by midday tomorrow at the latest. And do not take the road you found me on. Go in the opposite direction.' He realised he was frightening her, but he'd rather have them all scared and out of the way than ignorant and in it. 'There are three men on their way here. They're coming from the same place I did, and I *really* do not want you to meet them.'

'How soon?' was all she could think to ask.

'Three days. I hope. Perhaps as little as two. Get a long way from here, and stay away.'

'I can't just forget about my walk.'

'It'll keep. The rock will still be there a week or two from now.'

'A week or two?' She was crestfallen. 'Have you any idea what I've had to go through just to get permission to walk across this bloody country? Another war could break out any time now. This may be the only chance I'll get.'

'Please,' he pleaded with her, 'these men are

extremely dangerous.'

'What about you?' she asked. 'How are you getting out of here?'

'I've got another idea.'

He turned his back on her and left without another word. It was certainly possible that he may have been able to convince the rest of her team and ridden out with them in their Landrover, but the ride he had planned in the morning was a great deal faster and had the added advantage when it came to crossing borders of being several thousand feet in the air. The last thing he needed now was to be slowed down by a border guard, however slick or efficient they may have been. He only hoped that Gail would take his advice to heart, and that she could convince the others that the delay was necessary. From what he knew of Jex, he didn't think that that one would have to be arm-twisted too hard into taking an extended break from the trek, but Tom was another matter entirely. He tried to tell himself that it was no longer his problem, that he had warned them and that was all he really could have done. It didn't ease his conscience one iota however, and it was with heavy, guilty steps that he trod his way across the town.

Nine

He met Elise waiting outside the surgery. She'd finished locking up and his delay with Gail had made him a couple of minutes late.

'I thought perhaps you had forgotten me.'

'Never.' She looked stunning, and Ian, who had heard a handful of Henry's tales of malingering amongst the local men, could fully understand their plight. The white, clinical outfit against her dark coffee skin made Ian feel literally hungry. Her hair was cropped close to her scalp, which served only to direct his gaze to her eyes: a wide, welcoming nut-brown. He spun on his toes and guided her arm through his in the manner, he thought with a smile, of Fred and Ginger off to paint the town any number of fantastic hues.

'Where to tonight, my sweet. Nothing but the finest wines in the finest establishments,' he joked, knowing full well there was a choice of exactly one establishment, and that the last time Siddi's had been described as fine had been with a shrug of acceptance.

'My place,' she surprised him. And when she registered his surprise she went on. 'Better food than Siddi's. Better wine than Siddi's.'

'And far better company,' he interrupted. 'Although I always thought you lived at the clinic.'

'Ha. Mister Funny.'

'Candlelit, I trust? Flowers? All the intimacies?' Even as he made light of it, Elise could easily determine the doubt in him. It was in his voice, and in the tension of his arm.

'You're perfectly safe with me Ian, as is your honour and that of she-who-waits-at-home. I am not a known corruptor of men.' She grinned widely and wickedly at this last and felt him relax under her touch and her words.

He had no expectations about her flat, yet was still pleasantly surprised by what he found. It was light and airy, sparsely furnished but plentifully populated with flora, and immaculately clean. And of all the miracles he least expected to see in the middle of this dust and heat, here was one that all but left him speechless.

The fish-tank was obviously her pride and joy. Five feet wide and three feet deep, it stood on a low, wooden plinth opposite her sofa. Tiny fish glittered and darted and seemed to reflect the light like a shoal of diamonds. Here and there larger fish moved with majestic languor around a few large, strategically-placed rocks. It was the most beautiful thing Ian had seen for a very long time. Elise was justifiably proud of it, and stood next to him while she pointed out the different types of fish.

'And hopefully,' she said. 'Yes, here you are, Alfie. I named him after the Michael Caine character. He's a rogue, but he's always in hiding.'

The blue-and-yellow Angel fish glided out from behind a rock and practically took his breath away. It dominated the tank with the beauty of its presence, and the tiny glitter-fish scattered before it as though ashamed by their own tawdry appearance. Ian felt himself to be in Heaven. An angel before him and another at his side.

'How?' was all he could manage to utter out in a breath.

'Henry brings them in from Kinshasa. I usually get some quite tatty specimens, but with a little TLC they tend to thrive here.'

'But it must have taken…'

'Years, yes. Henry got me the tank more than three years ago, after some serious hint-dropping. I was nagging him for a little bowl and a couple of goldfish, but Henry, well, you know…'

Ian did know. Henry had played the rôle of

father to her since she had been nine years old, and had been orphaned – a subject she'd skirted around deftly whenever it had been raised. Ian had long since given up the idea of getting any more information from her on that subject, and since it really was none of his business, had long since given up any notion to pry.

She left him gazing into the rainbow therapy of the tank, and while she made busy, productive noises in the tiny, spotless kitchen, he sank onto the sofa and let reverie overtake him.

When he draped his jacket over the back of a chair, Elise pretended not to notice the dull metallic thud of the gun in his pocket, and although she knew exactly what the sound represented, she was uncertain of the reason behind it.

Over dinner they discussed little. Ian allowing Elise to detail the difficulties of keeping tropical fish and only interrupting to make complimentary grunts about the meal which, as Elise explained, was Kudu steak, plentiful hereabouts, and reminiscent to Ian's palate of venison. It was with a very satisfied sigh that he dropped his cutlery onto his polished plate at the end of the meal. When she had finished, he gripped both plates and made to stand, only to be put firmly back into his place once more. He was her guest, he was informed sharply, and no guest of hers would ever wash a plate. Every precedent that Mama had ever set would be violated. Suitably chastised, he allowed her to continue her pampering, and tried not to feel too useless in the meantime.

Sat out on her slowly crumbling balcony, amongst more plant-life which Ian correctly surmised to have been placed to hide the peeling, whitewashed walls, they watched the sun concede gracefully to the night. If there was only one remarkable thing about Africa it was this, Ian thought, the incomprehensibly enormous scale of the sky. Since his arrival he had found in Africa a dozen things a day to surprise or delight his previously limited experiences, but this one thing would remain indelibly etched on his memory. The sheer size of the sky.

'Thank you, Elise, for a perfect evening.'

She returned his smile over the rim of her wineglass, but said nothing. And that single smile seemed to dissipate the remainder of his fears. He felt them drop away from him as a physical weight.

Time flowed past. Words did not. In perfect silence they accepted the nightfall. Ian felt for the first time a twinge of regret that their relationship could not, must not, progress beyond this moment. And then he felt obliged to resent himself for even considering resenting his other life – his Kathy-life.

Recurring thoughts of her while he saw himself on the brink of infidelity eventually goaded him into action, and he rose to leave. She stopped him with a glance.

'I've made up the spare room for you.'

He paused for a moment too long. 'I have one at the hotel. I'd best…'

'There is danger there,' she stopped him quickly, perhaps too quickly. 'There is none here.'

'I didn't know you even had a spare room,' he said with a grin.

'It's quite small, and I once considered making a study out of it, but that idea died a long time ago. I don't think I'll ever use it for much other than to throw boxes in,' she replied wistfully, before adding more practically, 'I've set down my old single mattress on the floor, and a pillow. It isn't much, but you should be comfortable enough.' Her eyes gave away her curiosity, but she was not willing to delve into territory that did not concern her. For the majority of her life she had been keeping others at arm's length, never letting anyone too close to her own past, and she now felt obligated to apply the same rules here. She would not pry, merely protect where she could.

She showed him to his room, and he noted with amusement that she had not misled him in the slightest as to the comfort of his accommodation.

He'd not slept on a mattress on the floor since the half-forgotten and long distant days spent in a shared house when he was still a student. He made a conscious decision there and then to spend the time before sleep claimed him to reminisce as hard as he could. The spartan surroundings should certainly aid recall, he thought.

There was a single sheet and nothing else draped carefully over the mattress. Anything else would have been not only uncomfortable but near-suicidal in this kind of heat. He stripped and slid naked beneath its coolness. Lying stretched on the mattress he set about wiggling his toes in anticipation of the memories he was about to invoke. And as he called up the first, in as much lucid detail as he could muster, so his body, in direct confrontation with his mind, gave the order to drop anchor, and his busy thoughts were dragged quickly along in its wake to sleep.

At first he hardly registered her presence, but as she slid in beside him on the narrow mattress she placed a finger to his lips and he waited, startled, half-afraid and immediately, self-consciously half-aroused, for her next move. Her next move, it was apparent, would startle him even further.

She whispered to him, all the while without moving her finger from his lips. 'Please. Don't say a word. Don't say anything.'

She drew the finger from his lips down to his chin and then his neck. Her lips replaced her fingertips as she pressed them against his mouth. He responded to her touch as though in a dream, his body coming alive to hers, and his mind gently smothering his doubts, as she now smothered his body with her heat. The taste of her in his mouth aroused a passion in him born not only of desire but also fear. And then, as if on a hidden signal, he was in her and she surrounded him, his defences finished, surrendered.

And now she attacked him with a barely-concealed fury of passion. Her hands on his chest, robbing him of breath. His head forced back into the pillow as she rocked above him. He had never borne witness to such intensity, and to be so close to her now was to stand on the brink of the volcano. Her fire was unquenchable, yet he dared not try to douse it.

In a swift, unthought movement he was in control of her now, her body moving, writhing beneath him. She brought up her hips to encircle him further, and he pressed his mouth to her breasts, seeking succour. Her frenzy began to subside as his slower rhythm overcame her own. In a trance she found her peak, and stiffened, suddenly aware of each molecule of her body, before descending the other side. And he followed her moments later, sinking into her; into a clear, mindless chasm.

They dozed. And woke. Talked softly and dozed again. Around them the night was perfectly still, and they were no more than a troubled eddy in the massive darkness.

The dawn light that washed slowly, whitely into the room revealed them in each others arms, a desperate clinging that neither of them wished to relinquish. But appetite overcame them, and this time their lovemaking was slower-paced; a stroll through and with each other, the race already run and won by them both. Slick with their own spent and escaping energy, they finally broke their embrace.

'I'd never seen your tan-line before,' she giggled softly into his ear. 'I shall name you "Little White-Arse". It's a tradition, you know.'

He grinned broadly. 'And a fine tradition it is too. Now, as for your name…'

'Not a chance, don't even think about it.'

'Hardly the fairest tradition I've ever heard of.' He raised himself to his elbows.

'My tradition, so my rules.'

He rolled to look at her. To study her and fix firmly in his mind the essence and memory of her.

'Come with me,' he said.

'I knew you'd say that.' She rolled herself

upright and stepped off the bed, her nakedness arousing him anew. She left the room that way, unclad and silent.

He fell back into the mattress, unsure of what he'd said or done wrong. His thoughts fled to Kathy and his all-too-recent betrayal of her. He was morally stymied, he knew. He loved Kathy – simple fact. Was he also in love, or falling in love with, Elise? Could he love two women? The answer was of course a simple no. In all the world's history his situation had only ever led to the ruin of one or all of the parties concerned. And who was he to buck odds like that? Resigned, he rolled off the mattress and grabbed up his clothes.

She was waiting for him in the front room. A pot of coffee stood on a low, ornate table in the centre of the room, within easy reach of the sofa where she sat, dressed in her nurse's whites. He took the mug she offered him, and perched himself on the edge of the seat.

'I meant it, you know.' He spoke to break the weighty silence. 'You really should come with me.'

She took his hand and spoke without raising her eyes to his. 'I've dreaded you leaving, Ian, even more than I dreaded your reaction last night. But I can't go with you. It's impossible.'

'I don't see why…'

'Of course you don't.' And now her eyes lifted

and flashed at him a look filled with both anger and determination. 'How can I possibly leave what I've struggled so long to build here? This is my place, and I'm among my own people. I don't know where you're going, or what you think you can achieve by running away, but I'll tell you this one thing,' she paused, and then said sadly, 'a running man will always be alone.' Her eyes brimmed, but no tear fell.

'Be that as it may, Elise, you simply can't stay here and pretend nothing has happened. It's too dangerous. At the very least I want you to get away from here for a short while.'

'I've met one of your friends before now, Ian. What makes them so dangerous now?'

'It's impossible to explain now, there's too little time, and besides…' he trailed off, unsure of how to continue.

'Besides what?' She had no intention of letting him off that easily.

'Besides which you wouldn't believe a word of it.'

She considered this, and seemed almost ready to accept the fact that he was going to offer no explanation. But then decided she hadn't finished with him after all. She had the sudden suspicion that he was going to try to force her onto the arriving plane. That *she* would be the one leaving and not him. 'Are you going to try to stop them? Is that why you're carrying a gun?'

He gave her a surprised look. He *was* surprised. But he hid it quickly enough. 'No. If I had any chance of killing them it's long since past. And I couldn't even if I wanted to. I don't have the heart it takes to be a killer.'

'Then why the gun?' She refilled her mug from the pot on the table, sounding for all the world like this was a conversation she had every day.

'It's for you.'

'Me?' She stopped pouring. This wasn't even remotely funny.

'I somehow knew I couldn't convince you to come with me. Just hold onto it. I shouldn't think for a second you'll need it.'

'It's not me they're after, right?' she half-joked.

'Right. I don't expect them to even stop here, but they just might. If they come looking for you, trying to trace me, just stay hidden. If you *do* get found, don't fuck about with them. That gun's a last resort, and I hope to God you don't have to use it, but it may save your life if it should come to that.'

'You're beginning to scare me now.'

'That's the idea.' He stood and bent over her, taking her head in both his hands and raising her face to his. 'I want you so scared that you'll be safe.'

'I don't know how to use a gun.'

'I'll show you.'

Ten

The tiny Cessna landed with a couple of minor bounces that made Ian's stomach lurch just to watch it arrive. He wasn't altogether comfortable on anything smaller than a Jumbo, and even then he usually felt the need for a little Dutch courage before stepping onto one. He was flat sober now though, and his mouth was parched in trepidation. Elise stood at his side and watched the plane taxi along the rough strip to a halt about sixty feet from them. The engine revved briefly and then rattled to a halt.

Henry White, at five and a half feet tall and weighing a little above seventeen stone, nevertheless presented a formidable figure. He unleashed a broad, confident smile upon them both and stuck out his hand for Ian. They shook and Ian stepped back while Elise planted a kiss on each of the older man's rubicund cheeks. Ian hadn't been close enough to catch the other man's powerful breath – he hadn't needed to. Henry White was clearly drunk.

Ian helped Elise unload what few medical supplies Henry had garnered on his travels, while the obese pilot sat slumped and sweating in the shade of the airstrip's single unmanned shack. When they had finished loading her car – a battered and extremely dusty old Renault – the three of them climbed in and headed for Siddi's at the insistence of Henry. He was dry as dust, he claimed.

Over the next two hours, Ian watched in growing horror as the doctor grew steadily more drunk. Henry had listened to what little of the story Ian was willing to impart, and had finally agreed to fly him out – at a price, naturally enough. Ian had agreed to the exorbitant cost almost too eagerly in his hurry to put some distance between Henry and the bar. But try as he might, his new-found pilot was as determined to get even more drunk as was Ian to remain sober for the first time on any flight. His terror sunk claws into him, refusing to be uprooted.

'He flies better this way Ian, believe me.' Elise tried to set his mind at ease, and naturally failed.

'She's right, Ian,' offered Henry. 'You'll get a far smoother ride when I've got a couple inside me.'

A *couple*, thought Ian in exasperation. He'd already seen the third glass of beer disappear beneath the onslaught of the fourth and fifth, and Henry showed no sign of slowing down.

'Besides, you wouldn't get me up in one of those things sober. Bloody death-traps.' He let fly an enormous guffaw of laughter at the sight of Ian's horrified expression.

He left the two of them, his beauty and her drunken beast, and made enquiries at the front desk about Gail and her team. They had left early that morning, he was told.

'Did you see which direction they took?'

He was answered only with a shrug, John's hands raised palm upwards to his shoulders as he shook his head.

'Never mind, it's not important,' Ian lied with ease, and returned to the bar. He hoped to God that Gail had taken his warning seriously – he thought she must have, and then tried to put them out of his mind. He had more important matters to attend, such as ensuring the safety of Elise and of somehow getting Henry airborne.

Eleven

The colonel stopped jogging at the sight of the Landrover. He motioned to Carl and Sylvester, and gestured at the wreck. They approached it together at an easy amble, and were only partially surprised to find the driver's seat empty.

'He was extremely lucky there,' Carl pointed out helpfully.

'It would have been a shame to lose him like that,' added Sylvester, 'and so soon. Do you think he could have made the rest of the journey on foot?'

'Not a chance,' said the colonel. 'Not with the amount of water he'd need, and burning it off so fast.'

'Found the sat-phone,' Carl's voice echoed out from the passenger side, where he'd slipped and slid his way into the gulley to pull open the door. 'He totalled it.'

'Of course he did,' the colonel replied softly.

'He could hardly have carried it, now could he?'

When they'd cleared the first hill outside of the encampment, the colonel had suggested they speed the pace up a little, stretch themselves for a while at least. Sylvester and Carl had readily agreed, and they had all opened out into a comfortable jog. Now, some seven or more hours later, finding the remains of Ian's Landrover in the gully, the only man showing any sign of exertion was Carl, whose forehead was a little shiny with sweat, but that, mused the colonel, had been his almost constant appearance for the last five months anyhow.

Each of them had started the journey with the absolute minimum requisites – the clothes they stood up in, their passports, and a canister of water apiece. Nearly sixty miles further, and each man still had water to spare; even Carl, whose prior consumption of the life-giving liquid had been a source of amusement to them, in that other life.

'What do you think?' Sylvester addressed his question automatically to the colonel.

'Impossible to tell right now. Ground's too hard to make out any tracks, but I think it's safe to assume he walked out on foot. Out here there aren't many other options so, considering the distance he'd already covered, he must have ditched here in the middle of last night. There's no way of knowing how long he may have been unconscious for, or even if he *was* unconscious. So,' he paused briefly, and stooped to gather up a handful of road-dust. 'Let's assume he remained conscious, took a few minutes to smash up the sat-phone, and then lit out. We won't catch up to him today, unless he's suffered some injury. As for his water, I suspect he'd have finished that some time back.' He ground the dust between large, calloused hands and let it trickle through his fingers. A light breeze scattered it around his feet. 'Rain's not far off now.' There was still not a cloud to be seen.

Twelve

It was into this open blue sky that the little Cessna now sped. Henry at the controls, by all appearances sober, though that was far from the truth. Ian sat, knuckles gripped whitely on his knees, in the passenger seat.

His farewells to Elise could not have gone more disastrously wrong. He had practically broken down and begged her to come with him, and she had eventually fled in angry tears, trying not to hate him for going back on his promise. She had wanted no regret, no resentment. In her heart, she only half-believed in any of Ian's foretold dangers, though her head reminded her to take at least a little more notice of her surroundings for the next week or so. She felt prepared and unafraid, perhaps exactly the opposite result of what Ian had been trying to achieve, but that could not be helped. She simply could not run with him. She had nowhere to run to nor anything she feared to run from.

He regretted his behaviour now, several thousand feet too late, and yet still believed that he could have convinced her had he shaped his argument in a better fashion. Around him the tiny plane shuddered as its wayward pilot put it into a gently banking turn. Inwardly, Ian matched the aircraft shudder for shudder. The fat man at his side was sweating profusely, though this was no sign of fear, rather his natural torrential state. He handled the Cessna like a parent would an unruly child, coaxing and cursing it in equal measure. But his hands at the controls remained as gentle and as delicate as those of a concert pianist. When they had once more levelled out, Ian allowed a little of his fear to slip from him.

'You handled Elise extremely badly Ian, but then I think you already know that,' Henry said, dropping the plane into auto-pilot and relaxing back into his seat.

'Yes, I'm well aware of that, thanks,' Ian replied. 'But I leave her in your capable hands now, old man.'

'Ha.' He emitted a snort. 'As long as she remains in the capable hands of Mama, rather than my less-trustworthy own, she'll be safe as houses.'

'Are there many of you left, Henry? Flying

doctors, I mean.'

'Ah. A change of tack,' Henry grinned wryly across at him. 'From what scent are you trying to throw me, I wonder?'

Ian enjoyed the older man's language. As far as Henry was concerned, why employ only one word when so many existed to be commanded, conjured up at will.

'No scent, Henry. Simply curious, that's all.'

'None whatsoever, to be honest. Flying doctors are commonly associated with Australia, and with good reason. The whole landscape is different, whereas over here there are surprisingly few places to put even a little four-seater like this on the ground. I'm not so much a flying doctor, rather a doctor who happens to fly. Actually, you'd be more surprised at the number of doctors who'd rather pay to have their flying done for them.'

'Chauffeurs?'

'Of a sort,' he paused. 'Over here you can employ a black pilot for less than half the price of a white one. Same training, same experience, very different cost. So much for the death of apartheid, eh?'

'You're not kidding?'

'I wouldn't kid you. It remains the same all over. From labourers to computer programmers, the black dollar is about half the white, give or take a little.'

'And doctor's wages?'

'Not quite. The rates of pay are more comparable, but then there are many, many more black doctors in the African hospital system than white. The whites tend to stick to their own high-paying private patients, of whom very few are black, naturally.'

'And you've never been tempted down that road?' Ian asked, knowing full well that he and his team were perhaps the only whites to have crossed Henry's professional path in a great number of years.

'You think Mama would stand for that kind of behaviour? She calls me her pet white, you know that?'

Ian smirked despite himself. 'No, that I didn't know.'

Mary Mgumbe, or Mama to her family and close friends, had been with Henry for more years than either cared to count. She was a large woman, whose frame was only eclipsed by her personality, which was warm, bubbly, and occasionally overwhelmingly raucous. She had turned down Henry's offer of marriage many years ago, and he had never dared bring the subject up again. She liked to joke that she was his "Kundasa wife", inferring that many more were waiting in line in the wings, though anybody who got to know Henry would soon realise the esteem in which he held her. For him, there could not possibly be anyone else. She had stood firm by him when he had brought the nine-year old Elise home from the General Hospital, and their adoption of the skinny, overwrought child had been largely her idea. Elise had been the first to call her Mama, in half-sleep during one long, restless night in her childhood, and Mary had felt her stomach clutch. The name had stuck thereafter, at Mary's insistence.

She had told Henry at the time of his proposal, 'I ain't a white now, nor do I ever wanna be a White,' and had then dispelled Henry's initial shock and despondency with her enormous grin and welcoming, enveloping arms.

'I admire your principals, Henry, but a man has to eat, and also provide for his family. I can't see you doing that on a Doctor's wage.'

'It's easier than you think,' the big man replied. 'The plane is the only real overhead I've got, and that's taken care of by a mix of governments – an arrangement through various consuls. Besides, money is hardly a driving factor in my life.'

This, thought Ian, was an easy enough thing to say, yet that much harder in practice that Ian believed it near-impossible. Or was it simply that

Henry had dismissed the single most important element in Ian's career as a mere triviality?

'It's not just my flying you're afraid of, is it Ian?'

Henry's question had caught him all but unawares, and Ian needed a moment or two to recuperate.

'No,' he eventually answered.

'Something to do with your studies, out there in the wilderness?'

'Something like that.'

The overweight, profusely sweating pilot took a deep intake of breath, gathering himself, it seemed, for the answer to his next question. 'Is Elise safe, Ian? That's all I really want to know.'

'She's as safe as I could leave her, Henry.'

'That's not much of an answer.'

'It's all the answer I have,' said Ian sharply, and then added a small, guilty, 'sorry.'

Henry considered his next question with care, allowing a lengthy and uncomfortable silence to develop between the two of them. 'What went wrong out there?'

Ian turned in his seat and met Henry's eyes, his own fear heightened by that which he saw there.

'We discovered too much, Henry. We took it too far.'

Thirteen

The house that Penny McCleane liked to call home was a seriously run-down affair in one of the few less-respectable neighbourhoods to which Bath could lay claim. Two storeys of red-brick terrace in need of a paint-job and re-pointing and no doubt countless smaller tasks on the inside. The house reminded Kathy of a child's teddy-bear. It was worn and scuffed and tatty-looking, yet somehow undeniably welcoming. The woman who answered the door was, to Paul's eye, a striking antidote to her surroundings. She belonged in a palace. Her fluid grace made her surroundings seem even harsher, and more unrelentingly drab than they really were. The dirty air shied away from her presence. She dropped the scrawny cat she had been holding to the ground and held out her arms to embrace Kathy. After a short time, Penny let her go and stepped back.

‘And who might this be?’ she enquired, glancing meaningfully at Paul, who grinned toothily and extended his hand.

‘Paul Scaife. I’m an old school-friend of Kathy’s’. He found the old woman’s grip surprisingly strong. Her dry, warm hands pulled him through the front door and into a house that he knew would take him a long time to forget.

‘Are you allergic, Paul?’

The first thing that struck him was the smell. It wasn’t unpleasant, but it *was* animal – lots of them.

‘Allergic?’

‘To cats.’

‘No. No, not at all. I love cats.’

‘Really? How lovely. You’ve certainly come to the right house, in that case. Come in, come in, come in.’

As Penny turned back into the house, Kathy brushed past him. ‘Cat lover? You? Since when?’

‘Since I met the Princess here, naturally.’

‘Creep,’ she hissed, and followed Penny into the depths of the house, leaving him floundering at the door.

He made himself as comfortable as he could in the cramped living-room while Kathy was in the kitchen with Penny, ostensibly brewing tea, and less ostensibly putting a tiny distance between the two of them, so that Kathy might satisfy her Aunt's curiosity.

He'd been sat on the sofa for less than a minute when he caught Penny staring at him. It was an innocently curious look, and he could feel no enmity in it whatsoever. He raised his hand in a half-wave, which she returned quickly before vanishing again. He got up from the sofa, which felt suddenly less comfortable, and paced about the room, unconsciously shying clear of the kitchen door, staying out of eyeshot. The room, probably the whole house, was crammed with Penny's life. A life in the shape of photographs and trinkets, memories and memorabilia. There were nearly two dozen framed photographs on the upright piano which stood against one wall, and these drew him magnetically.

He picked his way among them, mentally tiptoeing through the memories of strangers. Here a girl of twelve standing chest-high to a striking figure in a RAF uniform. Possibly Penny with her father, he thought, though it was impossible to tell, the years having erased any clue. Here a picture of two women dressed like hippies, standing in a field amongst many similar flower-children. A festival, obviously enough. Perhaps even Woodstock, and he thought he might ask the Princess about it later. And here a more recent photograph. In this one of the women was obviously Penny, dressed formally, the background a function of some kind, maybe a wedding, or even some kind of award ceremony, it was impossible to tell. Her companion in this shot could have been the same one pictured at the festival, but her shoulder-length blonde waves had been cut drastically short, and her soft features replaced by a particular hardness, especially around the eyes.

He continued through the photographs, the professional in him unconsciously tutting at the poor lighting in one and applauding the accidentally efficient framing of another. The further he pried, however, the more his criticism receded, and he found himself drawn into her life, intrigued by what he saw and what the snapshots led him to assume. There was no wedding photograph, for one thing. Every woman of Penny's age would have had a wedding photograph, and Penny was too handsome a catch to have remained a spinster all her life. Yet, with the evidence now in front of him, Paul suspected that she had never taken the plunge herself. He hadn't looked earlier, but he suspected now that Penny bore no ring of betrothal. A more obvious suspicion seeped slowly into him, and he ran his fingers and his mind over the previously studied pictures. And then he realised he'd found Penny's life-partner. The close-cropped blonde woman. The second hippie in the festival photograph. Another very handsome woman, he noted, and wondered who she might have been. They certainly made a striking couple.

'A photographer, eh? How racy.' Penny cornered the younger woman.

'He photographs furniture,' Kathy replied, a little too acidly.

Penny ignored her. 'Handsome fella,' she half-mumbled, staring at him through the kitchen door. Apparently she'd made him uncomfortable, and she returned his little wave and turned back into the kitchen.

'Is he a friend of wotsisnames?'

'Ian. As you well know. Yes, he's a friend of Ian's, and a friend of mine, too. Emphasis on the "friend".'

'And where is Ian? Still gallivanting around abroad?'

'Africa.'

'Nice for some.'

'He's working, Aunt Pen. If anyone's got a right to a gallivant or two, it's him. He works very hard.' She struggled to keep the petulance from her voice.

'I'm sure he does, dear.' Smug sounding, before she called out in a sing-song, 'sugar for you,

Paul?'

'No, he doesn't.' Kathy replied for him.

Penny said nothing. Her archly raised eyebrows spoke volumes as she grabbed two steaming mugs and swept out of the kitchen. Kathy drew an inward, exasperated sigh and followed in her wake.

Paul held out both hands for his mug and clasped it gratefully. He threw Penny a curious look when he noticed the half-naked picture of a girl wrapped around his drink.

'She gets dressed again when the mug cools down.' Penny's eyes glinted mischievously. She carried on with scarcely a pause. 'You'll stay for dinner of course, won't you?'

'Well, we've already...'

'We'd love to,' Paul interrupted. 'If it's not too much trouble.'

Kathy shot him a look of pure irritation. But the decision had been taken out of her hands, and she resigned herself to it with as much inner grace as she could muster. At the very least, she thought, it would make a change from her usual diet of TV dinners or canned Ravioli.

'May I use your phone line, Aunt Pen?'

'Promise me you're not calling Africa.'

'No, Auntie. I've just got to get my e-mail. It's only a local call, and it shouldn't take more than a minute or two.'

Penny waved her silent with a tiny show of irritation. 'Yes, yes dear. I know what e-mail is. I'm not *completely* behind the times, you know.'

'Sorry.' Kathy looked a little abashed. But then Penny seemed to have that effect on her pretty much no matter what she tried to say or do. 'You don't happen to have a printer I could use as well, do you?'

Penny looked condescendingly at her, eyebrows raised this time in mock disbelief. 'I'll tell you what,' she began, 'you just write down your address and password and I'll sort it out for you after dinner. Agreed?'

'Sure.'

Penny had left for the kitchen before the affirmation had made it to Kathy's lips, taking for granted her agreement in the matter. For the next hour and a half, Penny busied herself out of sight, interrupted occasionally by one of the legion of cats which made less of a nuisance of themselves than their number suggested. Kathy and Paul took turns fussing over the latest arrivals – two snow-white kittens with outsize magnets on their collars. The magnets enabled the cats to come and go as they pleased, but the kittens seemed to find all sorts of new and interesting uses for them, such as trailing clutches of spoons or forks from pillar to post, and

Paul had to rescue his car keys on one occasion, as they were dragged bouncing across the carpet behind one of the puffballed creatures.

Dinner came and went, and early evening settled over them, Penny clasping an enormous glass of port and regaling Paul with assorted tales from her glory days. He couldn't seem to get enough of them, and pressed her constantly for greater details.

Kathy felt too aware of how much time was passing, and when Penny suggested they stay overnight she was surprised to find herself readily agreeing. Resistance is futile, she mimicked in her head.

'About that email?' she asked.

'Already got it, dear. I'm printing it out now.'

'But how?'

'Webmail, sweetie. All you need is a name and password and you can access your mail from anywhere in the world. Very straightforward, really.'

'Since when did you become such a technogeek?'

'I like to keep up. You can have the print-out in the morning. I assume you're on the way to the cottage?'

'You assume correctly. Was that just a wild guess?'

'Hardly. A cottage with no phone line. That's the main reason for your visit, I take it?'

'One of them, admittedly. But then I do get guilty when I think of the number of times I could have stopped to visit, but we always drove straight on to the cottage.'

'You don't need to feel guilty on Ian's behalf. I know he's the one who'd rather not stop here.'

'Well…'

'Well?'

'Well, you do rather tend to intimidate the man.' And also me, when it comes right down to it. Kathy left this last unspoken.

'Intimidate him? Little old me?' She laughed heartily, abruptly. 'His wires are extremely easy to pull, that I'll admit.'

Paul grinned with some private amusement. 'That much has never changed,' he said.

'Aunt Penny doesn't need your encouragement, either.'

Paul looked at his feet.

'I don't really dislike the boy that much, Kathy. It's just that sometimes he can be so…'

'So what, Aunt Penny?'

'Well,' she searched for the word. 'So wet, I suppose.'

'Wet?'

A muffled guffaw from Paul. A spiky, hurt

look from Kathy which effectively stifled him.

'Oh come on, Kath,' Paul began to defend himself. 'Ian can be...'

'Enough. The pair of you. No more slagging off Kathy's fiancé. Subject closed.'

Paul clammed up abruptly. Penny grinned widely and mischievously, but dutifully changed subjects.

'Are you one for the great outdoors, Paul? Or would you consider yourself solely a townie?'

Paul thought he could see where this was leading, and although he understood that Penny knew about the existence of the cottage, he wondered how much Kathy would be comfortable giving away. Then he mentally checked himself. The simple fact that he knew next to nothing about it himself made him a reasonably safe keeper of secrets.

'I've always been a country boy, but the nature of my work keeps me in the city.'

'Photographing furniture?'

'Furniture? Ah.' What on earth had Kathy been telling her? 'Only occasionally furniture. Mostly fashion, and very rarely some glamour work when I'm desperate for cash.'

'It must be nice to have your hobby as your living.'

'The two meet rarely, truth be told. Fashion

and glamour are as far removed from my real interests as the sun from the moon. Architecture and portrait studies are what really drive me, but there's very little living to be made from that. Unless you're called Lichfield, of course.'

'You've brought your equipment with you, I assume? You're going to love the cottage. Quaint rustic architecture amidst all that dramatic scenery. Simply love it.'

'You've been to the cottage? I was under the impression that it was their little secret.' He sloshed his whisky as he gestured lazily toward Kathy.

'Ah, I see.'

Paul didn't, and proved so with an inquisitive raising of eyebrows.

'No secret really. Edie wanted to leave the place to me in her will, but I convinced her to leave it to someone more deserving. I would have found the place depressing without her, and besides, Edie had no family of her own, and loved Kathy easily as much as I do.'

'There really is, sorry, *was* an Aunt Edie?'

'She's told you nothing, has she?' Penny looked accusingly at Kathy, who assumed an air of innocence.

'I was under the impression that Edie was a work of fiction.'

‘Honestly, Kathy. Are you really that ashamed of me?’

‘Of course not,’ Kathy blurted out in reply. ‘It’s simply not his business, is it? I could never be ashamed of you.’

‘But you would have mentioned me on the way here. You would have talked about my husband, or lack of one. You would have gossiped a little if you had not, unconsciously, been afraid of making Paul here uncomfortable with me.’

‘I can’t argue as professionally as you, Aunt Pen. I never have been able to, but I have never, ever been ashamed of you. You take these things too far sometimes.’

‘Yes, I do. You’re quite right.’ Penny gave her a twinkling smile. ‘Edie, Paul, was what I had in lieu of a husband. She was my grace, my light, my life. We were together since college, inseparable. Until three years ago. She just couldn’t give up her ciggies.’

‘My father was the same. Not a pleasant way to go,’ Paul said sadly.

‘I don’t suppose there really is a pleasant way to go. But I have a mind full of wonderful memories of her, not to mention a crate’s worth of photographs, which both comfort me an awful lot more than the thought of that empty cottage. We caused quite a stir in our heyday, I can tell you.’

'I can easily imagine,' he said softly. 'But didn't you suffer much discrimination?'

'Funnily enough, we rarely received the kind of abuse usually reserved for single-sex couples. I think it was probably due to the openness with which we conducted ourselves. That, and the fact that we were breaking no law. There weren't, I suppose, that many people who could get away with leading an openly homosexual life in those days. Look at poor Mister Wilde, for example. A tiny bit before my time though, I'll admit.'

'Yet you said you were breaking no law? I was under the impression that Oscar Wilde was slung in Reading gaol for exactly that reason.'

'Because he was a man. One rule for you lot, one rule for us.'

'How did that work?'

'It was all thanks to Queen Victoria.'

A brief pause, before Paul said, 'still don't get it.'

'When homosexuality first came to her attention, she was as appalled as your average hetero, and she agreed to pass a law against homosexuality between males, no matter their age or standing, but when it was brought to her attention that it was not only men who suffered from this "malady", but women also, she simply did not believe it. She couldn't see the point, and therefore passed no law against it, effectively legalising lesbianism.'

'Are you sure she didn't do it on purpose?'

'I'm not even a hundred per cent sure of those facts, but it makes a good story, and that's what counts.'

Evening passed into nightfall, and a slow procession of cats made their way from their hidden daytime corners and out into the dark. Paul watched them as they left in sporadic groups of twos and threes, and some alone. He could see no common element to link them. Siamese, tabby, chinchilla. There a night-black, a snow-white, a mixture of the two.

'You have an awful lot of cats.'

'They cost a bloody fortune in food and vet bills, but Edie and I could never resist the latest offerings from the rescue centres.'

'I can't see that you'd have much time for anything else. They must take all day to take care of.'

'Not at all. A cat is a most self-sufficient creature. Feed and forget them. And when I go away, I have a very helpful little au-pair who looks in on them.' She paused thoughtfully for a moment, and then looked around to recharge their glasses. 'So how come you've been invited to the little hideaway, Paul?'

He looked helplessly at Kathy, unsure of whether to answer. She waited for Penny to refill his glass before taking the initiative.

'Ian called this morning. He wanted to meet me there.'

'Well, that explains absolutely nothing, Kathy. Thank you.'

'It wasn't your standard Ian message. I think he's in some kind of trouble, and I thought Paul might be able to help.'

'And how might our Paul help?' Penny leaned forward and gave him a friendly pat on the knee.

'I didn't really want to face this alone.'

'That sounds like an enormous amount of trouble. Did he not give you any more details?'

'Not really. I think he expects us to find the answers we need in his diary.'

'Which is what I'm printing for you now, I presume?'

'It is. You presume correctly.' Kathy went on to describe the basis of Ian's message.

'Curiouser and curiouser,' said Penny. 'But that's enough for tonight, I think, it's past my bedtime. I've made up a couple of rooms.' She addressed this to Paul. 'Kathy will show you the way.'

She plunked down her empty glass, kissed Kathy on the way past and bade Paul goodnight.

They looked at each other in silence for a long while after that. Eventually Kathy broke it.

'Shall we?'

'I suppose we should. How long do you think tomorrow's journey will be?'

'Three to four hours, I imagine.'

'I feel like I'm embarking on a Nancy Drew mystery.'

'I always preferred the Famous Five, myself.'

Later, alone in Penny's study on a fold-out camp-bed, he tried desperately to wrestle his mind to sleep, but his mind was having none of it.

The multitude of cats prowled outside.

Kathy's mind raced every bit as furiously as Paul's.

Penny was the only one who got all her sleep that night.

Fourteen

The Landrover was kicking up a healthy cloud of dust behind it, as Jex careered along the return path to Gail's marked rock. She had taken Ian seriously enough the previous night, but something inside her, some unknown doubt, had prevented her from discussing their conversation with the others. In the cold light of day, when her judgement appeared to her to be sound and solid, she had come to her own decision. Had she warned the guys they would no doubt now be scurrying for the shelter of a further, larger township, and her walk would have been postponed indefinitely as their discussion went around and around like a Catherine Wheel. She was impatient to continue her journey, and to this end had taken the decision into her own hands. She knew she could rely on Tom, even had she repeated Ian's warning to him. He seemed afraid of nothing. Jex, on the other hand, was an unknown quantity, and may have abandoned them entirely had he been enlightened to any potential danger. It would have been extremely difficult, perhaps impossible, to find a replacement driver at such short notice and in such a remote backwater as Kundasa. No, it was better this way. If there was any truth whatsoever in Ian's warning, Gail still believed that they were unlikely to encounter the men reportedly chasing him, and if in any case they should, her team was ensconced snugly and safely inside an enormous, moving metal cage. They need not even slow down. The more Gail considered their options, the more her confidence grew. A single cloud appeared in the sky above them, as if willed there.

They arrived at the rock some twenty minutes after the colonel. He had at first been intrigued by the large white X, and the three of them had postulated its existence briefly, before Sylvester had spotted the distant dust-cloud and alerted them. They broke for the bushes lining the gully side of the road and waited, the colonel hardly daring to believe his luck when the Landrover lurched to a halt beside the marked rock.

He watched the team step down from the outsize vehicle, and waited patiently to see what came next. Carl lay next to him in the dirt beneath the bushes, flat on his stomach, staring intently at the Landrover and its curious occupants. Beside him lay Sylvester, on his back with his hands behind his head, to all intents enjoying a mentally-drawn day at the beach. To the colonel's surprise, the three safari-goers appeared to be setting up breakfast. He watched as the first man, the dark-haired one, arranged his pans and plates around him and then, on an unseen signal, the others strode off into the bush to locate, presumably, firewood. Now would be a good time to act, while they were separated, yet something held him. A fascination crept over him. The lepidopterist captivated by the glowing flight of his soon-to-be-prey. A hand on Carl's arm was enough to signal the man to be patient. He didn't trouble Sylvester, who seemed lost in a reverie of the no longer cloudless sky.

Jex, to the constant amusement of Tom, was proving to be a procurer of some skill, even though this was his first visit to Africa. Jex prided himself on his ability to fit in practically anywhere with ease, and this pride was only swollen on the occasions when he managed to surprise the others with his latest prizes. And today he had excelled himself, having gotten up particularly early and cajoled the hotel manager into providing for them an unparalleled breakfast spread. He deliberately took his time with the cooking of it, anticipating every grunt of appreciation from Tom and waiting expectantly for Gail to salivate. He actually expected to *hear* her mouth water.

'Smells good,' a new voice said, startling him.

Jex whirled around in surprise, but recovered quickly enough as his shocked senses took in this dusty apparition that had appeared from nowhere.

'Andrew,' said the dusty man, extending a hand. 'Andrew Marten. Sorry if I made you jump. Wasn't expecting to see anyone at all much before Kundasa, to be honest.' He smiled a wide smile, and noted the tension visibly leaving Jex's shoulders.

'No, no. Sorry. It's just that I was expecting someone else.' He shrugged out a smile and grasped the strangers hand. 'I'm Jex. Shouldn't have been that surprised, really. This road's getting to be a regular Piccadilly Circus.'

'I take it I'm not your first encounter today, then?'

There was something behind the visitor's apparently innocent enquiry, but Jex could not have put his finger on it had he tried. The man's appearance was dishevelled enough to have suggested a lifetime spent on this road, but his gestures, his composure and his welcoming eyes dispelled any lingering suspicion Jex held.

'The first today, yes.' He found himself becoming increasingly at ease with the man. 'But we picked up another guy night before last. He'd crashed his Landie.'

'He was okay? Not hurt at all?' The visitor asked eagerly. A fraction too eagerly.

'No, he seemed all right. A little shaken maybe, but mostly fine.'

'Ah, thank goodness. That must have been Ian.'

'You know him?'

'We've been very worried about him. He was supposed to get in touch, let us know if he'd got the supplies we sent him out for.'

'He didn't mention you at all,' said Jex, and as the words fell from his lips his own suspicion was rearroused. Why *had* Ian made no mention whatsoever of either his task or his colleagues? Or perhaps he had, of course. Simply not within Jex's earshot. 'We dropped him outside the mechanic's. I'm surprised he didn't call you then, or even from the hotel.'

'Oh, he may have…' The colonel waved away the subject, and stepped closer in to Jex. 'Phone's old and unreliable anyway, on the few days it chooses to work at all.'

'You hungry? We've got plenty to spare.'

'That's very kind of you. Thanks.'

The colonel moved around him, as if to take a seat, moving out of his line of sight. Behind him then, and one extremely strong hand clamped over his mouth. The colonel's other hand pressing the needle into his neck in one invisibly swift movement. As Jex's eyes rolled up into his skull, the colonel laid him gently on the ground alongside his cookware. Then he went over to the marked rock and sat down on it to wait.

Tom was the first to see him sitting there, and he put a hand on Gail's arm, slowed his own pace. Gail looked up ahead, immediately tense, fear replacing tension when she saw Jex's prone body. Was he possibly asleep? Just as possibly dead.

Tom started forward, but before he could break into a run, Gail grabbed at his arm. 'Wait,' she said.

'What the fuck?'

'There's more of them. Ian said there were three of them.'

'Ian?'

'He warned me about three men. Told me that we should get away from Kundasa. It's Ian they're after.'

'What about Jex?' His anger reflected in his raised voice, and the man on the rock swivelled around to gaze at them, though he made no other move.

'I don't know. I don't want to go up there.'

Tom looked at her closely. She was petrified, rooted to the ground. He hadn't the faintest idea what sort of trouble she'd managed to get them into, but he knew that his only course of action was forward. If Jex needed help, if Jex *could* be helped, then that was what Tom would have to do. 'I don't want you going up there either.' He spoke in a determined growl. 'Wait right here.'

'They're dangerous, Tom.'

'*I'm* dangerous, Gail.' He shook off her grip. 'Stay here.' He moved to meet the stranger, the danger, head on. He half-wanted to reassure Gail, to tell her not to worry, but he left the thought unvoiced. She would worry anyway, regardless of anything he said, and perhaps it was better that way – if the outcome of this encounter went against him, then he'd rather have her worried. Worried enough to run like hell at least, and Tom knew she could really run when she put her mind to it – she'd beaten him in more than one friendly race. Besides, knowing that she was worried simply drove up his anxiety, and therefore his adrenalin, to a point where his own doubts vanished. The adrenalin drove a new, frightening strength into him, and the sight of Jex helpless on the ground served to keep it at a strident pitch. His focus seemed to relax, and swell into this new strength. It was a feeling he was not unused to, this hardly being the first, and undoubtedly not the last, fight of a life spent fighting for every inch of the man he'd become.

The colonel rose at his approach, turning as if to greet an old friend. A smile played about his lips, his posture was relaxed, welcoming. And he was taken completely by surprise when Tom's punch landed squarely on his chin. The colonel dropped stone-like to his backside, the heels of his boots kicking up tiny puffs of dust as his legs shot out from beneath him. Tom loomed heavily above him, the muscles in his arms and neck bunched and tight, a look of scarcely-concealed fury in his eyes.

'What happened to my friend, shithead?' Tom forced out between clenched teeth. The words an animal snarl.

'He's fine, truthfully.' The colonel rubbed his chin, not looking nearly as afraid as Tom would have liked. 'He'll wake up soon.'

'What did you do to him?'

The question went unanswered. From behind the Landrover Carl and Sylvester made their unspectacular entrance. Their appearance naturally did not go unnoticed by Tom, who took a step back from where the colonel sat and waited, wary.

'No Ian, I take it?' Sylvester addressed the colonel, who had drawn his legs up but remained sitting. Tom noticed that the younger man had not enquired after the colonel's health, which seemed odd, after the punch he'd taken.

'These good people dropped him in Kundasa.'

'Perhaps they'll extend us the same courtesy,' Sylvester said, without a trace of a smile.

'After,' said the colonel.

Sylvester raised his head and met Tom's gaze. 'You like a fight then, do you?'

Tom gave nothing in reply. He was not fool enough to underestimate this wiry little man, but he didn't think he'd have nearly as much trouble with this one as with the mountainous black man in the background of his vision. Still, Tom had beaten bigger before today. He stood his ground as Sylvester advanced.

As his opponent stepped into range, Tom raised both bunched fists. This was enough misdirection, and as Sylvester raised his own fists, Tom snapped out a vicious, lightning-fast kick to his groin. Unbelievably, his kick was turned aside by Sylvester's knee, who promptly followed through open-handed to send Tom sprawling. He regained his feet quickly, spinning for Sylvester, and lashed out another kick, this time for the man's temple. Which should have been enough to finish any opponent had he connected, but Sylvester had ducked and reappeared on Tom's blind side, giving him a push in the back which, although gentle, caught him horrendously off-balance, and sent him staggering once more. Tom's confidence vanished faster than steam. Worse, he felt the nagging pull of fear, which he vaguely recognised as something he'd long ago left far behind.

"He's quicker than a snake." The thought flashed into Tom's mind with similar speed, and he unconsciously switched from attack to defence. If his actions were so swiftly and easily repelled, then his only possible chance lay in reaction. He took a couple of backward steps before settling into an easy, relaxed stance, somewhat mimicking Sylvester's own, who for some reason decided to oblige him and moved in for the attack.

'Got a little something for you,' Sylvester sneer-grinned.

Tom saw the silver flash in the other man's hand, and at first took it to be a knife. As his opponent stepped in, however, he saw the weapon clearly. A hypodermic needle. Was that what had happened to Jex? The thought of that needle anywhere near him appalled Tom. Though needles by themselves held no fear for him, this was only because he was more used to their being wielded by a smiling, reassuring nurse rather than the homicidal little madman who was now coming straight at him, grinning like a lantern. What was in the hypodermic? Could be just about anything. Central Africa led the world when it came to disease and contagion. The Kinshasa Road, or The AIDS Highway as it was colloquially known, was only a few hundred miles hence. It couldn't be AIDS, thought Tom, if the contents of that or a similar hypo had lain Jex unconscious or dead in an instant. Other options presented themselves in his mind and were crossed out an instant later. Ebola, malaria, yellow-fever, flu. The only certainty he held onto was the fact that he absolutely, positively did not want to find out first hand. Sylvester lunged.

His first clumsy movement, and Tom responded with savage proficiency, grasping Sylvester's wrist at first lightly, and then using their shared momentum to whip his arm downwards and out in a wide arc, bringing Sylvester crashing to his knees with his arm pointing skyward behind him. Tom stepped over the kneeling man's legs, continuing the same smooth movement, and twisting his arm beyond the point of no return. He heard a cracking noise, like a stepped-on twig. Felt it beneath his grip. Watched Sylvester's fingers slacken and drop the hypodermic into the dust. He dropped the arm, its wrist broken and useless. Stepped away from his kneeling, beaten opponent, and faced his remaining audience of two.

'How about you, fatso?' Tom jibed at Carl. 'You wanna go around?'

He was not in the habit of taunting anyone who stood over a head taller and weighed half as much again as he did, but he felt today warranted some special merit as his shittiest day to date, and was now deep in the mood for some dark celebration.

Carl remained silent, standing with his hands in his pockets, at the far side of the campfire, where Jex's hard-won breakfast remained unprepared. The colonel had his back against the painted-kiss rock, his eyes trained with amusement not on Tom, but on Sylvester.

Tom looked sideways, as the wiry man got slowly to his feet. He was clutching his broken wrist fiercely, as if he were afraid it might detach. Sylvester began to massage his wrist, grinding his fingers deep into the flesh of his arm, a slight grimace on his face. He raised the wrist in front of him, turning it back and forth to the accompaniment of tiny crackling noises which made Tom blanche. What he was witnessing should have been impossible. He couldn't begin to imagine the amount of pain that Sylvester appeared to simply shrug off. The broken wrist was able now to move of its own accord, and Sylvester dropped the other hand to his side. He flexed his wrist back and forth, rotated it left and right, flexed his fingers and thumb and then curled and uncurled them into a fist and back. He glanced at the colonel with raised eyebrows as if to say "How about that?" The colonel responded with a flat smile and a nodding head, suitably impressed. Nowhere near as impressed as Tom, however.

'What the fuck?' Wide-eyed, he backed slowly away from Sylvester. Backed as far as the Landrover, which was when he decided he needed an advantage. He dashed around to the far side of the Landrover, yanked open the rear passenger door and scrabbled wildly around for any kind of weapon. He surely had only seconds before… there! He grabbed his prize and wheeled around. Sylvester hadn't followed him, nor had Carl moved to block his exit. They were exactly where he'd left them, all eyes on him, mocking, amused. He was about to change that. A mix of fear, anger and adrenalin coursed through him, and he came around the front of the Landrover, hefting the tire-iron, its flat weight comforting in his hands, ready to finish the job this time.

'Let's see you fix a broken fuckin' head.'

He swung the iron at Sylvester, who leapt backward out of range. His swing had been wild anyway, a warning shot. His next would be no warning. There was cold, bloody murder in his heart now. An alien, brutal lack of feeling. A numbness. He could see no other way of escape. He had to get both Jex and Gail out of the way of these monsters, and the only way to do that was to go through them. Which was exactly what he now planned to do.

What happened next he found unfathomable. Sylvester seemed to go limp, the next second tensing, head thrown back, arms out, eyes shut, as though electrified. He seemed to swell before Tom's eyes. His outward size didn't change – he simply seemed to fill up somehow. Sylvester was shuddering with the effect of whatever was happening to him, and at the last moment, when he seemed swollen to bursting point, it all suddenly stopped. He drew in an enormous draught of air. Then snapped his eyes up at Tom, his face otherwise expressionless.

When Sylvester came at him this time, Tom may as well have been fighting smoke. He got in one good swing, at least in his opinion, before the tire-iron was ripped from his grasp. A blur of motion, a sudden pain in his temple, and then blackness devouring him. He couldn't be sure of the final sensation before he succumbed to the dark. It felt like a bee-sting, or perhaps a pinprick.

Gail saw Tom crumple and watched the wiry man who bent over him. She was rooted to the spot, only her fear confirming what her eyes took to be real. The wiry man was treating Tom gently now, easing him onto his back, and propping his head on something Gail couldn't make out, so he looked as though he were sleeping. Could he be only sleeping? And if so, why? Why hadn't they simply killed him? They seemed only too capable of that, certainly. She stiffened as she felt their eyes upon her.

The three of them held her gaze steadily, peering at her as though she were some sort of curiosity in a shop window. She felt herself begin to tremble. The huge black man started toward her. She turned and ran.

More famed for her walking rather than her running, Gail nevertheless turned in a good speed. She'd not yet met a man who could catch her in a race, though admittedly she tended not to meet that many sprinters in her line of work. She had quite some stamina, though, that had never been in any doubt. But no plan yet, simply headlong flight. She glanced over her shoulder and wasn't surprised to see her pursuer dropping back already. She hoped to gain enough ground in her sprint to allow her to settle into a steady jog, which she could keep up damn near all day.

Her circumstance and surroundings would work against her, though. In the past she'd successfully completed three marathons – twice in London and once, a favourite memory, in New

York. There was a world of difference however, between pacing yourself comfortably in the middle of a pack of a thousand or more runners, in the relative coolness of the Northern Hemisphere, with water and glucose energy drinks on demand and the emergency services keeping an ever-watchful eye on the competitors, and running full-tilt through the African bush with the sun rising higher, soon to be scorching, and an enormous psychopath lumbering along in your wake. She needed a viable plan, and fast.

The boots weren't helping either. As comfortable as they were for hiking twenty miles a day, she would have given almost anything for a simple pair of low trainers. She thudded through the scrubby grass, arms and legs pumping adrenalin, glanced behind again. Hard to say, but she didn't think she'd made any ground at all since she'd last looked back. He was pacing her, yet he looked to be loping along in a gentle trot. She put her head down and willed her body to move faster. She had to give herself the space and time to think. Had to.

Gail angled for the road, a hundred yards to her right. At least the ground there, though hardly perfect, would be less treacherous underfoot. She'd make better time, and she'd have a better chance, though admittedly a damned slim one, of being spotted, or even rescued, by any passing travellers.

That's your whole plan? She cursed herself for a fool. Fool to have come back here. Fool not to have taken Ian at his word. Double-cursed-blasted-bloody fool for getting Tom and Jex into this mess, perhaps even getting them dead. Hot tears started into the corners of her eyes. She met the road, pounded out into the middle of it, glanced back once more. He was right there.

Not ten yards behind her, closing rapidly. Oh, that wasn't possible, surely. Please don't let it be possible. Her breathing became harsh and laboured suddenly, and she fought to choke down sobs of terror. She could hear him now: could make out his easily-measured pace, the sound of his footfalls surely too relaxed, like those of someone out for a gentle jog. The tears really started to flow then. Her vision became blurred and she missed a step, stumbling forward, momentum carrying her onwards, angling out, arms stretched in front of her, beginning to fall.

One immense arm around her waist, lifting her bodily from the ground, sweeping her literally off her feet and into the air. A second arm now taking her weight at the knees, she was hoisted child-like into the massive embrace of her pursuer. She looked up into the black man's calm, untroubled eyes.

He hadn't even broken into a sweat. Gail wriggled about in his grip like a petulant child, and was rewarded only with soothing, shushing clucks from her unlikely father-figure.

'What are you going to do to me?' Her question was no more than a whisper.

'You'll be fine, you'll see,' he shushed her once more.

'What about Tom?' She desperately wanted to believe him. Needed to believe that everything would turn out fine. How could she trust any of them though, after all that she'd witnessed, all that they'd suffered?

'Both of your friends will be fine also.' Carl felt like adding "trust me," but couldn't really see the point of that. In truth, the only reason that he'd set off after Gail had been lack of choice. The colonel's impatience or Sylvester's quick temper would simply have made a mess of this encounter. Carl knew exactly where his skills lay. He was a champion pacifier, and he firmly believed in debate before action. He would reason with the young lady on the way back, make her see their point of view, make a willing supplicant of her. He couldn't envisage a single problem with that. The power of reason, he firmly believed, was an unstoppable force in its own right.

Of course, reason is usually meted out by the

power with the biggest stick, and when Gail began to kick and scream and tried several times to sink her teeth into him, he decided to postpone their chat. He lifted her into the air, draping her over one shoulder in a fireman's lift, her arms flailing the vast landscape of his back. With his free hand, he dug into a pocket for his hypodermic. He uncapped it with his teeth and, without breaking stride, plunged the needle into the flesh of Gail's buttocks and depressed the plunger. She yowled magnificently, redoubling her attack on him briefly before sinking gently away into darkness. It took Carl less than ten minutes to return to the camp, by which time he was convinced he could hear tiny snores following behind him.

The six of them proved a tight squeeze in the Landrover, but they made very good time into Kundasa, where they headed straight for Siddi's. The colonel kept John N'Gobo busy, allowing Sylvester to slip behind the counter and apply his needle to the hotelier's neck. Carl they left babysitting the Landrover out front. Once Mister N'Gobo was safely and comfortably settled in his own back office, they set about transferring the walking team to the upstairs rooms, where they could recuperate for a few more hours. There was no sign of the hotelier's wife, and the colonel presumed her to be shopping or out visiting friends somewhere. There was no rush; she would turn up at some point.

Once they had reassembled in the tiny lobby, the colonel took polite charge. The immediate plan, he explained, was to locate Ian without unsettling the locals in the process, and to this end he managed to persuade Carl and Sylvester (who only managed weak resistance to the idea) to wait in the bar while he did the detective work.

His first stop was the surgery, which he found deserted. As an only occasional visitor to Kundasa, he had no idea whether or not to be surprised, immediately decided against it, and made his way to Stef's bar.

He strolled quite nonchalantly through the gloom of the narrow room, raising not a single eyebrow from the handful of customers as he grabbed a proffered bottle of beer from Stef and continued through to the back room. He found Jan sitting exactly where Ian had left him twenty-four hours previously. He took the same chair opposite the slovenly Afrikaaner.

'I'm looking for a friend of mine, Jan. A gentleman I believe you'd know.'

'And I look like Philip fucking Marlowe, do I?'

'His name's Ian.'

‘Like I said,’ the fat Boer switched his eyes back to the television. The price of his slightest attention was the customary beer, and even this little formality had been overlooked by this unwelcome stranger.

‘So,’ the colonel leaned forward, arms on the table in front of him, ‘you’ve not seen him recently? Like in the last day or two?’

Jan tore his eyes away from the television and allowed them free reign to burrow away angrily at the figure opposite. They didn’t like what they saw. The older man with all his intruding questions hardly looked dangerous to him, but there was something about him, a hardness in the man’s eyes, perhaps, that made Jan uneasy. He wanted the man gone, the sooner the better.

‘I’ve got nothing to say to you.’ Jan kept his voice hard, uncompromising. ‘I don’t know your friend. I don’t know where he is,’ he paused momentarily, ‘and I’d appreciate you leavin’ me alone now.’ He dropped his eyes from the flat reflection of the stranger’s.

The colonel’s hand snaked out, and wrapped itself around Jan’s meaty fist. The Boer jumped, shocked, and would have pushed up out of his seat if he could have, but the colonel’s grip was a vice and it was tightening quickly, sending arrows of pain shooting up Jan’s captive arm. He could feel the pressure of his knuckles grinding against one another.

'Motherf...aah.' Jan breathed out between gritted teeth. He balled his free hand into an enormous fist, with the intention of smashing it into the face of his tormentor, but the pressure in his hand intensified suddenly. An unbelievable heat shot through his hand and arm, and he felt a crack which may have been his little finger breaking, but he couldn't be sure. Didn't want to be sure. His hand felt like a ball of liquid fire, nothing solid left in it at all. He slumped where he sat and looked at the colonel with pleading in his eyes. The gaze he met was not normal, barely human at all.

There was no anger, nor even pleasure, in the colonel's eyes. He stared at Jan blankly, waiting patiently for the man to succumb. He didn't have to wait long.

'He was here yesterday,' Jan croaked out, and felt the pressure in his hand ease immediately. He pulled on his arm, but the colonel wasn't yet ready to free him.

'What did he want with you, Jan?' The colonel's voice was soft, coaxing.

'Ammunition.'

'For a rifle?'

'That's right.'

'Anything else?'

'Pistol.'

'A pistol.' It wasn't a question. The colonel seemed simply to be taking the information on board, turning it over. 'He say why he needed these items?'

'Didn't ask,' Jan grunted. Feeling was starting to return to his numbed appendage, and with it a hot, throbbing pain.

'Of course you didn't,' the colonel said tenderly. He spoke to Jan now as though to a wayward child. 'And where will I find him now, Jan?'

'The hotel, I think. That's where I delivered the stuff.'

'That's much better, Jan. You see how helpful you can be when you put your mind to it?'

The Boer winced. 'Bastard. You broke my fucking hand.'

'Don't worry,' the colonel said gently, 'I'll give you something to take away the pain.' He met Jan's rabbit-scared eyes. 'All of the pain, I promise,' he uttered, patting the big man's ravaged hand.

'He was here yesterday, according to the register. I checked out the room, but it looks like he didn't bother spending the night here,' Carl informed the colonel when he arrived in Siddi's bar. He had been waiting with Sylvester, who had been struggling through a bottle of lager for nearly an hour, making little headway.

'The only thing my body is crying out for is water.'

'So have some water,' the colonel replied helpfully.

'I've already had well over a litre of water. What I'd really like, right now, is this beer.'

'What's the matter with it?'

'I don't think there's anything the matter with it. I think there's something the matter with me.'

'I doubt that very much.'

'Every time I take a sip, I just feel like puking,' Sylvester moaned. In his opinion it was his inalienable human right to enjoy a beer without feeling instantly sick.

'Your body trying to tell you something, do you think?'

'Telling me I'm never going to have any fun again, is that it?'

'Well,' the colonel answered thoughtfully, 'perhaps not the fun you're used to.'

Siddi's bar was typically empty, the three of them making up the sole clientele of the place. Their road-dusty appearance fitted perfectly with their drab surroundings. The colonel joined them at the table, stretching out his legs luxuriantly, and uttering a tiny sigh of contentment. Sylvester regarded him with a tiny trace of disgust.

'I don't see how you can be so self-satisfied. I'm sitting here with a broken beer-gland, and all you can do is look smug. Do you have any idea whatsoever how irritating that is?'

'You're just going to have to let it go, Sly. I don't think your body is going to let you hurt it anymore.'

'It's not the body I mind so much, Andrew. It's the non-stop flaming tick-tock in my brain. It won't shut up. I can't stop it racing about. It's bloody irritating, frankly. A beer or two to slow the pace down. Surely that's not too much to ask?'

'I don't know,' Carl chipped in with his slow drawl. 'It's like finally having the time to put your house in order. No more questions all the time. Just a world full of answers.' He glanced up at the pair of them. Andrew interested, and Sylvester looking startled. Perhaps he had a right to look startled. Carl, although always lucid and pertinent, rarely let slip more than one short sentence at a time. He grinned at them broadly, unleashing the pearly smile that had seen more than one woman fall devastatingly hard. 'And the answers don't seem to stop coming. For the first time in my life I feel motiveless.'

'How do you mean, motiveless? The goals we've set are motive enough, surely?' the colonel asked. For one whose entire life had been mapped out by goals, achievable and otherwise, Carl's outburst seemed nonsensical.

'Not the same thing, really.' His slow words beginning to speed up a little – a hint of agitation stirred them into life. 'Goals and objectives can be achieved now with so little effort, so little time or manpower, that the motive, the struggle to answer the questions thrown up along the way, is lost. Any real challenge now seems elusive.'

'It's taken all the fun out of it, in other words,' said Sylvester, clutching his bottle of beer tightly on the table, but not raising it to his lips.

'You need your unanswered questions the way Sly needs his beer. Or at least you think you do.' The colonel got up from the table in one sudden movement. He paced quickly to the bar, slipped behind it, bending low and searching for something. When he returned to the table it was with three bottles of spring water. He twisted off the caps and set the bottles on the table. 'Give your body a break, Sly. Try listening to it. Really listening.' He raised one of the bottles to his mouth and took a good long pull, filling his cheeks and throat with the liquid of life. 'You can taste the molecules themselves. You can tell the hydrogen from the oxygen. When water tastes like this, what need do you really have of beer anymore?'

'It doesn't stop the ticking.'

'That you'll get used to. As for you with all your answers, here's a question or two for you.' He glanced meaningfully at Carl. 'Why us? Why now, at this moment in time? What made us get so lucky? What are we heading for? And by that last I don't mean the four of us.' He spread his arms wide, as if to embrace all humanity, 'I mean *all* of us.'

Carl rolled his eyes and, addressing Sylvester, said, 'here we are at the dawn of a new humanity, and Mister Marten here tries to fob us off with an epithet or two.' He narrowed his eyes, his speech quickening along with his heartbeat. 'The only question left is a moral one, colonel. Do I, or we, have any real right?'

'Yup,' Sylvester agreed. He launched the beer bottle over one shoulder. It arced casually through the air, losing not a drop, before it crashed into the mirror behind the bar, shards of glass splintering down to the floor, scattering minuscule reflections of light into the murky air. 'Actions and reactions. Consequences.' The memory of a conversation on a fishing-trip with Ian. Possibly the root of his bitterness: his anti to Ian's pro, and their roles now reversed. 'More answers simply means less choices. We have no choice now. No choice but to continue what we have already started. Hell, if we all ceased to exist right this minute there'd still be Gail and

Tom and Jex.'

'And Jan,' said the colonel.

'The Boer? The fat one?' asked Sylvester. 'You sure that was wise?'

'It's like we've already discussed. We cannot allow ourselves to discriminate.'

'Sure, I know. It's just... I don't know. He always made me uncomfortable.'

'I think there will be a whole lot more discomfort before this is over.'

'If it's ever gonna be over,' interjected Carl. 'It's a mammoth task we've undertaken, that's for sure.'

The three men were silent for a time, each seemingly lost in their own reverie. When Sylvester finally broke the silence, it was to ask, 'What about Ian? Where do you think he's got himself to?'

'He'll be heading home, to Kathy,' the colonel answered.

'He had to get out of here somehow. Kundasa is not exactly listed on any major bus routes.'

'He may have got hold of some other transport. Though I'm damned if I know where or how.'

'The doctor,' Carl broke in. 'He flies in and out. Fastest exit you could make.' He studied the frowns on the other men's faces. 'It's what I'd do,' he added with a shrug.

'There's an airfield here?' Sylvester asked.

'Gotta be something.'

'Hmm. How about we go visit the surgery again. If Ian's chosen to fly out with the doctor, then there's a slim chance he's still in the neighbourhood.'

They studied the colonel, nodded, and stood up from the table as one.

'Let's get on with it,' Sylvester said, leading the way to the door.

Fifteen

Penny watched the tail-lights redden as Paul braked at the end of her street, and gave them a final little wave as they turned onto the main road. A brace of felines, one tabby and one tortoiseshell, eyed her as she made her return trip from the gate. She brushed past the two tiny observers, and they followed her back into the house, snaking in and out of her ankles.

Upstairs, in her study, Ian's diary was still open on her computer screen. Penny unwrapped a new ream of paper and dumped almost half of it into the feed tray of her printer. She set the printout running once more, before returning to the kitchen for her breakfast and the horde's daily meal.

When Penny had dropped the package in her lap that morning, Kathy had been surprised at the weight of it. Ian had never been much of a one for writing everything down, but that seemed to have changed over the past eight months. His diary must have run to well over a hundred pages, nearer two hundred, she thought. Kathy had stowed the package in the back of Paul's car, alongside the mousecage. Penny had been amused and slightly intrigued by the two little white mice.

'How thoughtful. You brought some cat toys.'

'You can be quite cruel, Aunt Penny, can't you?'

'I think it's terribly sweet of you, dear. Not many people are thoughtful enough to take their mice on holiday.'

Kathy pulled a wry face. 'Hardly a holiday.'

'Whichever. I'm sure you and Paul will have a good time up there. Attractive fellow.'

'Enough, Aunt Penny.' An exasperated look from Kathy. 'You really are incorrigible.'

'And you're very sweet for noticing. Now get in the car and don't keep your young man waiting any longer.'

'He's *not* my young man.'

'Whichever.' Penny waved her away with a hand.

'It's whatever, not whichever. Honestly, if you must speak like a teenager, and an American one at that, you really should try to get the lingo right.'

'Too much Buffy, I'm afraid.'

Kathy had pulled open the car door, and now

stopped short, brought herself back up to lean on the roof. 'Too much what?'

'Buffy the Vampire Slayer, dear. I'm quite the addict.'

Kathy shook her head. 'We'll look in on you on our way back. Okay?'

'Whichever,' said Penny, grinning mischievously.

With a final exasperated wag of her hand, Kathy slumped into the passenger seat and let Paul take her away from her lunatic relative.

Once her animals were sated, and Penny herself had gorged on two meagre slices of toast and the compulsory cup of tea, she wandered back to the study. The printout was still running, probably less than halfway finished. She grabbed the finished sheaf of papers and made her way back to the living-room, where she had an enormous wing-back leather chair placed near the window, where the light was best for reading.

She settled herself into the chair, papers on her lap, cuppa within easy reach. Penny started to read.

Sixteen

The surgery was still closed when they arrived. Sylvester peered through the grubby windows and reported no signs of life inside.

'What do we do? Come back later?'

'Locate the nurse. She's local, and the chances are she's already been contacted by Ian.'

'Can you remember her name?'

'I never knew it. We'll just have to ask around.'

On the street outside Stef's bar, two men sat at a table, playing the world's slowest game of chess in between tugs of beer and tall stories. Carl approached them alone. Despite his imposing enormity, Carl had by far the most approachable manner, and therefore the greatest chance of quick results. He meandered up to the two men, who were lounging back in their seats, their game temporarily forgotten. Both looked to be in their sixties or thereabouts, but to Carl the white man appeared to wear his years far less comfortably than his companion. The white man's eyes were rheumy and bloodshot, offsetting the redness of his drinker's nose. His black companion, however, still held a twinkle of youth around his eyes and mouth, as if he was constantly on the verge of hearing the best punchline of his life. Carl found himself somehow envying the old black man. He looked up into Carl's smiling face, 'What can we do for you, son?'

'I was looking for the doctor, but he appears to be out.'

'Always seems to be closed, that one. The nurse wasn't there?'

'No. Whole place was locked up.' Carl grinned his effortlessly pleasing smile. 'Don't suppose you can tell me where to find her?'

'Emergency, is it?'

Carl couldn't tell if the old man was suspicious or not. He certainly didn't look it. Just passing the time in the commonly unhurried manner that was the norm in the non-existent hustle and bustle of Kundasa. 'Not yet, no. But I don't want to push my luck, you know?'

The old man scrutinised him gently, any hint of suspicion vanishing from his features like an early mist. 'Well, I heard the doctor coming in this morning, so Elise probably went to meet him. I'd have thought they'd both be back by now.' Distracted by a sudden thought, the old man bent forward to the table in front of him and shifted his Bishop a couple of places. With a grunt, he leaned back again in his chair, ignoring the suddenly anxious movements of his red-nosed friend, who now bent over the board with renewed interest.

'Mind you, if she's not at the surgery by now, you should be able to find her at home. Second floor of the most ugly building in the next street. Tell her Alby says hello.'

'Sure. And thanks.'

'Don't mention it.'

Carl sauntered slowly away, his pace increasing only slightly when he reached the corner around which Sylvester and the colonel waited.

'Got her?'

'Got her.'

They made their way across the dusty street to the two-storey building where their quarry waited.

She'd seen them coming. From her kitchen window she could see them cross the street to her building. She watched the tops of their heads disappear in through the front door. A mild panic set in. There was no way out of her flat bar the front door, and that would lead her straight in to their arms. She glanced around wildly, her eyes falling on the pistol Ian had left for her. But that was crazy thinking, surely? Dangerous as Ian had warned her they might be, she could scarcely imagine anything more absurd than three killers stalking Kundasa in broad daylight. And coming for her? Surely not possible. Not outside of a Stephen King shocker, at least. She grabbed the pistol up, checked the safety, and tucked it into the waistband of her jeans, against her spine.

There was no spy-hole in her door, and she could only imagine the three of them on the stairs outside, as she listened to their approaching footsteps. Only one chance, she thought. She'd have to embrace the notion of attack as the best form of defence, try and catch them off-balance at the very least. She slipped her right hand behind her, resting it on the butt of the pistol, her thumb on the lever of the safety-catch. With a sense of timing that surprised even her, she swung the door wide even as the colonel's hand was raised to knock.

He was alone on the landing, a salesman's smile in his eyes and on his lips, his companions presumably guarding the bottom of the stairs. Just one against one then, she thought, and reckoned her odds had improved slightly.

'Elise, I'm a friend of Ian's. I'd like…'

She snapped the gun up in front of his face

before he got any further, and wagged it beckoningly. 'In,' was all she said.

The colonel did as he was bid. 'You're in no danger whatsoever from me, I can assure you,' he said placidly.

'I can see that.' The gun remained unwavering at his face. She slammed the door shut behind him, and would have locked it, had the door ever possessed such a luxury.

'He told me you'd be coming.'

'So I see. But honestly, the pistol is hardly necessary. I just need to see Ian.'

'You're too late.'

'He left already?'

'Uh-huh.'

'With the doctor, I take it?'

'Yes. That make a difference?'

'Not really. I'll catch up with him sooner or later.'

'What the fuck is going on?' Her gaze was pure steel, even though her insides felt like jelly. 'You mind telling me that?'

'To tell you may take a lifetime, Elise.' He took a step closer, his forehead pressed against the muzzle of her gun. 'Better to show you, I think.'

She saw the needle in his hand, and instinctively jumped backward, upsetting the table-lamp at the side of the sofa. She levelled the gun at his head again, thumbing back the hammer as Ian had shown her. 'Fucker,' she spat.

'No.' The colonel raised his arm, as though to ward off a blow.

She continued to lift the gun, until it arced above the colonel's head and was pointed at the ceiling. The arc continued, and she bent her arm to bring the gun tightly up underneath her own chin. The look in her eyes was one of mild surprise. The colonel's face reflected nothing but horror.

Without a moment's hesitation, Elise squeezed the trigger. The explosive report of the pistol deafened the colonel temporarily. He could hear nothing, but he saw it all. The top of Elise's scalp seemed to lift off in a bloody fountain. Red and grey matter arced out above her in a thick, gritty spray, and her body collapsed slowly in front of him, as though her legs had been kicked out from beneath her.

'No,' the colonel breathed again. His voice came out as little more than a whimper this time. A tiny breath of fear and regret.

The door practically left its hinges, banging back against the wall as Carl flew in, Sylvester hard on his heels.

'What in Christ's name have you done?' Carl was staring shocked at the scene before him. The white upholstery speckled with red-black droplets.

The pool of darkening blood spreading out beneath her head, where it lay canted at an obscene angle against the sofa. Her legs were twisted beneath her flattened body. Bright sunshine flooded the room, illuminating everything, and only serving to make the scene that much more grotesque.

Sylvester grabbed the colonel's shoulders, spinning the man around to face his accusing eyes.

'What happened? What…' he began.

The colonel held up a hand. 'Not what you think, Sly. I didn't pull the trigger.'

'Suicide?' from Carl.

'In a way, yes.' The colonel slumped down then, resting himself on the arm of the nearest chair. For the first time in days he looked weary, even drawn. 'Still my fault, though. I told her to do it.'

'Told her? Just like that?'

'No. No, not just like anything. I just kind of thought it at her. Didn't mean to. It all happened too quickly. Like I wasn't in control of my thoughts. Sent the thought out before I could stop myself.'

'What are you saying, man?' Carl again.

A moment of composure from the colonel before he replied. 'I'm saying that it wasn't my thoughts. I mean, I saw them happening, but I was like an outsider. I got the image, the potential future, and then it simply happened. It came true.'

'It defended itself, didn't it?'

'*Yes.*' A shout, rather than an answer. 'Yes. It defended itself.'

'We've gotta go now. Right now.' This time it was Sylvester's urgent voice, and he sounded terrified enough to wake all but the sleepiest dead. 'We're stuck in the middle of a fucking murder scene, and all you can do is discuss the fuckin' details. It's time to leave. I mean right fuckin' now. C'mon.'

He grabbed at the colonel's sleeve, like a nagging child just aching to get onto the dodgems before the next passenger change. Carl was away, apart from them, apart from everything. A murder scene was something new and unwanted to his senses, and he had no idea how to react. Sylvester, on the other hand, took immediate action. It was up to him now. Everything was up to him. The colonel offered no resistance to his sleeve-tugging, and Sylvester practically whirled him out of the door. Carl refused to come out of his daze, yet allowed Sylvester to manhandle him out onto the stairs in the colonel's wake.

'C'mon, c'mon,' Sylvester kept muttering under his breath, rounding his charges up and guiding them down the stairs like the persistent sheepdog he was. There was no police force in

Kundasa to speak of, only an occasional visit, too sparse to be called regular, by one or two men from Kinshasa, nearly two hundred miles away. But still, a single loud gunshot in this tiny place had exactly zero chance of going unnoticed, and whatever defence systems as Kundasa possessed would take no time at all to react to it. Time was of the absolute essence here, Sylvester knew, and they had exactly none of it left.

Down the stairs. Fast as possible, and out into the street. Deserted, thank Christ. The three of them half-walked, half-ran back to the relative safety of their bolt-hole at Siddi's.

In his private quarters behind reception, John N'Gobo slept on, undisturbed by dreams. His wife had not yet returned from whatever errands she had been running, and the three men took the opportunity to arrange their necessarily hasty departure. They made their way upstairs to where they had left their charges sleeping peacefully. The colonel slipped into Gail's room.

'Go check on Tom.' Carl said to Sylvester, before entering Jex's room.

Sylvester did as he was bade, only too glad that both Carl and the colonel seemed to have snapped out of their despondent funk. His mind was more at ease now that he wasn't the only one capable of making a decision. He slid into Tom's room, eyes flicking everywhere at once, warily taking in the entire scene. The last thing he wanted was a rematch with Tom. He had no advantage now.

To his immense relief, Tom was sleeping soundly. Sylvester pottered about the room for a short time, before finding himself a seat by the window, and settling himself there for a well-deserved few minutes break. He could hear Carl's low tones through the thin wall, making reassuring noises. It had been around an hour since they had left Tom, and he would probably be coming round soon. Sylvester wished to be gone by then. He got up from his chair and approached the bed.

Tom's pulse was good. Strong and steady beneath Sylvester's fingertips, perhaps a little quicker than was natural in sleep, but then this was hardly the most natural sleep. Sylvester dropped Tom's arm gently to his side and exited the room on cat's feet.

Carl was sitting on the edge of Jex's bed when Sylvester entered the room. The enormous and imposing bulk that was Carl was chatting in a soothing, reassuring manner to a groggy, shivering Jex. The lights in the room were off, the curtains drawn, and the sunlight that managed to filter through lent the room a soft, dream-like ambience. Sylvester was reminded of his childhood for some unfathomable reason. Perhaps it was the way Carl addressed Jex, in much the same way his own father had sat on the edge of his bed and spoken to him softly, all those lifetimes ago. Or perhaps it was the seemingly perfect stillness of the scene. Sylvester used to view his childhood as little more than a series of static scenes such as these, golden-washed. Even these memories were changing now, enhanced almost hourly with an increasing clarity.

'How are you feeling now?' Carl's voice, like honey poured over chocolate.

'Like… shit. Can't. Stop shivering. So cold.'

Sylvester sympathised. He'd hated this part.

'And hot.'

Yeah. Almost exactly like the flu. It hurt like hell at first, what with the hot and cold sweats, and the feeling that you daren't move a muscle, for fear of it being the last movement you were ever capable of making. But give it a while, kid. Live through this part. Then you'll know heaven. Sylvester drew into himself, searching, not finding, losing track of the emotion or feeling he so desperately sought. Or is it hell you'll know? Perhaps neither. Perhaps, like me, you'll simply become all too familiar with limbo.

'It'll pass, don't worry.' Carl's honey-soft voice again, though this time Sylvester was only half-certain that the reassurance had been addressed to

Jex and not himself.

Jex seemed to notice him for the first time. Unsurprising, as Sylvester had been hovering at the doorway, unsure as to whether he should breach the scene ahead of him or not. He nursed some half-formed fear that should he do so he would find himself transported back to the land of his childhood, that the man on the edge of the bed was nothing more or less than his father in disguise, beckoning him back to the past.

'He telling the truth?'

It took Sylvester a moment to realise the question was even meant for him, let alone to form a reply. But finally, form one he did.

'Sure. It passes. I've been there.'

'Figured.'

'It gets better, believe me.' He wished he'd sounded at least a tiny bit comforting, but Carl seemed to have cornered that particular market today.

'I was thinking we could take young Jex here with us. He could bring the Landrover back for his team.'

Carl's observation snapped Sylvester out of his dream-world, and he stepped into the room. 'Fine idea. What about the other two?'

'If we can get one of them compos mentis before we leave, they can take care of each other.

Leastways till Jex gets back. You think that'll work okay?'

'Yeah. Happy with that.' Sylvester looked not remotely happy with anything. 'The colonel with Gail?'

'Uh-huh. Don't expect she's come round yet. How was Tom, while we're on the subject?'

'Sleeping like the proverbial baby.'

'How long's it been?'

'Around an hour, maybe less.'

'Think it's always that way? Same time for everyone, I mean?'

'Hard to tell, really. It may vary. You think it matters?'

'I'm not sure.'

Sylvester watched with interest as Carl seemed to lose himself in this latest thought. Jex was sitting up now, arms around his midriff, looking ready to puke. Sylvester felt for him, he really did.

'What I mean is,' and here Carl paused, looking at Sylvester as a dying man looks at his nurse for reassurance, 'will they *all* wake up?'

Sylvester looked at his feet. There was no answer to that one. Only a feeling of hope.

'Elise was bad enough, man. That's all I'm saying. I don't want to have to witness that kind of shit again. Like ever again.'

'We've just gotta be more careful. Watch what

we're doing.'

'And watch what we're thinking?'

'Yeah. That too.'

'Can I have some water?' Jex interrupted. He sounded pitiful.

'I'll get it,' said Carl. 'What do you think, Sly? Ready to leave in about ten minutes, thereabouts?'

'Fine. I'll go see how the colonel's getting on.'

Seventeen

The sun had plodded past its zenith by the time Paul had heaved the Landrover into the last short leg of their journey. The only real clue to the sun's whereabouts was the clock on the dashboard, as the clouds above managed to conceal all, occasionally spitting at them, as if reluctant yet to release their gargantuan store of water.

The M4 motorway had given way first to A-roads, and then their tributaries, the B-roads, though to Paul's mind they rated no higher than F's. The last tiny town, consisting of little more than two streets, a small river no better than a stream, and an area of swampland where the annual bog-snorkelling championships were held, was behind them now. The higher into the Black Mountains they ascended, the higher Paul's spirits rose. At the boggy bottom of the valley, Paul's mood could have used a snorkel of its own, but now, rising above and leaving behind that low valley mentality, he managed to pick himself up dramatically.

This may be just the thing his city-nurtured soul needed. A spell in the harsh and unforgiving territory of the countryside, where the arm was mightier than the lens. The next week or so would rejuvenate him faster and better than any health club or detox centre. The six-pack he only recently mourned would return like an absent friend. His pallor would disappear to be replaced with that healthy outdoor glow you could read about in some of London's "Just-For-Men" health magazines. He mentally pictured himself as a 21st Century Grizzly Adams, and he thought he could feel his stubble grow just that touch more wiry as they neared their destination. The coming days would see him splitting logs and repairing wooden things. The image was still a little unclear, but it would come, he knew. And for some reason as yet unclear to him he would be accompanied on his vividly-imagined walks through hill-top woods, and across crags and other manly terrain by a border collie, appropriately named "Wolf", or somesuch. Getting hold of the collie was obviously the first hurdle. Oh yes, and a roll-neck woolly jumper.

'It's here. Turn here,' and then, 'Jesus Christ,' as Paul stamped too heavily on the brake, shaken out of his daydreams.

He swung the Landrover into the tiny rutted track, which looked as though this vehicle was its first, unwelcome visitor of the industrial age. The only evidence of the track's existence were the two deep, parallel ruts which were separated by knee-high grass and surrounded by two hedgerows which had obviously longed desperately for each other over the years, so arduously did they try to bridge the gap through which Paul now tried to force the Landrover. He slowed to a crawl, the better to seek out all of the rutted track's more interesting features, and they ambled along the lane gently, and sometimes not so gently, gaining headway as though fighting for it.

It was worth the fight. The hedge-hidden track finally gave up its prize. It opened out onto the yard at the front of Edie's cottage. It was a sprawling, two-storey whitewashed building, with large windows, a huge wooden front door and a chimney which promised an open hearth beneath. There was also a barn off to the right of the main house, huge, dark and potentially forbidding. At just to one side of the front door, to Paul's amusement and inner satisfaction, stood a huge knuckle of wood, patently ancient, torn from the body of some enormous and legendary oak, ready for chopping. The grizzly in him managed to stop just short of roaring with pleasure.

'Well, what do you think?'

Kathy's voice gently diluted the setting before him, but nothing in the world would have removed its magic. He had stepped back an entire century, and it was one of the most ideal, romantic places he had ever seen.

'S'perfect,' was the most he could manage.

Kathy looked at him, her brow wrinkled with a mixture of concern and confusion. He must be horrified, she thought. Probably wondering how on earth a peaceful, law-abiding city-dweller ended up in a place like this. She also considered it very gallant of him to try to spare her feelings at a time like this. But wait until he sees inside, her mind comforted her. He's in for a pleasant surprise.

'C'mon, perk up. Let me show you around.'

'Sure.' Paul drew the Landrover round to the front of the cottage, and they jumped out. He made his way round to the back of the vehicle, and was already opening the tailgate when Kathy called out to him.

'Leave all that. We've got plenty of time for unpacking. Come and have a look round with me.'

Paul didn't need a further invitation. He left the keys hanging in the back door of the Landrover and joined Kathy at the huge wooden front door. From her pocket, Kathy pulled what seemed to

Paul to be an unnecessarily large bunch of keys. As she fussed and fiddled through them he realised that there were, in fact, only a small percentage of keys to sundry colourful objects on the rings she was wielding. Looking at the state of her keyring and all the various paraphernalia it held, he was only thankful that he would never be called upon to root through her handbag.

The oak yielded, and they stepped inside. Kathy reached around the large door, and snapped the lights on. It was still broad daylight outside the house and the place was well lit by that alone.

Kathy pre-empted him. 'Just checking. The electricity is always paid well in advance. Ian always makes sure of that.'

Paul had moved past her into the middle of the room, his eyes widening as he took in each new feature.

'But it doesn't hurt to check.' She left the lights on, and followed him into the heart of the room.

Paul turned in a slow circle, his mind classifying and pigeonholing each item of furniture into the various catalogues from which he knew they'd arrived. Here a table from Ikea. There a lamp from Ocean. He recognised just about every item he had spent the last eight years photographing for a living. He was surrounded, it seemed, by the detritus of what Ana would have called Heaven. For Paul, other descriptive terms sprung to mind.

'A little over-the-top, you think?'

Paul tried to answer her question. Really tried. But the words failed him. A fake sheepskin in front of the open hearth tried to remind him. The white leather suite joined in the chorus. The almost-Tiffany lamps in the alcove muttered their assent, and the Bang and Olufsen upright entertainment centre tried to bully him into speech.

But he found none. His supposed worries about spending a long weekend with nothing but an open hearth for cooking and a tin bath to wash in were exactly that: supposed. In reality, it had been the stuff of dreams. A couple of days of discomfort that would have fuelled near-endless dinner party small-talk. But *this*? This was a nightmare. Everywhere he looked stood yet another testament to the luxury he was expected to endure over the coming days. He could have had all this in London. Why cross practically the entire country for this? Where was the challenge his soul cried out for?

Kathy showed him the remote control for the electrically-operated curtains. He could have wept.

'You're going to tell me next the fire runs on self-chopping wood.'

'What are you on, Paul? I swear. I drag you to

a cottage that's the last word in luxury, and you have the gall to stand there with a face like thunder. What's missing, for God's sake?' Kathy thrashed around for something *she* could have complained about, and there was exactly nothing. 'You're worried about the kitchen, is that it? Let me show you the kitchen.'

He knew it would be immaculate. Somewhere deep inside him, Paul knew it would be perfect. So when Kathy showed him around the spotlessly beautiful kitchen, complete with stainless steel work-surfaces and matching accessories, the look of anti-consumerist horror on his face was taken for awe by Kathy.

Oh come *on*! Where were the hardships?

'Don't you like it?' Kathy was perplexed.

'What's not to like?' Paul answered in a low, non-committal tone. He turned round twice in the centre of the space-age kitchen. 'What's not to like?' he asked again, giving Kathy a wide smile, his arms spread out crucifix-like as he spun around. 'It's gorgeous, Kath. It's nothing like I expected.' He pinned her with a gaze. 'When you told me about the lack of facilities in this place, I was thinking it was probably no more than a shack. But this… This.'

'Yeah, it's none too shabby. But you still have to chop your own wood if you want a real fire.' She shrugged.

'Well, that's something, at least.'

She shot him a quizzical look.

Paul looked at his feet. 'I was expecting something a little more challenging, you know? Something to tell your grandchildren about.'

'Or a tale of hardship for your bourgeois friends around the dinner table?'

How long had she been reading his mind? And wasn't there something he could do about it? Surely that was illegal?

Kathy fought back her giggles. 'Did you take yourself for some modern-day Robinson Crusoe? Is that it?'

He kept his gaze firmly on his feet. It was all he could do to stop his bottom lip from poking out in a pout.

'You were thinking you'd be Tom Sawyer, off on the last great American adventure, didn't you?'

Paul stuck his hands in his pockets, and shuffled his feet. This was a game he did not want to play, no matter how much she baited him.

'Tarzan, even? I can see the temptation there, mind. Does that make me Jane?'

'That's not what I…'

'Grizzly Adams.' She jabbed one finger at him and placed a finger from her other hand on the tip of her nose.

'Oh, for fuck's sake.'

'I got you, didn't I?'

He let Kathy get her little victory dance out of her system, gave her his best withering look, and marched outside to the car. When he returned a few minutes later with a couple of their bags, she had apparently had enough of her celebratory jig and was now busying herself about the kitchen, waiting for the kettle to boil.

'Bedrooms?' he asked, in a low, resigned voice.

She showed him upstairs to the guest bedroom. At least this was a little more to his liking. Evidently, she and Ian were counting on only rare visits from anyone, and very little effort had been expended on the second bedroom. Paul presumed, by the amount of junk in there, that they were using it more as a storage room – a place to sling their empty boxes and the like. She swept a couple of boxes from the double bed and tossed them into a corner, where they made their home on top of an ancient, leather couch.

'This a little more like it, Grizzly?' she smirked.

'Yes. Okay. Joke's over.'

'Come on, now. How could you not have known? You didn't really expect Ian not to surround himself with his little creature comforts. He doesn't do camping.'

He heaved one of the bags onto the bed. 'It's nice, Kath, okay? This one's yours.'

She took the second bag from him and led the way back downstairs, pausing only to hurl her luggage through the open door of the master bedroom.

Unloading the remainder of their luggage took Paul very little time, and as he grabbed the last item, the cage that housed Mickey and Minnie, Kathy joined him in the living-room with a coffee mug in each hand.

'Just stick them on the floor there.' She pointed to the right of the hearth. Plonking the steaming mugs on the table in front of the sofa, Kathy trotted up the stairs to her room, returning less than a minute later with her Aunt's printout in her hand.

Paul looked up at her from the sofa. She was clutching the sheaf of papers to her bosom, a look of trepidation on her face.

'Hey you. Relax. It's only a diary, remember?' He patted the seat next to him, gave her a grin that was supposed to reassure her.

'It's not though, is it?' Her voice lowered as she herself lowered onto the cushions next to him. 'This is the reason for the warning.'

He looked hard at her, unable to fathom what she was thinking or feeling.

'You want to read it out loud? We could take it in turns.'

'Yeah. Okay.' She placed the pile of paper on the table in front of her. Lifted up her mug and took a mouthful of coffee. Then grabbed the top sheet and held it up before her eyes.

Clearing her throat noisily, and trying very hard to keep from trembling, Kathy began to read.

Eighteen

Gail had surfaced from her non-dreams in a fury. The colonel was standing, facing out of the window with his hands clasped behind his back, ostensibly admiring the view outside, when she snapped suddenly upright, gasping and spluttering as if getting over a near-drowning.

'What the fuck have you done to me?'

The colonel didn't move. He remained both stationary and silent at the window. It crossed his mind momentarily to answer the girl. To offer either reassurance or explanation. But he let the moment pass. She was strong enough to come out from under hissing and spitting, so she was strong enough to handle this with the minimum of input from him. His attention wandered, once more outside. From here, the view he was treated to would have bored anyone else within minutes, perhaps seconds. For Andrew Marten however, the minutiae of the scene held an endless fascination.

Opposite the hotel window stood a two-storey apartment block, obviously built in more optimistic times. It was, at best, less than half-occupied, he guessed. And that was another funny thing, wasn't it? He wasn't guessing. Somehow he knew. He knew exactly which apartments were taken and which still laid unclaimed. He only had to glance, just the once, and the clues stood out clear as day. Top row, second from right, and he could see the thick layer of dust laid down on the sill behind the curtainless window. The dust was simply icing on the cake. The fact that there were no curtains told the story well enough.

'I said…'

'I heard what you said. I simply chose to ignore you.'

He could see the history of each brick. At first he felt it must be an illusion, optical or otherwise imagined. Yet even as he imagined himself misled, the secret history gave itself up to him. He could see the hands that had placed each brick, pushing firmly into the mortar. Could feel the sweat running down the backs of these ghostly labourers. Feel the heat of the kiln where each and every brick had been fired.

'What did you put in me?'

'It doesn't have a name.'

'Huh?'

He turned to face her finally. She was sat up on the bed, her legs straight out in front of her, fists clenching and turning in the sheets at either side of her. Her hair was tangled and hung about her face in loose strands. Her eyes glared angrily out at him.

Behind her, he saw Sylvester pause in the doorway, surveying the scene ahead of him. He'd obviously decided to let well enough alone, entrusting Gail to the colonel's care. He switched his attention back to the girl.

'I said…'

'Yeah, yeah, the drug with no name. I heard you the first time. I simply chose to ignore you.'

For the first time in what seemed an age the colonel discovered he was smiling. This is how it was supposed to happen, he thought. This was much more like it. Elise's death had disturbed him much more than he would ever have let on to the others. But already he could feel the guilt lifting from him, being dragged up and off his shoulders like a black shawl. He would never let himself get so careless again. That one unforeseen and very unexpected death had done more to undermine his resolve than any of the arguments he'd had with himself over the previous months.

'It's nothing that will hurt you, I promise.'

'And I'm supposed to believe that?'

'Well, perhaps not immediately, but you'll find out soon enough, one way or another.'

She pushed a hand up through her hair, quite pointlessly, the strands simply rearranging themselves into another cloud of disarray.

'Where are Tom and Jex?'

'In the next rooms.' The colonel pushed himself away from the window, starting toward the bed. 'They're fine. Fast asleep, I should think, but otherwise perfectly all right.' He reached the end of the bed and, seemingly at a loss as to what to do next, sat down on the end of it.

She looked at him, drinking in every detail she could, studying him as one might a venomous snake. 'And what do you intend to do with us?'

'Everything we wanted to do, we have already done.'

As confused as she was, this served only to upset her even more. Frustration bloomed angrily inside her, and she felt the first wetness of tears in her eyes. 'What did you do? Please tell me. Oh God, what did you...'

'Hey kid, you okay?'

'Jex.' She threw herself up off the bed, arms out, launching at him. Her legs gave out the moment they hit the ground and she fell heavily into Jex and Sylvester, who had lunged through the door when he realised what Gail was up to.

'You've got to give it a little while yet, Gail. The feeling will come back to your legs soon enough. Just take it easy for a bit, okay?'

'Jex?'

'I'm fine, Gail. Honestly. Tom too.'

He eased her back down onto the bed, the concern in his eyes badly hidden by the comforting tone of his voice. 'You've got to rest up for a little while, love. When you're ready, you can go next door and help Tom. He's still fast asleep.'

'Yeah. Okay.' Her voice was resigned and weary, yet still suspicious.

'I'm going to leave with these guys…'

A sudden start from Gail interrupted him. He could see the worry in her face. Worry didn't cover it, he thought. She looked scared. Extremely scared.

'It's okay. It's okay.' He held up his hands, palms out to her. 'I'm going to bring the Landrover back from the airport, that's all. I need you to stay and take care of Tom. I'll try to explain everything when I get back.'

He dropped to his knees in front of her, taking her hands in his own. 'And when the both of you are up and about, you should find John. I think he's going to need your help too.' He looked up at the colonel, still perched on the edge of the bed. He jerked his head toward the door and the colonel, obedient puppy that he was, got up and left the room, taking Sylvester with him.

When they were alone, Jex said, 'look, I know how you're feeling.'

Doubt in her eyes.

'Disoriented, confused, fed up and generally shitty. It *will* pass. I'll be back as fast as I can manage, but it probably won't be until the morning, no matter how many laws I break.'

She relaxed the tiniest bit.

'I don't think it's any use looking for bad guys where there aren't any. I don't think any of this is that simple.'

He'd run out of things to say. He had neither homily nor epithet to spare that would seem in any way appropriate, so he kept his mouth shut.

'I'll be okay, Jex, I suppose.' She looked at him with anything but certainty in her eyes. 'It's you I'm worried about. You'll be alone with those. Those...' She supposed she had meant to say "men", but somehow the word didn't seem all that suitable.

'I can't tell you not to worry, I know that. Because you'll worry any which way. Besides, I've made up my mind. I can trust these men so far, and we do need the Landrover back. So just wait here and try to be patient. That's the best I can do.'

She saw the apology in his eyes, but it didn't help. The last man who had asked her to wait was laid up next door, to all intents and purposes unconscious, but just as possibly stone cold dead, for all she knew.

'All right. Just get back quickly. In one piece. That's all I'm asking.'

She lay down on the bed again and rolled away from him onto her side. Jex, taking the hint, left the room without another word.

Kinshasa airport was a little over two hundred miles distant, perhaps four or five hours away. Jex sat in the rear of the jolting Landrover with the colonel, who appeared to be sightseeing. Sylvester manned the controls in the driver's seat while the enormous bulk of Carl, too large for anything but the front passenger seat, passed the time fiddling with the dashboard buttons. He'd exhausted the limited attractions of the cigarette lighter, the air-vent and the de-mister, and was now busy tuning the radio all the way across the dial and back again, switching wavelengths as the whim took him. He was beginning to get on Sylvester's nerves.

Jex had begun to sweat almost as soon as he had got into the Landrover. He felt his stomach cramping, and then he was shivering uncontrollably. He couldn't speak. His mouth was the only part of him which remained dry. The colonel stared placidly out at the passing scrub, offering no comfort, no solace.

They travelled that way for an interminable time, their silence only disturbed by the squawks and wails Carl was wringing from the radio. Eventually, after the umpteenth sweep of the airwaves, Sylvester reached out a hand and placed it gently on top of Carl's own. Carl seemed to snap out of his reverie at the touch.

'Enough already, Carl. Please. It's starting to drive me nuts.'

'Yeah. Sorry.' He contemplated the dials again, and turned the thing off. 'Feel like I'm getting obsessive about everything. Know what I mean?'

'I guess we'll get used to it.'

'Hope so. I mean, it's not like I'm even that interested in the radio. But once I start on something, it's impossible to stop exploring it.'

'Yeah. That's obsessive.'

Sylvester tried to concentrate on the road ahead, but his gaze kept straying to the rear-view mirror, where he could see the ghostly-pale reflection of Jex grimacing back at him. The young man was obviously not having an easy time of it, and the colonel's daydreaming was doing exactly nothing to help him. He began to wish he'd squeezed Carl into the back seat with Jex. Perhaps his obsession could have been turned onto Jex's welfare. Two birds with one stone, he thought.

Now that Carl's fidgeting had abated, he turned his full attention back to the road ahead.

For Carl's part, he spent the time fighting his obsessive urges. He clasped his shovel-sized hands in his lap and stared out of the windscreen. Even the dusty road over which they sped threw up more than enough for him to concentrate on. As the road flicked past beneath them, so his stare hardened, to the point where he had to remind himself to blink. His hands clenched tightly. Small cords stood out along his neck.

Sylvester noted all this and more. For his part, being in the driving seat offered at least a small respite from the turmoil in his mind. But he wasn't looking forward to any future periods of inactivity, such as trying to sit quietly on a plane. He did his best to push these thoughts away from him. He had enough to concentrate on, surely?

The colonel's mind was wandering across its own internal landscape. Long ago he had trained it in the manner of Matteo Ricci, and the vast cityscape he now dreamed his way through was his only lasting treasure. Everything else was a shadow in comparison. He'd spent decades on this structure. Each building in his internal city housed its own specialised subjects. Memory was a gift to be treasured. The mind was, in the end, the greatest part of man, so he believed. Alzheimer's disease, in is opinion, was the worst curse of mankind. A crueller affliction he could not possibly imagine. It was partly the fear of losing something he treasured so greatly that had been the force that had driven him for the past twenty years. He wondered how he was going to manage the coming years without those fears to face.

'So what happens next?'

Jex broke into the colonel's dreaming, and the city dissolved around him as he dragged himself slowly and reluctantly back to the real world.

'To us or to you?'

'Both,' Jex said, shuddering from a sudden chill that only he could feel.

'You're going to have another hour or two of flu before it dies down. You'll feel pretty tremendous afterward, though. Ready for anything. And the rest of us,' the colonel continued in his smooth, even tones, 'are going back to England for a brief respite, before we go our separate ways.'

'I don't really understand any of this,' Jex whined softly.

'I'd love to enlighten you, but to be perfectly honest it's all new to us as well.' The colonel found space for a smile and placed a comforting hand on the younger man's shoulder. 'Relatively new, at any rate.'

The colonel hardly expected Jex to be satisfied

with this answer but, although it fell short of the whole truth, it was the most he was willing to divulge to anyone until he was certain of all his facts.

Thankfully, Jex pressed him no further, and they spent the remainder of the trip in silence. The colonel returned to his window-gazing. The landscape continued its toil past his eyes. And then, glancing upward, he saw the first contrails in the sky.

'Look up, guys,' he addressed the two men in front. 'Our gateway to the network.' The beginning of the beginning, he muttered silently to himself.

PART TWO

BREAKTHROUGH

Nineteen

I'd intended to be just fashionably late for dinner, and the nightmarish parking conditions in Soho made it easy to keep that intention. I strolled into 'The Sleeping Dragon' around quarter-past eight, and was shown up to the first-floor restaurant by a fragile doll of a Chinese waitress. For whatever reason, Londoners had deemed Tuesdays the popular night out, and the place was packed.

I couldn't see Andrew Marten anywhere, and it wasn't until he rescued me from floundering at the door that I could see why. The beard was as new as beards get, and he'd lost weight. The once-heavy jowls had vanished far into his hollow cheekbones. He looked like he hadn't slept in a year which, for all I knew, could have been the truth. I hadn't seen him for over two. He recognised me, though.

In hindsight, I'm hardly surprised. Andrew's capacity for names and faces is astonishing. He never appears to forget a thing, and he's made mention many times since that day of memory being man's greatest gift. A gift he obviously treasured highly.

He plucked me from the midst of a throng of Chinese businessmen who were on their way to the second floor where, if this establishment was designed along similar lines to the majority of Chinatown restaurants, there would be both a conference room and a karaoke room, where deals struck would be celebrated with a song and a glass of sake.

Andrew led me to the table he had reserved by the window, waving an arm to indicate I should sit. I did so, giving the view outside the window a cursory glance. Summer had started late as usual, and as usual Londoners were making the most of the mild, light evenings. The best place for people-watching is street-level, where you can make out the expressions on everyone's face. I wasn't here for that reason, however, and the tops of their heads held little fascination for me. I turned to give Andrew my full attention. The short message he had sent me had fired my imagination, and I was intrigued to hear what would come next.

'Evening, Andrew.' It was a weak start, and for some inexplicable reason I found I was nervous. Nervous of a man I'd met only once – at a celebratory cocktail party after the launch of some tome or other. A scientific-business crossover, if I remember correctly. That would have explained the presence of us both. 'The Science Of Successful Business', that was it. Dusty, was my impression, but then I hadn't exactly studied it that thoroughly.

'Good to see you again, Ian.' Andrew's voice still possessed a light Mid-American burr despite his twenty or so years in England. He gave me a good healthy smile, full of good healthy American teeth. 'Would you mind ordering for the both of us? Chinese food is still a mystery to me.'

This surprised me doubly. Andrew Marten struck me as a very worldly man and besides, The Sleeping Dragon had been his choice, not mine. I looked the menu over with barely more interest than the view, and made my decision as quickly. Andrew seemed impressed nonetheless.

'Well,' I said, handing over the menu to the waiter, who was eager to be about his business. 'I got your message. Sounds interesting.' A lie. The only thing the message had sounded was vague. The one interesting word it *had* contained was "opportunity", and that's a word I rarely ignore.

He looked hard at me. With eyes like Andrew's, I get the impression that's the only way they could look. Hard. Penetrating. A visual assault.

Then he turned coy. A few seconds silence that seemed to stretch into minutes. He toyed with his empty wine glass, and then laid his hands flat on the table in front of him.

'I'll come straight to the point, Ian. I'm starting a project that needs some serious financial backing. I've done my homework, and I believe you're the backer I need.' He looked up at me again. Those eyes.

'So tell me,' was all I could think to say.

'We're talking a lot of money, Ian. And I've no idea of the scale of risk.'

'Sounds dangerous.'

'Financially risky.' Andrew raised his hands, as if to shrug, then put them back on the table. 'But like I said, I've done my homework. This isn't only about the money.'

The waiter returned with a bottle of house red and filled both our glasses. In our few moments of silence, something occurred to me.

'Your homework,' I said. 'You mean you've done your homework on me, don't you?'

'Uh-huh. You're an impressive moneymaker, Ian. Your own brokerage at twenty-two, a self-made millionaire at twenty-five. You're…' he searched for a moment, 'thirty-four now, and worth nearly forty million. Is that about the size of it?'

If anything, that was a conservative estimate,

but I was quietly impressed. Talk to a man about himself…

'Dot-coms?'

I was impressed. 'I was lucky. Got out well ahead and well up on the game.'

'Very modest.'

It had been my single greatest triumph. I'd made an absolutely obscene amount of money before the bubble had burst, and it seemed at the time like I'd been the only one who had seen the crash coming. That hadn't been modesty. That had been sheer embarrassment. Nobody was supposed to be that lucky.

'But like I said, it's not just about the money. You and I have something in common.'

The first course arrived, and I showed Andrew how to deploy crispy duck and spring onions to best effect in his pancakes. He was relaxing now, visibly less tense, and that helped relax me too. We began, two relative strangers, to have a good time. I needed to hear more.

'Such as?' I asked through a mouthful.

'Such as what?'

'We have something in common. What?'

'Alzheimer's Disease.'

That threw me.

'Senile Dementia, they used to call it. I prefer Alzheimer's Disease though, don't you?'

'To what?'

Now I'd thrown him. English humour. Indecipherable to most Americans, and just about the only evidence left of the cultural differences between us.

'Your father suffers from Alzheimer's, doesn't he?'

I stopped halfway through preparing my next pancake. That had really hit a nerve. Andrew's homework hadn't stopped at my bank balance, apparently. 'Yeah. Ten years of forgetting my name, and it won't get any better.'

'Mine too.'

'And that's what we have in common? Both our Dads have Alzheimer's?'

'My father suffered it for eight years before he died.'

'I'm sorry to hear that, but I'm still not getting the full picture here, Andrew.'

'Memory. Retention of facts. How to stop deterioration of the mind.'

'And that's the project you're working on?'

'Right.'

Now I was getting it. Or at least beginning to. Alzheimer's Disease was a common complaint, and there was no treatment, no cure. Certain symptoms could be alleviated, but there was no way to stop the eventual deterioration of the sufferer. What had

Andrew Marten been up to? How far had his research taken him? A treatment perhaps. Something to ease the sufferer's final years. He surely couldn't be talking about a cure. Could he? So I asked him.

'It's a possibility, yes.'

A cure for Alzheimer's. The market was already enormous, and could only grow bigger. Financially, this was huge. So there had to be an appropriate financial risk. That wasn't the only factor, though. Andrew had done his homework on me, that was for sure. There is some evidence that Alzheimer's is hereditary – I wasn't guaranteed to develop it, but I had a better than average chance. I'd seen what Alzheimer's had reduced my father to – he'd forget to dress, to eat, to wash. His concept of time had evaporated. It is a truly horrible disease. And now here was Colonel Andrew Marten, telling me it didn't necessarily have to happen that way. That was bait I had to take.

'How much do you need?'

'Half a million pounds minimum.'

'And maximum?'

He shrugged. 'I can't put an upper limit on it. Sorry, but it depends on time and circumstance.'

'Any idea how long it could take?'

'Somewhere between six months and two years. But again I'm guessing.'

'So why choose me?'

'I thought we'd covered that already.'

'Sorry, Andrew. It can't be that simple. Any potential backer these days would jump at the chance of getting into pharmaceuticals. So what's the something else you're not telling me?'

'Discretion. Privacy. I need someone who's acting alone, not a blasted great corporation. One man can keep a secret.'

'How far from legal is this project of yours?'

He arched his eyebrows high and opened his eyes wide, assuming what he thought to be a look of complete innocence. He wasn't fooling either of us. He packed his expression away carefully.

'It's a little wide of legal,' he finally admitted. 'Not too wide to break many laws, but not strictly ethical either. Think Dolly.'

'The sheep?'

'Similar ethics, different approach.'

We were silent for a time. The main course arrived on red dishes edged with gold, obviously torn from the same material as the restaurant walls.

'What's your field of science?' I asked him.

'Genetics.'

'Figures.'

We munched some more, while my brain ticked slowly around.

'Who else is involved?'

'At the moment, just myself. But I'll need a small, select team.'

'You already have one in mind, presumably?'

'Two others. Carl Jones, and Sylvester Candy. I've worked with Carl before.'

I'd never heard of either of them, but then there was no reason I should have.

'Tell me about them.'

'I worked with Carl at USAMRIID, he…'

'yousamwhat?'

'U.S.A.M.R.I.I.D. United States Army Medical Research Institute of Infectious Diseases. Carl's one of their chief virologists. He specialises in Level Four, what we call the hot ones – Ebola, Marburg, all that kind of nasty shit.'

'He doesn't work there anymore?'

'Indefinite leave of absence. I asked him to join me on this project. He agreed, and he's here in London by now, I should think.'

I tried to catch him out in a lie. 'I was under the impression we were the only ones who knew.'

Andrew raised one hand in a stop motion. 'He doesn't know the first thing about the project or its aims. He only knows that it's important to me.'

'And that was enough for him to drop everything and come over here for you?'

'Sure.'

'He's admirably loyal, I'll say that much.'

'We go back aways.'

'What about Candy?'

'Never met him.'

I wondered if he'd been accepting résumés for these positions. That was no doubt unfair, but I was hardly in a position to take the man at his word for now.

'He comes highly recommended by Carl. Sylvester was, is, a civilian. There are plenty of civilians at USAMRIID, don't be surprised. Carl worked with him several times in some pretty intense situations, apparently. He rates Candy among the best lab-men he's ever had.'

'What does he do?'

'Senior lab technician, and we need someone for the grunt work. There's going to be a lot of it, believe me.'

'And that's the team?'

'One more.'

'Who?'

'I was hoping you could help me there.'

A brand new waiter was spilling coffee into my saucer while our original one cleared away the debris of dinner. Andrew ordered a brandy, so I joined him. I felt I deserved one. I was still unsure, but I suppose my subconscious had already spent the money required. The brace of waiters left us. We cuddled our glasses as closely as a winning hand. Eventually, I called him.

'The fourth member. How do I help you?'

'Administration. Costs in, costs out. A bean-counter, or a secretary. A note-keeper. You must have someone you can trust?'

'Sure.' I sounded disappointed. Tried to keep it out of my voice and failed. 'I'll get someone.'

Around us, the usual restaurant babble had died to no more than a whisper. I'd hardly noticed the place emptying around us. Two other tables remained occupied, one obviously unmarried couple mooning over each other, and a trio of po-faced Chinese businessmen in the far corner. The remaining waiters were sat at the bar, cloths draped over their knees, chatting in stage whispers to the barman. Andrew caught the eye of the nearest one, and he brought us the bill. Andrew settled it, leaving a Texas-sized tip.

'I'll leave you this, Ian,' he said, handing over his card. 'Take a couple of days to think it over before you call me, okay?'

I said I would, and we parted on the street with a handshake. I watched his back for a few seconds, before the crowd swallowed him whole. I had the feeling I wouldn't sleep that night but, mercifully, I was wrong about that. Amongst other things, it would turn out.

Twenty

I took Andrew's conversation home with me that night, and picked it to pieces. There was no room in my mind to doubt him. The colonel was as serious as a moving bullet. I decided against coffee as I needed no help staying awake – my mind was far too busy for sleep.

I lay in bed at first, scrunching my eyes shut and waiting for dreams, before I gave up, sat up, and started on "Titus Groan". It was something I'd promised myself I'd read before I died, and I'd started it perhaps twenty times before tonight. It usually did the trick, and I'd find myself asleep before I knew it, but not tonight. Not even a mallet to the skull could have blanked me out tonight. I had the urge to check the market.

Insane thinking, but somehow comforting. Andrew had been right about me to a certain extent. I'd spent every moment of my time since college chasing money. I'd made an awful lot of it, and it was something I was very, very good at. But now he'd thrown something new into my lap. Something that seemed to have a purpose all its own. Not money for its own sake, but a real purpose. I couldn't possibly hope to spend all I'd made in one measly lifetime anyway. Maybe I was secretly counting on the Buddhists being right about reincarnation. But even if they had a point, there'd be only the slimmest chance that I'd come back as my own inheritor.

Sleep did claim me, finally, just when I thought I'd have to get up and go looking for it. But it was fitful, to say the least. I tossed and turned the entire night, watching past acquaintances, turned macabre, dancing against the background of my monochrome life. It felt wasted. Even the colourful nightmares felt wasted. They would surely have served an artist better. A man like me had no need for images such as these. There was nothing I could do with them. A change of life, then. Could it really come to so much so suddenly? Perhaps it could.

The following morning was about as grey as mornings get. A tangible mist pressed against the windows as I made coffee and toast in the kitchen. And that made me smile. Here was I, money spilling out of my ears, still living and cooking like a bachelor student. The money meant nothing for one reason only – I'd done absolutely nothing with it. Money to me was like a muscle that needed constant exercise. I was determined to make it grow bigger, but what was I going to do with it in the end? What was the point of it all? Maybe that was what Andrew had given me. The goal at the end of one journey. Perhaps the start of a whole new journey. But the journey could hardly involve me if I simply decided to finance it.

I had to be involved on a larger scale. Not only to keep an eye on where the money was spent, though that was a valid reason and probably enough to ensure my involvement, but also to give myself a real reason finally. A reason for all that money to exist in the first place. Self-justification. Or plain selfishness.

My receptionist-cum-secretary Holly was already in place when I meandered into my office. She was looking pleased with herself, and I put it down to the fact that she'd arrived ahead of me for the first time in the four years since I'd hired her. If there had been an archetype for the dizzy blonde, Holly would have fitted it perfectly. To me she had been a godsend though. What little filing our tiny offices produced she handled with consummate efficiency. She could lie about my whereabouts and engagements with grace and good humour, the perfect foil. And she was unquestionably pleasant eye-candy, something to lift the spirits of a new client, or an old one. Chauvinistic as that sounds, she was most definitely the right woman for the job. In many ways, she reminded me of Christina, my college nemesis.

Apart from my office and the reception room, the firm boasts one other office. It was a shade smaller than mine, and not so well lit, as befitted the office of my junior partner, a bright spark named Kevan (with-an-A) Wilson. I'd badly needed someone to share the load for a very long time now, and Kevan had come my way out of the blue, practically gift-wrapped. If I was to entrust the running of my office to any man, I could not have chosen better.

But that was a decision I'd yet to make. The way I saw it, I had three options. I could wrap the company up, take the money and run, and turn Kevan and Holly out onto the streets – with excellent references, naturally. Alternatively, and this struck me as the most sensible plan, I could assign Kevan to the colonel's project, while I took care of the business. Definitely the best option, I thought. Kevan was fiercely loyal, scrupulous, and the perfect candidate to take on the job of looking after my investment.

The third option was a little trickier, and I needed to talk to Kevan about it. I had a lot of faith in the man's abilities but when it came right down to it, with not a little fanfare of trumpets, he simply wasn't me. A head for maths was essential in this business, and Kevan had maths in abundance. That wasn't enough however, to ensure you rose above the rest of the field. What that needed was that elusive "something else", that indefinable Midas touch.

Think of the devil. Kevan appeared in my office just before ten, following his stealth-knocking technique. He had to clear his throat before I was even aware of his presence.

I can see the Thames from my office window, and one corner of Canary Wharf and a bit of the old Dome. It's a view I enjoy immensely, especially Canary Wharf. I can imagine Paul up there, snapping away at some exotic, underdressed beauty. I admire the starved artist in him, though God knows I'd never admit it to his face. Everybody has their weakness though, their Achilles heel. Mine is money, as I'm all too well aware. I'd feel naked, helpless without it. But for Paul it's always been women. A man who's lost without women, but can do nothing except lose women. You can't help but love the man.

'Holly said you wanted to see me?' Kevan

queried in a tiny voice.

I left my feet where they were, pointing comfortably at the river from the safe perch of my desk. Kevan was personable enough, but I got the feeling he hadn't been bullied at school nearly enough.

'Let's go out, Kev. A spot of brekkie, my treat.'

I watched his jaw slacken momentarily before he caught himself. 'Oh. Okay. I'll get my coat.'

We'd socialised exactly once before. I'd taken both him and his mousey little wife to my favourite yuppie-encrusted hangout and we'd all had a thoroughly miserable time. The mousewife, Anne, had been allergic to everything on the menu, and had sipped unhappily at her Beaujolais throughout the indifferent meal. Kevan, it turned out, was also allergic – to fun in any form. Still, fun was not what I had in mind for Kevan.

I helped myself to croissants, it being over two hours since toast, and slurped coffee – pricey, frothy stuff. Kevan settled for just the froffee. "The Lowdown" was an immaculately expensive café-bar squashed in at the base of one of the Wharf towers. When he could afford it, it was also one of Paul's favourites. There was chrome everywhere. What wasn't chrome was smoked glass.

Kevan treated the silence between us with

reverence. Silence to him was something both fragile and precious, something he'd never break. I simply had my mouth full. When I finished the croissant I'd also finished deciding.

'Kevan.'

He was looking at me expectantly. Doe's eyes in headlights.

'There's a project I need your help on. I'm going to be backing it alone, and it's quite a lump of cash I'm going to risk, so what I need…'

He was trying to nod at the same time as drink his coffee, so I let him take a second to organise his reactions.

'What I need is a full-time insider on this project. I need you to look after my investment for me. Liase with these people, watch the money, that sort of thing.'

I could picture him trying to explain this to his wife.

'I want you on-site, naturally. There'll be an awful lot of administration I'm afraid, but nothing you're not well used to.'

Had Andrew told me where the site was? Did he even have anything lined up? I was damned if I could remember.

'Maybe some travel.'

Mathematically, anything bar the infinite can double, and Kevan's look of trepidation now did exactly that.

'And I'm not sure precisely how long the project will last.'

Not a word. Not a sausage. Not a dicky-bird.

'What do you think, Kev?'

I knew exactly what he thought.

'Well. Er...'

It was in his eyes.

'I...'

It hung about him like an odour. In all his mannerisms, his shrugs and eye-rolling.

'You couldn't tell me where, I suppose?'

The ghost of the mousewife was next to him, sitting and glaring at me. 'You'd dare to throw my husband at the real world, would you?' her eyes said. 'You'd cast him from his office, his refuge? Who are you planning to move in there when he's gone?'

'It's just that...'

'Oh, bollocks.' I got up from the table and went straight to the bar. It wasn't quite eleven yet, and the barmaid seemed to be trying to make me aware of this obvious fact. But after growling my order in what I hoped were non-arguable tones, she relented and poured the whiskys I'd ordered. I took a heftily-priced can of diet Coke with them.

'Change of plan, Kevan,' I practically barked at the poor sod when I regained my seat.

'What's this?'

'Whisky and Coke. It's good for you, trust me on this.'

'Change of plan?' He picked up his glass, gingerly, as though it might have bitten him.

'Change of plan.' I could hardly believe I was saying this. 'I need you to look after the office while I'm away.'

'Away? Where are...'

'The project, Kevan. The one I was talking to you about not two minutes ago.' I consciously tried to ease up on him. 'I'm going to do the legwork on the project, and I need to leave the office in safe hands. *Your* safe hands.' I pointed at him with the hand holding the Whisky and Coke, waggling the glass in front of his face.

'Well, that's a huge...'

Responsibility. Yeah, I know.

'...responsibility. But you know I'd be only too glad to step...'

Into the breach. I knew that too. I waved the rest of his muttering away. What had I been thinking, trying to send a man like Kevan into a situation full of strangers? It would have been easier, and fairer, to simply have him put down.

So option three it was. We sat in that bar for three more hours, Kevan actually pulling out a notepad and pen in an effort to capture everything

I needed him to remember. He managed to sip through nearly one whole whisky to three of mine, and I knew I'd done the right thing for both of us. He was going to love the cosy pressures of the office, and I was finally going to get the adventure I felt I deserved. I drank to that. Alone, naturally enough.

Twenty One

It was Friday when I next met Andrew Marten. He'd apparently enjoyed his Chinese so much that he'd booked the same table for our return match. I was uncharacteristically early, and was nursing a whisky minus the coke when the colonel made his entrance. I didn't see him until he'd reached the table, because he'd been eclipsed by about the biggest man I'd ever seen, in or out of the movies. There was an American Footballer called William 'The Fridge' Perry. That kind of size. Somebody nobody ignores.

'Ian,' the biggest black man in the world shoved a dinner-plate of a hand towards me. 'Carl Jones. Pleased to meetcha.'

'Likewise.' My hand, and part of my forearm, vanished inside his immense grasp.

The colonel grinned broadly at me as they both sat. He suggested I order for them again and I happily obliged. Carl turned out to be an aficionado of Chinese cuisine and, as he was happy with my choices, I liked him immediately.

'You've decided to join us, I take it? You're on the team?' Carl asked me halfway through the main course.

'Yep. That's the idea.'

The colonel was surprised, but nowhere near as surprised as I'd been two days previously, when the decision had formed whole-made in my mind, in an instant. Until that moment I'd been convinced that I'd been undecided, if that makes sense. But now that the decision was out in the open, for better or worse, I felt calm. Satisfied. Resigned to it.

'Well, that's the team settled,' Andrew raised his glass to us.

'You mentioned a fourth man,' I pointed out. 'Sylvester something.'

'Candy.' Carl said. 'Sylvester Candy. A good, reliable man. I can guarantee you'll like him.'

'Really?'

'Sure. Everyone likes Sly.'

I was intrigued, but I thought I'd reserve judgement for the moment I met the man. Carl spent a few minutes singing his praises. How trustworthy he was. Solid, reliable, and one or two other terms of praise I wasn't keeping track of.

For me, the rest of the meal passed in a happy

blur. I introduced Carl and the colonel to Irish coffee at the end. They both seemed to appreciate that.

'So it's just a matter of when we start, then,' Carl said.

'Ready when you are.' I raised my glass to him, completely unsure of what ready might even mean, let alone my own state of preparedness.

'We can begin Monday,' the colonel said, 'if you're sure that's not too soon.'

'I'm sure,' I said, and wasn't.

Andrew pushed a good-sized wad of paper across the table to me.

'What's this?'

'Call it a business plan, if you like. It's really just a big wish-list. Give you some idea of where the money's going to go.'

'I'll look it over this weekend.'

'That's the idea.'

'We'll be setting this up as a business come Monday, I take it?'

'Of course. Everything kosher and above board. I think you'll like the idea once you've read it through.'

'Still giving me the option to bail out?'

'Only good manners, after all.'

We needed more coffee, or at least I did. Irish for me, straight for them. I sipped and mulled quietly for a time. Andrew and Carl seemed happy enough to let me.

'So give me a brief overview,' I said, waggling the sheaf of paper at Andrew.

'Covers our needs, that's all. Premises, equipment, licences, stuff like that.'

'Licences?'

'Animal licences. Complicated.'

'Yes, I can imagine.' I couldn't, of course. I had no idea what he was talking about, and I hadn't any wish to. Still, that could wait until next week, when I'd gone through the small print.

'Salaries?'

'Valid question,' the colonel answered. 'But we're not running this operation in any conventional manner.'

'I held my palms out to him, and the gesture seemed to say 'Well? Explain.'

Carl stepped in. 'Sylvester and I have enough savings put by to last us a couple of years. The colonel here, too. We've agreed to work without a salary until the end of the operation. Then we'll demand a percentage of the profits, naturally.'

'What percentage?'

'Twenty-five percent,' Andrew interrupted. 'A straight four-way split.'

I looked hard at him. It was my businessman's look, and it had served me very well in the past.

Twenty-five percent of this potential market was a ludicrous amount of money to promise your employees, which was effectively what Carl and Sylvester amounted to.

Andrew returned my stare. He'd have made a very good businessman if that look had been anything to go by. 'First off, Ian, it's fair. Four of us. Four-way split. Secondly, presuming we succeed, there'll be more than enough money to go round, now matter how big your appetite.'

That was a low blow. Low, but accurate.

'And lastly,' the colonel continued, 'it's the only way I'll do business.'

I gulped at my Irish. He was right, of course. I couldn't see, really, beyond my ideas of making money. I was still struggling with the bigger picture. I'd been given a chance to do some real good in the world, and I was on the brink of blowing it all over petty cash. I don't think I've ever been quite so tactfully humiliated.

'Sounds fair to me,' I said, trying to save at least a little face. 'Just one thing, though.'

They waited silently enough for me.

'I can't set up a business with employees who are paid nothing. The Revenue would be on me in a flash.'

'A business whose employees are also stockholders is not an uncommon practice, Ian,'

Carl reassured me. 'We will simply invest our savings in the company shares, and draw what we need, our so-called salaries, as stock dividends.'

'Why make it so complicated?' It *was* unnecessarily complicated, and I needed to know why. 'I've shown enough interest in this project to satisfy Andrew, and I can afford to fund the whole thing, you know that.'

'One,' said Carl. 'It's a show of good faith on our part. To show you it's no scam, if you like. Two.' He held up a second enormous finger. 'It's a guarantee to both you and the colonel that we're in this project to the end.'

'Okay, if that's what you want. It won't be too hard to set up the paperwork.'

There was a lot of handshaking at the end of the evening. I enjoyed shaking hands with Carl – it was like plunging your arms into a warm cement-mixer – comforting and dangerous at the same time. Even the restaurant manager was grinning broadly. He must have seen many business deals brokered at his tables, and the signs of a successful transaction seemed to please him immensely. I worried for a moment that he might invite us upstairs to sing.

Twenty Two

Talcum powder. It was a terrific idea.

I'd gotten up late on Saturday, nursing a small hangover. I hadn't drunk an awful lot at the meal the previous evening, but I seemed to get a hangover these days at the drop of a glass. Some people are just susceptible, I guess.

At around midday I'd climbed out onto my terrace – not the brightest move in the middle of January – and sat on the freezing metal chair from where I could gaze over the river. No, I can't see my office from here – that's half the point.

I had with me a litre-sized cafetiere of coffee to keep my mug topped up, and the colonel's so-called 'business plan'. A swig of coffee to fire up the grey cells, and then I turned the top page and started reading.

Our bogus business was to be centred around talcum-powder, of all things. Many cosmetics were tested on animals before getting anywhere near human skin, so that partly justified our need for a licence. The real reasons were subtler, though.

We had one colonel who had left the American army in order to set up in private business. Carl and Sylvester would also be greatly missed by their respective camps. The absence of the three men was enough to raise suspicion anywhere. But once they surfaced again in private enterprise, those suspicions could be easily allayed. The call of the mighty dollar was the first great understandable motive to Western civilisation. Buck-chasing was a valid, almost noble, reason to give up a life in the Civil Service. And certainly more believable than a sudden religious calling. The other very good reason for hiding behind talcum powder was the simple lack of interest. Hell, it's not as if we're cloning people here. Talc? Who gives a shit? It was perfect.

The colonel's wish-list was nowhere near as long as I'd expected. I had to find, effectively, a quiet location, with potential for development into a laboratory which, according to the colonel's notes, was a lot simpler than I would have imagined. I was, in fact, amazed what one could build a laboratory out of nowadays. The rest of his list consisted mostly of numbers of scientific glassware we'd need, chemicals and solutions and containers (even Tupperware, believe it or not). There was another column alongside all of these items containing an estimate of their cost, except for one or two items towards the end, which were listed 'Live Subjects'.

There were forty-four pages in Andrew's report, but the majority of it looked as though it had been drawn up by one of life's cheaper solicitors. Piss and wind, mostly. The real meat was hidden so deeply that anyone but the most avid trainspotter would have given up long before any of our legal sidestepping would have been spotted. In short, I was pretty pleased with the whole idea. It took me less than three mugs of thickening coffee to finish the report, and I dropped the sheaf of papers onto the table with something approaching relief. I was in, that was for sure. I'd been royally hooked.

What the hell was I going to tell Kathy?

Twenty Three

'Well?'

'Well what?'

'Well, what did he tell you?'

Kathy dropped the papers onto the table in front of her. 'The truth, mostly. He said he was getting involved in a project, swore me to secrecy, that was that. Not that I wasn't paying any attention to him, but the idea of secret projects left me cold. It all smacked of boy's own adventures, and I'd practically forgotten all about it until he left for Africa.'

'He didn't tell you he was going to be working on a cure for Alzheimer's?'

'Not exactly. He just told me it was in the pharmaceutical line, and reassured me there was a lot of money in pharmaceuticals. He seemed to think I'd find the idea of even more money reassuring.'

'You can never have too much, I suppose.'

'Ian could never get enough. That's half the problem.'

'What problem?'

'Look, I really don't want to discuss it. You read for a while. I think it'll sound more natural in a male voice anyway.'

'Could we just take a break for a while? You want more coffee? You hungry?'

'Okay, yeah. Good idea. Let's get out of here for a bit. We'll get some food at the pub.'

'You've got a pub here?' He'd seen nothing on their trip to suggest civilisation was just around the next corner. Perhaps just a county or two away.

'Not far. A couple of miles cross-country, but about twenty by road, so let's walk. I think you'll like it.'

'Sure. We gonna take that with us?' He waved at the pile of paper on the table.

Kathy's lip curled. 'No. Think not.'

Less than an hour later they crested a hill and the pub came into view. The Good Shepherd clung to the side of the next hill like a barnacle. So embedded in the hill, in fact, that it was impossible to judge where the rock ended and the pub began.

Paul pushed the door wide and stepped into the welcoming gloom. A pub was a pub no matter where you were, and you walked into them as though they were your own home. That was the theory, at least, and it had held him in good stead thus far.

It was different this time. As soon as he had opened his mouth to order at the bar, the conversation around him seemed to change into something unintelligible. In the gloom he could make out groups of twos and threes seated at tables. Here and there men drank alone and silent. A good fire was going in the grate, and the chimney had apparently not been swept in many years, its unwanted output adding to the gloom of the bar.

The barmaid, or possibly the landlady, was friendly enough. They managed to order a couple of ploughman's lunches, although it was nearer dinnertime, and then found themselves an unoccupied table as far from the fire as it was possible to get.

'I thought that was only a myth.' Paul spoke in a whisper.

Kathy regarded him. 'What was?'

'Welsh, Kath. The instant we came in they just started speaking in Welsh.'

'They *are* Welsh, Paul. What language did you expect them to speak? Honestly.'

'There's no need to raise your voice, Kath. And I'm not kidding. I heard at least two or three

English voices in here when we came in, but not a bloody sausage now.'

'You're being paranoid.'

'Not paranoi...' The food arrived, and Paul started on it with a gusto that surprised Kathy. She had not an iota of appetite, although she had been hungry enough on the walk there.

'Anyway,' she speared a pickled onion and swept it up in front of her face. 'That's not a problem we're going to be concerned with anyway. Ian will get here in a day or two at the latest.'

'And I suppose everything will be made clear then?'

'No idea. Is his journal not clear enough for you?'

'Clear as mud.'

'We've hardly started.'

'Yeah, I know. Change the subject.'

They ate in silence for a while. At least Paul ate, while Kathy pushed cheese and bread around her plate listlessly. There *was* no other subject. Around them the quiet murmur of the pub continued and Paul tried consciously not to stare at the regular denizens. Bar the landlady, Kathy was the only female in the place, and he was fairly certain that he was the only male under about fifty. Dark browns and greens surrounded him. Drab Tweeds and other cloths of similar ilk. For a few feet down from the ceiling the air was thick with a gunmetal-coloured haze of smoke from the various pipes and hand-rolled cigarettes that every occupant seemed to be puffing away at.

'You ever see "An American Werewolf In London"?'

'You baint be from around 'ere, be you?' Kathy chuckled. 'Yeah, I've seen it. Don't ee stray from the path.' She suppressed a giggle this time.'

'What was the name of the pub?'

'This one or the film one?'

'Film one.' Paul said through a mouthful of bread, wagging his fork around in a circle.

'The Slaughtered Lamb.'

'Yeah, that was it.'

'Afraid of the dark, Paul, is that it? Hairy monsters crossing our path home?'

He tried a withering look.

'I've brought a torch.'

'It's not even four o'clock yet.'

Kathy said nothing. Nature itself would answer his unspoken question. Mid-afternoon, in February, in this tiny Welsh valley, night would fall like a shutter. They'd both spent a lot of their lives in and around London, so she didn't want to spoil the surprise. In London, when dusk arrived, the inhabitants were protected from the gloom by an illuminated army of streetlights. You hardly even noticed the transition from day to night. Out here, however, things would prove very different indeed.

'Grizzly Adams, my arse,' she muttered, and forked out a bullet-sized chunk of celery just to pass the time.

Paul heard her, but her grin ensured he made nothing of it. He smiled himself. Things could have been worse, after all. Even if he found himself in hostile territory in the pitch black night, at least he was in the right company. He could think of more romantic venues, certainly, but that didn't mean the whole evening was bereft of potential.

Stop it. Stop it. I can't believe you even thought like that. That's just fucking *you* all over. Can you not behave like a gentleman for five minutes? Or even a day or two? It can't be that difficult, it really can't. Think about Ian. Now there's a bloke who really knows how to conduct himself. What if your situations had been reversed, eh? Would Ian have been behaving as badly as you? Practically salivating at the sight of her? Her red-brown hair? Her immense, impossible eyes? No, of course not. Because Ian knew how to conduct himself as a gentleman. A proper one, not the pseudo-gent wraith you're in danger of turning into.

I'm not Ian, though. Sorry Ian. Terribly sorry, old chap.

Kathy wondered where he'd gone. Typical Paul, really. The man could daydream at the drop of a nightcap – one of the reasons their relationship, so long ago now, had failed. He had never been there, even when he had been. His mind was always off exploring planets and spaces she'd never been privy to, much less invited to. It had driven her crazy at the time, and it was something she'd thought she'd never get used to, but when their relationship had feathered out to friendship she found her own reactions changing. She'd still no idea where he went in his dreams, or why, but she began to understand why he needed them. She could understand why he dreamt, if not what. And had they still been together, it would have been enough. Had he been less handsome, perhaps – his hair less dark, eyes less than striking blue – could it have worked then? Stop that thought, Kathy. You've got a perfectly serviceable future husband in Ian. Couldn't really ask for better than Ian, actually, short of the fact that he'd been about three thousand miles away for the past six months. Bar that, of course, everything was peachy. Still, it was nice to have Paul around, if only to remind her of who she was really missing.

'Kath?'

'Uh-huh?'

'You want another drink? Or are we done

here?'

She looked around. The pub had lost more than half its clientele, and outside the windows, well, outside the windows there was nothing. It was pitch black outside. Night had thumped down, as she'd predicted yet not really, wholly, expected.

'Not really.' Somewhere in the middle of her dreaming their plates had been cleared away. She had the vaguest half-memory of nodding her thanks to the landlady. 'We'd best be getting back anyway, don't you think?'

'Sure. Best we not stray from the path, either. Got your torch?'

The return journey seemed to take twice as long as the outward one, which probably wasn't that far from the truth. The moon was nothing but a slice in the sky overhead, and the only real light they had was supplied by Kathy's torch. So with linked arms they strode, stumbled, felt and fell their way home. Kathy uncorked a bottle of red wine once they were safely inside and waited while Paul struggled manfully to light the fire. It was his Grizzly Adams moment, after all, and she felt it would have been churlish to interrupt him with, say, the bottle of lighter fluid from the kitchen drawer.

'I want you to read the rest of it.' Kathy placed

their glasses on the table and prodded half-heartedly at the pile of paper. 'Like I said, it'll sound better, more natural, you know, in a male voice.'

'You just trying to get out of doing your fair share?'

'Don't know. Maybe.' Her eyes pleaded with him briefly. 'Look, I'll make a deal. I'll cook, okay? Dinner, breakfast, the lot. I just don't want to read that thing.'

'It really can't be that scary, Kath.' Paul stood up from his barely-raging fire and approached the formidable sheaf of papers on the table. 'It's only a bloody journal.'

'Yeah, I know,' she said, and sat herself in the corner of the sofa. 'You read it.'

Twenty Four

Kathy turned out to be less of a problem than I'd been anticipating, or perhaps she simply hadn't been listening to me properly. We're at that stage of our relationship where she's expecting me to pop the question. A stage I'm pretty sure most relationships reach, some sooner rather than later. We've been together seven years now, more or less, and I am sorely tempted. But I'm going to wait until this project is out of the way. That way, I reckon, I can devote myself full-time to a marriage, and a family. I might even retire, who knows? I think the colonel's plan has sown more than a few seeds of dissatisfaction with my present life.

So over dinner on Sunday she managed to convey a modicum of curiosity about my latest venture before losing interest entirely. It scarcely mattered at any rate – my decision had already been made. Callous that may sound, but it's just my way.

Once I get my teeth into something I find it next to impossible to concentrate on anything else.

So we met the next day, the colonel and I, over breakfast in The Lowdown, both of which he seemed to like.

'I've got a solicitor who can draw up a business contract for us,' I informed him.

'That was quick work.'

'Oh, he doesn't know about it yet, but that won't be a problem. He's quite tame – I've put enough work his way to ensure his discretion.'

'Useful chap. Now,' he folded his paper napkin, blotted his mouth with it and then threw it onto his empty plate. 'What say you and I spend a couple of days house-hunting?'

'You think it'll take that long?'

'No telling.'

'I suppose not.' I'd finished my breakfast and now looked around unsuccessfully for something to fiddle with. 'What are the specs for the sort of place you're after?'

'Wasn't that covered in the plan I gave you?'

'Outlined, certainly. But it would help if you gave me a little more detail. Something to help our mental images match.'

'Well, something like a barn conversion, or a farmhouse with a barn, even better. Needs to sleep three or four. Preferably four, as Sylvester, Carl and myself will be staying on-site, and you might need a room yourself on occasion. I wouldn't suggest it otherwise, but every now and then these things tend to run over a little.'

I shrugged. It would certainly be interesting to spend an evening or two with these people, but there was no way I would commit to living full-time in any sort of laboratory.

'We need an extra couple of rooms for offices, mine and Carl's. One for yourself if you're not going to be doing the paperwork from here. A separate barn, now I've thought about it, would be ideal. We can rig up a lab in a barn with the minimum amount of fuss.'

'Is that all?' I asked. I watched his expression closely for signs of having missed my English irony. It's all-too-well documented that they have none in The United States.

'Indoor swimming-pool, Olympic-size, unheated, for cold storage of various cultures.'

I raised my eyebrows at this. Sounded dangerous.

He laughed out loud. Touché.

'Okay,' I stood up. 'Let's go hunting.'

We found one that same day, of all miracles. It was larger than we needed, with seven bedrooms, two reception rooms – whatever they're for, and the rest. It also had a barn. Stuck in the West Country, on the edge of the New Forest, it would be an awful commute, but the colonel loved it on first sight, and he wouldn't have to travel to and from the place all the time. It had been standing empty for an unspecified number of months, so I sicced my pet solicitor onto the agent to haggle on my behalf. He was very good, I'll grant that much. It took four days to get the papers in my hand, and the following week the colonel moved his team in.

I left them alone for the first week of their occupancy. They were professionals after all, and probably didn't need someone like me around until they were settled in. What use would I have been anyway? I wouldn't have known the front of a lab from the back, and when it came to DIY I was more amateur than artisan. Besides, I had enough on my plate at the office, settling Kevan down to his new duties.

Andrew had left it to me to oversee the more mundane, yet very necessary factors. I had to organise the reconnection of gas and electricity, and the installation of three phone lines and an ISDN line for the internet connection they wanted. The boring bit. Slightly more fun was the ordering of their computers and I chose to deliver them myself early in the second week. That was the first time I met Sylvester Candy, too.

Twenty Five

'Good morning,' I waved at Carl, who was stripped to the waist, making the most of the rare May sunshine. He was sawing something or other up. I stepped down out of the rental van and approached him.

'Ian. Good to see you, my man.' He thrust another of his incredible handshakes my way. 'Everything is coming along nicely, as you'll see soon enough. The colonel's fast asleep, so let's go meet Sly first. He's in the barn.' He waved a hand that way, ushering me on.

'Asleep?'

'He keeps some pretty crazy hours, so me and Sly are hammering and sawing as quietly as we can,' Carl grinned broadly. 'Sly!' he shouted as we pushed open the barn's enormous door.

'Up here,' a voice sounded from somewhere in the rafters toward the back of the cavernous barn.

Its owner was invisible.

I stood in the doorway and looked around the place. When I'd seen it a fortnight previously it had been dusty and dingy, with straw scattered everywhere, and old tools abandoned haphazardly. It had also smelled. Animal smell, mostly, but also engine oil: machinery smells. And the roof and walls had both let in plenty of light through their many cracks and fissures.

The last week must have been strenuous, to say the least. The floor had been concreted, and the walls sealed, with an internal plasterboard skin. The paint-job, all white, was half-finished already, with what Carl explained to me as a thick coat of rubber-based paint, which would be applied several times over, effectively making the structure airtight. Where the panels met, he pointed out, they would apply a thick neoprene gel, which turned out to be a colourless sealant – a little like the gunk you'd line the edge of a bathtub with. There was a chalk line across the floor about ten feet inside the door. I asked Carl about it.

'What you've got, see, is one structure, the lab, inside another, the barn. That line will be the front of the lab, and the space between the lab door and the barn door will be a decontamination area. We're also going to put up a false, flat roof on the lab, say eleven, twelve feet up. Before we do that, though, we've got to weatherproof the outside of the barn.'

'You make it sound straightforward enough.'

'It's gone pretty smooth so far. The only outside help we needed was for the concrete floor. We had a team lay it down on the second day, and had to wait two more for it to set. When the walls are finished, I'll seal the floor too.'

Sylvester dropped to the floor at the far end of the barn and approached us at a trot, his hand held out in greeting to me. I took it.

'Nice to finally meet you. Heard a lot about you,' he rattled out in quick fire tones, his syllables running all over each other as he spoke.

He was a compact man. Wiry, bordering on skinny. And pale too, as though he hadn't seen sunlight for a very long time. Straggly black hair fell in a mop over his shoulders, and I assumed this to be one of the privileges of working as a civilian in a military organisation.

'Carl showing you round the place?' he asked as he hopped from foot to foot.

'I've only just got here, but what I've seen so far is pretty impressive.'

'We eating yet?' He shot his next question at Carl.

'I'll get something started. You wanna show Ian round the rest?'

'You haven't seen the house yet?'

'Only the outside.'

'Come on, then.' He spread his arms and swept us both out of the barn.

The farmhouse, from my first sighting of it, had looked beautiful. The yard we were crossing was dusty, and would turn easily to deep mud with a day or two of rain. There were signs here and there of its previous life as a working farm. A roll of chickenwire leant against the barn, and there remained a run-down pen of sorts at the end of the yard, where another barn-like structure loomed. This one, however, consisted only of a roof and two side walls, the front and rear open to the elements. I had no idea what it may once have housed, only that it probably hadn't been livestock. Somewhere to park the tractor and the ubiquitous four-wheel drive, I supposed.

The farmhouse itself was whitewashed, and boasted a slate roof, as opposed to the thatching so beloved of the tourist trade. They would have been delighted, however, by the front door. It was a stable door, the top half of which was swung wide open. Very authentic, I felt. Carl reached in and unbolted the bottom half, leading us straight into the kitchen.

'I'm gonna whip up a little breakfast here,' he announced. 'Sly, you let the colonel know, would ya?'

'Sure. I'll catch him on the tour. Let me show you round,' he added to me.

I followed him through the kitchen into the living room, off which led another two doors. Sylvester led me round, jabbering away like an estate agent all the while.

'We're stripping out the three downstairs bedrooms – they'll be offices for Andrew and Carl, and yourself, if you need it.'

'What about you?'

'I'm not the office sort.' He gave me a grin. 'Don't need one, really. Any paperwork I generate is already covered either by yourself or the colonel. The upstairs bedrooms we'll be leaving as they are, and there's a bathroom on each floor.'

Sylvester sprang up the stairs ahead of me, pointing at things I either didn't see or didn't appreciate. I struggled to keep up with him. A lightning inspection of the upstairs rooms ended at the colonel's bedroom, the last in the corridor. Andrew Marten was sitting on the edge of his bed, gazing out of the window. He turned to greet us as we entered. There was a suggestion of grogginess about his eyes, and I guessed he'd just rolled out of sleep, fully dressed.

'Ian. Sly. This'll be my breakfast call, I take it?'

'When we first talked about the lab, I

imagined chemicals and solutions and all sorts of bottles and bell-jars. I hadn't imagined the need for all this air-tight apparatus.' In truth, the part I hadn't imagined was a decontamination unit. That had spooked me. When the colonel had first told me of Carl and his connection to USAMRIID, I had taken it solely as evidence of the man's established professionalism. But a decontamination chamber? What else did we have in common with USAMRIID? If I was going to be working within ten miles of one of those awful viruses I wanted to know about it.

We were sitting around the kitchen table, swallowing post-breakfast coffee. The colonel put paid to my apprehensions without being aware of it.

'The laboratory is sealed from the outside world so we can be sure of no contamination. Any factor we can't control can screw our results.'

'Like Fleming and his penicillin,' Sylvester chipped in, 'except his was a luckier break than most.'

'Keeping the outside world on the outside has always been one of the most difficult tasks,' the colonel continued. 'The most likely contaminants will be ourselves, and whatever we bring into the lab, so the decon chamber is what we use on the way in. It's not much more than a glorified scrub-up room, but it should be pretty much all we need.'

While the colonel cleared up the breakfast ruins, the rest of us unloaded the boxes I had brought down. Sylvester's eyes lit up at the sight of all that hardware. Electronics and computing were his first love, I was to learn later, but there seemed to be nothing he couldn't turn his hand to. He was supercharged, that man. I couldn't believe how much energy God had managed to pack into such a tiny frame. Sylvester stood a little over shoulder-height to me – I guess around five-foot five or six – but what he lacked in stature he more than made up for in sheer drive. We hit it off, as Carl had promised, famously.

It was dusk by the time I finally left them. I'd had a pretty full day of it, and wasn't looking forward to the four-hour return journey. I climbed up into the cab and swung the van slowly round and out of the yard, the colonel and his team watching me go, waving me off. I felt, now that I had seen them in action, that we had finally started something.

Twenty Six

For the next three months I pretty much left them to it. The colonel kept in touch by phone a couple of times a week, but there was little to report. Every couple of weeks I'd drop in on them, occasionally with the pretext of bringing them some new piece of kit, but more often than not empty-handed.

I stayed with them a few times, occupying the fourth bedroom after long evenings spent talking in aimless circles with Sylvester. His company grew very quickly on me, and he was never boring, seeming to know a little of everything, and not a few bawdy jokes and stories. Our talks were accompanied by either wine or whisky each time – what he liked to call "bachelor fuel".

We swapped life stories, and he made me feel horribly unaccomplished. He'd graduated at twenty-two, and had spent the next two and a half years globetrotting on a budget of next to nothing. He'd taught English in South American rainforests and African deserts, picked fruit in the Australian Outback, and built irrigation systems in India. His last great dream was China, which he'd not yet visited, and he was planning to use his share of the proceeds from this project to do the trip in comfort. I envied his experiences, but his modesty was enough to prevent me envying the man himself.

Carl Jones and Andrew Marten seemed to live in each other's pockets for most of the time although, unlike the colonel, Carl had a fairly rigid self-discipline. He was an early riser, and never too late to bed in the evenings. He could put his work down, leave it behind him, while he got on with the day-to-day business of eating, sleeping and relaxing. He believed that his downtime from working was as important as the work itself. Claimed it kept his mind sharp.

The colonel, on the other hand, seemed unable to switch off. His work dominated his every waking moment, and engaging him in conversation unrelated to it was a haphazard endeavour. He'd drift off into some unfathomable internal reverie, only snapping out of it when you addressed him directly, and then only with some reluctance. And he had been having trouble sleeping, according to Sylvester, who worried about him constantly.

'He's heading for a serious burnout,' he informed me late one night.

Carl had excused himself to bed a couple of hours previously and the colonel had only just returned from the laboratory, heading straight to his office where he would shut himself away until the small hours, hammering away at his keyboard and chewing the ends off all his pencils.

'It's been the same routine for at least a month now. He can't keep it up. Nobody could.' Sylvester was speaking in little more than a whisper, although the colonel had no chance of hearing us from his office. Even if he could, our voices would have been nothing but white noise to him, washing over his head, unimportant and unrelated to anything he cared about.

Carl and Sylvester made allowances for his workaholic tendencies, taking on the more mundane everyday tasks themselves, such as the cooking of meals and washing of clothes.

'He can't cook for shit anyhow,' Sylvester explained with a smirk.

I collared Carl the following morning, when he was making breakfast.

'Should I be worrying about him?'

'He's always been the same, Ian. I'd only worry if he stopped. The only thing that keeps him happy is his work. I doubt the colonel has a carefree bone in his body.'

I was only a little happier after that morning, but I learned to accept the colonel's way of doing things soon enough. I suppose I had little choice in the matter really, but I hoped the colonel's relentlessness paid off sooner rather than later, for all our sakes.

As the months passed, and the money dripped slowly out of our budget, I looked to Andrew more and more often for results I knew I couldn't have. I deliberately tried not to push the man, but my natural inquisitiveness got the better of me in the end. He stopped taking my calls – preferring to delegate to Carl or Sylvester, which didn't improve my mood in the slightest. And it wasn't as though I had anything to truly worry about. All the money I had poured into this project amounted to a tiny proportion of my net worth. It wasn't like I couldn't afford to lose the project, far from it. So why did I find it taking up such a disproportionate amount of my time? Time which I spent needlessly worrying?

And then four months in, somewhere in the middle of September, the first breakthrough came. Jokingly, we referred to it as the "Night of the Mice". Very James Herbert.

Twenty Seven

'Didn't he talk to you about any of this?'

It took Kathy a moment to realise that Paul wasn't quoting from the journal but was, in fact, asking her a direct question.

'Yes, of course he did. But like I said before, only generalities.' Sometime in the last hour she'd joined him on the sofa, and now she turned to face him, drawing her knees up in front of her. 'But he's been so distracted for so long. I suppose he's been worrying about the money he's been spending. That would be too much like him.'

'Even though he claims it's a drop in the ocean?'

'Look after the pennies, that's his motto.'

'My mother used to say the same thing.'

'You never listened, though.'

'No.' Paul grabbed up the coffee mugs and

repaired to the kitchen. Kathy spent the next twenty minutes unsuccessfully trying to find an acceptable radio station on Ian's state-of-the-art monstrosity. Expensive as it may have been, it was still unable to tune into a half-decent show. Kathy supposed that was hardly the manufacturer's fault, however. She settled for an Alanis Morissette CD, her favourite wailer.

'Smells good,' she said, settling herself against the edge of the kitchen doorway and accepting the glass of Merlot he held out to her. 'What is it?'

'Pasta with stuff in it.' He spread an arm wide and offered up a grin. She feared he might take a bow. 'A perennial bachelor favourite.'

'Pasta surprise, huh? I don't recall you having any Italian girlfriends.'

'I don't learn all my skills at the hands of women, no matter what you may think.'

'I'll bet you cook up a great Swedish number though, don't you?'

'I won't even dignify that with a reply.'

Kathy gave him a puzzled look. 'But haven't you just...'

'Don't,' he warned.

'Have it your way.'

She watched him mill about the kitchen for a while, hunting out interesting ingredients and adding them to the pot randomly.

'You're making this up as you go along, are you not?'

'Uh-huh.'

He had his concentrating face on, a frown at the top of his head and the tiny pink tip of his tongue pressing on his top lip. She decided to let him be for a while, taking what little pleasure she could in watching him work. After enough time as she considered decent, she refilled their glasses.

'You ever meet them?' He broke both the silence and her daydreaming.

'Who?'

'The colonel, Carl, Sylvester. Ian's mates.'

'Christ, no. That was business. You'd never catch Ian mixing me up with business.'

'You never pushed him on it?'

'In the very early days, sure, I'd push him on most things. But you know him as well as I do. Tight as a clam.'

'Get the table made up, this is nearly done.'

'Yessir,' Kathy performed a very brief curtsey and left.

Paul tasted his mixture, stirred it a little more, and let out an inaudible sigh. This was his idea of heaven. Good food, good wine, beautiful company, and all three trapped in a self-contained Eden miles from civilisation. If it had been any girl other than Kathy.

If it *had* been any other girl he wouldn't be in such turmoil now. Her presence did more than just warm him. He could feel the heat of her like an oven, slowly cooking him. Her heat burned through his skin, leaving him crispy on the outside. All his internal organs were melted and dripping, their fat spitting. He was the human barbecue, a spit-roast of confused desire. She only had to touch him to burn him.

'Hell, I'm toast.' He shook his head, holding back either a healthy laugh or a nervous giggle, he wasn't sure which. Self-consciously, he cast off the spell, and loaded up two plates with his "pasta surprise".

Kathy attacked the meal with some vigour. It shouldn't come as a surprise, Paul thought, as she'd hardly touched a thing at lunch.

'Remind me to feed and water the mice,' Kathy spoke through a mouthful.

' "Night Of The Mice". Dun-dun-dah,' he growled out. 'I can hardly wait for that bit. Sounds scary.'

Kathy didn't bother replying. Her eating slowed, and she couldn't meet his gaze, choosing instead to stare out at the blackness beyond the windows.

'Sorry. I know you must be worried.'

'It's not you, Paul. Your flippancy is the only

thing that's keeping me on the rails as it is. It's just...'

'Just what?' he asked, cursing himself at the same time for his impatience.

'Just that I wish I knew what I was supposed to be worried about, that's all. Be nice to have a target, you know. Somewhere to aim the worry.'

'Yeah, I do understand, believe it or not. But I hardly think it can be life-threatening, whatever it is.'

'What about the warning?'

'I think we should just wait and see what the journal has to say, and Ian himself when he gets here, before we get too paranoid, or jump to any conclusions we don't need, that's all.'

'Yeah, I know. Sorry. I just can't help worrying.' Her eating had slowed almost to a standstill, and she was aimlessly twirling her fork through the pasta now.

'I'll remind you.'

'What?'

'To feed the mice.'

'Oh, thanks.'

'And I'll keep you safe.'

She smiled to herself, said nothing at all, and finally forked some pasta into her mouth.

'Were there no warning signs at all before he

left?' They were in the living-room now, their glasses recharged and their stomachs full. Kathy had managed to eat most of her meal in the end, and had pronounced it delicious. Paul had considered it barely worthy.

He knew that he was now supposed to carry on his reading, but he felt like procrastinating a while longer yet. The journal wasn't going anywhere and neither were they.

'He seemed distracted for a long time, for months really. I'd thought it was me, to be honest. I'd thought maybe our relationship was going off the boil, something like that.'

'He mentioned marriage in the journal.'

'Yeah, I know. Never gave a hint of it to me though.'

'Always been a bit of a cold fish, our Ian.'

Kathy looked squarely at him. 'Every man I've ever known is a so-called cold fish. It's a man thing. It's what you do.'

'Well, no…'

'Well, yes. Even you, Paul. Sometimes especially you.'

He'd never seen it that way. At least he thought he hadn't. Sure, there were some things you simply couldn't discuss with a woman. Some things you couldn't talk about with anyone, but that hardly made him cold now, did it?

'That's the main reason we split, didn't you realise that at the time?'

'I reminded you of a fish?'

'Lack of communication, you half-wit. You know what I meant.'

'I thought women liked the strong, silent types.'

'You weren't supposed to be silent *all* the time, on *every* subject.'

Yeah. Jesus. Okay. Point taken. But he didn't voice this out loud. This was the last place he'd have expected an argument. And wasn't her timing simply the greatest?

'Why are you telling me this, all of ten years too late?'

'You think of a better time?'

What had gotten her so angry, so steamed up now of all times? It had to be Ian, of course. She was transferring all of her worry and frustration onto him simply because he was closer, attainable. Fair play. He couldn't say he wouldn't have done the same thing.

'I know what I am, Kathy. I don't need you to enlighten me on my bad points.'

'You need someone,' she said sulkily.

'I'm a typical man. Selfish and self-involved. Emotionally cold and ideologically unsound. I'm aware of all that. Are you aware of exactly what a typical woman you are?'

'You're not throwing this back in my face, not a chance.'

'It takes two to make a relationship work, Kathy. It only takes one to end it.'

Shit. That had torn it. He'd been doing so well too, he thought bitterly.

She said nothing. She didn't have to. Her arms were folded across her chest and her eyes burned at him. And then she seemed to let the moment pass. Paul wondered if she'd counted to ten in her head, but wasn't willing himself to push the matter further. He figured he'd done enough.

They stayed that way for a number of minutes. Her standing now, staring out of the window again, waiting for God-knew-what, while he waited on the sofa, with no idea of whether she would turn into a volcano or a fluffy cloud.

More time passed, incredibly slowly. Paul could feel the weight of the minutes themselves, kicking and slapping him as they thudded past on leaden soles. He felt there hadn't yet been a hole discovered big enough to swallow him now. The Grand Canyon, pah! A chicken-scratch. The Mariana Trench little better than a knifed-out groove in a schoolboy's desktop. A black hole perhaps, now *there* was potential. But where would you find a black hole when you needed one?

Eventually she answered his doubts for him. She sat down once more on the sofa next to him and topped up their glasses once more. Fluffy cloud had defeated the volcano, it seemed.

'You're supposed to be reading, remember?'

Without another word, he picked up a handful of paper from the top of the pile and did, for once in his life, exactly as he was told.

Twenty Eight

Summer was pushing on, relentless as ever. I still remembered 1976, the heatwave, and the Jubilee the following year. As a child, it had seemed never-ending, unstoppable. We don't seem to get those glorious summers any more – or is it just me?

I hadn't seen the team in well over a month. For whatever reason; reasons I can't recall now, I'd not bothered to take the trip south to visit. I probably had money on my mind – that was my usual excuse for remaining a hermit.

So I'd decided to invite myself down for a day or two. This wasn't strictly spur-of-the-moment. The colonel had told me in his last call that they were preparing an important experiment and he thought I might be interested in observing, or even taking part. This last part sounded worrying, and I questioned him on it.

'I didn't mean we wanted to experiment on

you, Ian. We have subjects for that. I mean we could use an extra hand for observation, that's all.'

'Observation?'

'Sure. It'll make more sense when you see the setup. Interested?'

'Yeah, 'course I'm interested. When do we start?'

'Come down Thursday. We'll be ready for you by then.'

So I found myself back at the farm. I had no equipment to bring this time, so I made the journey in comfort, in the Lexus I'd finally decided to pamper myself with. Andrew and Carl met me at the door, waving me through to the kitchen. Sylvester was hidden away in the barn, apparently making some last minute checks and whatever adjustments he felt necessary.

The kitchen table, an enormous and sturdy wooden affair, seemed to have become the centre of operations. It was covered in piles of papers, notepads and a fruitbowl containing every colour of biro and pencil your average five-year-old could wish for. Although I was hardly intimate with the team as yet, I could tell in a single glance where each of them sat, just by the arrangement of detritus in front of each chair. The strangest thing was exactly how un-strange I found this scene. It seemed the most natural thing in the world and,

God knows, I wished half my operations could run this cosily.

The colonel settled himself at the table and waved at the chair opposite, inviting me to join him. I did, while Carl sorted out some coffee for the three of us.

'Are you hungry?' he asked me as I gained my seat. 'I can whip you something up no trouble at all.'

'I'm fine, thanks,' I reassured him. I had the impression that Carl may have missed his true calling as a celebrity chef. He seemed to be constantly on the verge of "whipping something up". 'I grabbed a bite on the way down,' I added.

He didn't bother to answer me, expending his energy instead on throwing me a disappointed look before he brought the coffee over. We managed to kill an entire half-hour with small talk, the majority of which I've forgotten, which is probably a blessing. Andrew brought me roughly up to speed with their progress, of which I understood a little less than half. On the points I fell down, Carl reassured me that it would all make a lot more sense later, when I'd seen some results. Of course, as soon as he'd said this, Andrew jumped in and explained that there may very well be no results at all, effectively undoing all of Carl's good work.

A couple of hours after my arrival, around

three in the afternoon, Sylvester burst into the kitchen. It was the only entrance, I'd decided, that he was capable of making. The man had that much energy.

'Ready for the rat-race?' he jabbered breezily.

'Sit yourself down and have coffee,' Carl intoned, his voice a soothing, calming antidote to Sylvester's over-enthusiasm.

While Sylvester drank his coffee, he explained to me the coming evening's experiment. I could tell he was struggling to pace himself – to measure his words out carefully, but he soon lapsed into his usual hypersonic babble. I got the gist of it, though.

'We've got a dozen mazes set up in the lab. Each about half the size of a snooker table. Perspex top, interchangeable gates, and cameras. That was probably the most expensive part – twelve high resolution video cameras, one for each run. As you're gonna be joining us, we'll have three subjects each – we're using white mice. I'll go through the details on the clipboard later.'

'Just tell me what I have to do.' I aimed this at Sylvester, expecting him to rattle off another enormously forgettable list of tasks for me, but Carl stepped in immediately, outlining the details in his easy-listening tones.

'When you carry out an experiment like this,

it's best to try to keep as many common, non-variable factors as you can from the start. So all the mice are male, all the mazes arranged to the same route. Even the cameras are the same make and model. The only varying factor will be the injections we'll be giving them.'

'Injections?'

'Of course. You didn't think we'd been sitting on our butts down here, did you? We've got eleven viable compounds and one placebo – a mouse who won't receive any injection – who'll be our control subject.'

'It sounds like you've made some incredible progress. It's only been a couple of months.'

'There was remarkably little to do, to tell you the truth,' Carl continued. 'Ninety nine percent of the theory had already been carried out by the colonel here. All we really have to do is translate his theory onto the practical landscape.'

'Easier said than done, though, let me assure you,' the colonel said. 'Without Carl and Sylvester's practical minds my original ideas would have remained exactly that. Ideas, dreams.'

'Shall we take a bow?' Sylvester asked Carl, who replied with a grin. 'Seriously though, it's getting on.' He made a display of consulting his watch. 'Let's get a meal inside of us and get on with it, shall we?'

Which was exactly what we did. An hour later the colonel was showing me how to scrub up properly. There was even a little nail-brush which, considering I regularly bit mine to the quick, seemed pretty superfluous. I used it anyway, making my pink fingertips even pinker than they had been. Not to mention sore. Once the scrubbing had been taken care of, I was invited to don a gown of the sort I'd only previously seen on television, in the sort of trash that Kathy had been a fan of – hospital dramas and the like. Suitably scrubbed and garbed, we entered the laboratory.

Set out in four rows of three were the mazes. Each one was identical – about waist-high and topped with perspex, just as Sylvester had described. All the mazes were set to the same route, cheese at one end and mouse at the other. The tiny starting compartments were barely larger than the mice themselves, and above each compartment was a rubber seal through which the hypodermic needles would be pushed. Sylvester noted the look of trepidation on my face and volunteered to inject my subjects.

'What's the best way to inject a mouse?' he asked me.

'Uh, very carefully?'

'Right. Old joke.'

On top of each maze was a stopwatch, and a

clipboard on which we were supposed to make notes. The colonel showed me what he was after.

'This is only the first experiment,' he explained, 'so we don't need any in-depth analysis of the subjects' behaviour. Make the injection, start the stopwatch – this button,' he demonstrated, 'and lift the gate. This'll be mostly a watching game, unless anything extraordinary happens. Make a note of the time and speed of each subject, and then we'll start it all over again.'

'What do you mean by extraordinary?' I asked him. 'I don't know what ordinary mice can get up to, let alone extraordinary ones.'

'You know, exploding, growing wings, turning green,' Carl said in dead-pan tones.

'Anything that strikes you as odd, that's all,' the colonel reassured me.

Then he handed out the syringes, three each. Sylvester administered the doses to my charges, making sure I had the hang of the stopwatch and starting gates, before returning to his own end of the lab. I was in charge now of M10, M11, and M12 – the control subject. All our mice had codenames. When I pointed out the fact that they were all named after famously dangerous British motorways I was answered with a trio of American shrugs that seemed to say "Well, we hadda call them something." M12 received a placebo, the lucky blighter. This was the inert solution in which the colonel had cultured the drugs for the other mice. I could pretty much rest assured that M12 would eat his fill that day.

The cameras were all rolling, the injections administered, and all the tiny gates lifted, and then we waited, and the mice waited, and time held its breath momentarily.

Most of the mice took off soon enough, presumably glad to be out of their confined starting compartments, and drawn on by the smell of cheese which by then must have been flooding the maze. Only M2 remained where he was, and he was Sylvester's charge. The subject had apparently gone into extreme catatonia the moment he had been injected, and I could see the sadness in Sylvester's face as he watched the little creature stiffen and collapse without even venturing out into his private domain.

Sylvester Candy, supercharged little hardcase that he appeared from the outside, had a true soft spot for animals. He was aware of the nature of the colonel's work, and he had been the one to select and collect the subjects, knowing that there was an ever-present danger of losing one or more of them before the end of the project. All this prior knowledge could do nothing whatsoever to mask his unhappiness.

He watched the mouse for a few minutes more, his attention barely wavering to his other two charges but eventually, when there was no sign of change in the animal, he pulled himself together and concentrated fully on Ms 1 and 3. Carl had care of M4, M5 and M6, while the colonel looked over mice 7, 8 and 9. I watched Sylvester scribble a quick note on M2's pad, look at his watch and then scribble again before ignoring the subject for the rest of the experiment.

All of our little charges were wearing tiny collars, which transmitted their life-signs to a remote station. This computer kept track of the invisible signs of their progress, and displayed them on one screen for us. Twelve green heartbeats blipping across that one black screen. Eleven now: M2 having relinquished his tiny grip on this mortal coil. Remarkable technology, but I couldn't help wondering if the bloody thing would provide us with a colourful little pie-chart at the end of all this.

And then one of Carl's charges, M4, which had been progressing steadily through the maze, following its nose, dropped flat, apparently comatose. It was not dead, he knew that much. He could see from the remote monitor that its heart was still beating, and that it had simply fallen flat and seemed content to stay that way. Carl made a few notes, glanced at his watch, and moved on again.

The silence in the room enveloped me. It struck me that this was the only time I had seen these men truly at work. When I'd seen Sylvester hammering a nail or Carl sawing timber – well, that hadn't been their work, that had been simply preparation. Now I saw the three of them enwrapped in their true work. Sylvester's tongue on his top lip, Carl's face as untroubled as the colonel's was furrowed. Andrew Marten's frown seemed to burn out from his forehead. This was their natural state, I realised, and I felt oddly privileged to have witnessed it.

Then we heard the most peculiar drumming noise coming from the colonel's area, and Marten himself looked up at us quizzically when he realised we were all staring towards him. He muttered something under his breath, shaking his head gently, and returned to his studies. The rest of us stayed at our posts for the duration, but when we saw the replay on camera it seemed his subject, M9, had beaten itself to death against the walls of its maze, repeatedly butting its head and thrashing its body around. Its death throes were agonising to watch.

It was only a couple of minutes after this incident that one of my own subjects, M10, went into similar convulsions, and started chasing its tail and thrashing around, in obvious misery. It didn't last very long, and the animal's panic seemed to turn into resignation as it gave up the fight for life.

And then things started to happen all at once. M1 and M3, Sylvester's remaining subjects, both went into paroxysms and died, M1 shuddering and twitching horribly, and M3 bleeding profusely from the mouth and nose and anus. M6, Carl's only survivor if you didn't include the comatose M4, started scratching and kicking at one of the walls until its claws bled. M7 started retching blood and spluttering helplessly, while M8 seemed to grow dizzy and disoriented, and wandered in decreasing circles until it collapsed.

Everybody was scribbling away at various notepads. I scribbled too, although to be perfectly honest I had no idea what I was supposed to be scribbling. Did all this constitute extraordinary mouse behaviour? I supposed it could, as I couldn't imagine the natural death of a mouse would approach quite this level of insanity.

M11, one of the two remaining mice I was playing God to, showed no ill-effects whatsoever and M12, the control, was also acting normally. After a few more minutes I had Sylvester at my elbow, and he was peering in at M11 with me, but keeping a respectful silence and allowing me to make whatever notes I could dream up without interruption. All his mice had died, as had Andrew's, and he joined us soon after. Carl made a few last checks on his comatose 4, and then wandered over to maze 11 to join us. I was quietly glad of their company. There was little interest in M12, as he was behaving exactly as was expected of him.

M11 fascinated us, though. It took him exactly four minutes and twenty seconds to find the prize the first time around. If the drug we had introduced was to be proven more fully then he would have to run the maze several more times. Even if he managed to get straight to his target on the second run it wouldn't be proof enough of the colonel's drug – the creature might simply have a naturally good memory. We'd have to run a whole gamut of tests before the slightest conclusion could be made. It was a very complicated maze, though, and ordinarily we wouldn't have expected any creature to remember the correct route after only one attempt.

Nevertheless, following the rest of the day's tragedies we found that our hopes were extraordinarily high. Perhaps, in the manner of drowning men, we were clutching at straws. Even so, we all stood there silently, studying M11 on his route around the walls we had fabricated for him, not one of us expecting him to reach the end. Thankfully, ultimately, he realised his goal and disappointed our fears.

We said not a word between us as the colonel broke the airtight seal and lifted the perspex top. He retrieved the mouse and returned it to the starting point, and then slid the perspex back into place. We set M11 off to run again.

He barely hesitated. Only one wrong turn and he was once again at the cheese. It was marvellous. Sylvester couldn't stop grinning, while Carl shook his head from side to side and the colonel simply stood there with his hands folded across his chest, as if he expected no less from his tiny subjects. We looked at each other, and then we looked at the mouse again, and then we didn't know where to look.

Then without warning M11 threw up on the cheese he was attempting to eat. The tiny creature vomited and retched and then began to back away from the food as though it were an enemy. It looked bewildered, uncertain. The same could probably have been said of us, and not an eye wavered from the animal as it backed itself into a corner. Its pink eyes glazed and it pulled its lips back in a sneer-snarl, its body trembling and twitching. Then, after convulsive jerks and spasms, M11 went catatonic and died moments later, the remote sensor showing nothing but a single flat line in place of the heartbeat that had once held so much promise for all of us.

The passing of M11 was a horrible moment for us. Sylvester and I remained absolutely silent. I knew he was as shocked and as horrified as I was. The colonel spat terse instructions at Carl, to clean the place down and get it ready for another trial, and then he followed Sylvester and I through the sealed exit. We said not a word to each other. Sylvester and I exchanged a few glances – glances we would have kept to ourselves in other, lighter circumstances. The colonel looked as though he might explode at any moment. He was the first to leave the barn, and I could hear his heavy footsteps cross the yard on the way back to the farmhouse.

'He's as pissed as the rest of us.' Sylvester looked in my eyes as he uttered the words. 'By tomorrow he'll have forgotten it. And maybe you should, too.'

He was right, I knew, and I tried to excuse myself from the scene as fast as was conscientiously decent. I was following the colonel's footsteps across the yard a few minutes later. It's one thing to be in the company of friends with tales to tell, either of success or of failure. There is always, without fail, a good mix of the two, and at evening's end there is a feeling of closure, of balance. There was no balance now, however. Four men sharing the same singular failure, that was how it felt, unbalanced somehow.

The colonel and I shared the kitchen table while Sylvester quietly volunteered himself for coffee duty. The silence was almost unbearably heavy. Andrew Marten looked devastated and angry by turns. His lifetime's accumulation of work was sunk into the laboratory across the yard, and he was not a man to take such a setback lightly. I tried to avoid watching his glowering features – it was doing nothing for my mood whatsoever. Sylvester, more used to it than me, fared better, but he managed to stop himself short of whistling a ditty, out of respect for the colonel's blackened temperament.

The top shutter of the kitchen door swung suddenly, violently inward. The timing would have been comical almost anywhere else. The shutter caught Sylvester in the back, and he dropped two mugs of scalding coffee straight onto the table, where they exploded messily over me and the colonel. We both leapt to our feet, our chairs crashing to the floor. The colonel, much respect to his self-control, managed to avoid a stream of expletives and settled for an angry grunt. I let mine fly freely, however. Self-control had never been one of my stronger points.

Framed in the upper half of the kitchen

doorway was the imposing figure of Carl, who looked as though he'd been struck by lightning. The look of amazement passed quickly from his face, but his eyes remained wide, staring.

'M4,' he managed to get out in a gasp.

We stood still for a moment, regarding him stupidly, paralysed with incomprehension.

'Come *on*.' He turned on his heels and raced back across the yard.

There'd been no mistaking the urgency in either his voice or actions, and a nanosecond or two later we were scrambling through the door after him.

Carl hadn't bothered with the niceties at the lab's entrance, and we followed suit, crashing straight into the lab without stopping to wash our hands or wipe our feet. We clustered around the M4 maze.

'You must be joking,' Sylvester blurted out. 'He'll never do it.'

He was missing the most obvious point though, which Andrew pointed out.

'M4 was registered comatose. He was under for nearly an hour.'

Carl simply shrugged and replied, 'not anymore.'

He had arranged the maze in what looked to be a ridiculous fashion. There was an open route from mouse to cheese, that much he pointed out to us. The more unconventional part was that at the start both mouse and cheese were separated only by a single partition. The mouse was sitting right next to the cheese. Although he couldn't see the prize itself, the scent of it was going to be stronger in his nostrils here than at any other point in the maze. To get to the cheese he would have to move away from the scent, and that struck us as against any form of known animal behaviour.

We were proved immediately, wonderfully wrong. M4 must have realised immediately that he could not reach his goal through the partition and, as soon as Carl opened his miniature door, he raced out along the first corridor, away from the scent. His route took him around the entire perimeter in the most roundabout fashion Carl could devise. The four of us remained silent and transfixed as M4 made unbelievably short work of the maze. He made only one mistake, when he went running off along the wrong corridor. When this happened the colonel leaned back a little, folded his arms and donned a more comfortable, smug look that said, 'I thought as much.'

However, his contentment was extremely short-lived as M4, already halfway down the corridor, apparently realised his mistake, abruptly turned round, and raced off again. The colonel's face dropped just a little and it was Carl's turn to look smug, which he did with a certain degree of expertise. It took M4 a little under one minute to locate the cheese.

It was late afternoon, but we got so carried away with M4 that none of us noticed the time sliding by so quickly. The colonel's team constructed test after test for that little creature, and he staggered and amazed us all. By nine o'clock we had exhausted our imaginations, not to mention our subject, who seemed to want nothing more than to curl up and go to sleep.

We got drunk that night. Sylvester and Carl were so wired after their day in the laboratory that sleep meant nothing to either of them. They theorised and fantasised long into the night, and I was content to listen to them ramble on over our whisky glasses. The colonel joined us too, matching us drink for drink and only seeming to become more distant from us as each hour passed. Sleep wasn't really his thing anyway, unless he did it standing up, horse-like, I supposed.

Funny, really. I expected a lot more life out of him that evening. The project was his baby, and I somehow wanted him to crow about it – to get at least a little bragging out of the way. Perhaps give me some insight as to the future he had in mind for the project, or where he saw it going next.

Anything really.

How does that old saying go? Be careful what you wish for? Yes, that was it.

Twenty Nine

Kathy was squatting back on her heels on the floor next to the cage. Her head was bowed, her eyes closed. Her fingers were laced through the tiny bars of the cage, from wherein two sets of tiny, inquisitive eyes watched her rocking gently to and fro.

Cogs whirred slowly into place in Paul's mind, two and two reluctantly became four, and somewhere, somewhen, a penny dropped.

'Which one's M4?'

'The smaller one, I assume. He's the one Ian gave me before he left for Africa. Wasn't called M4, of course. Called him Mickey. So I bought him a Minnie for company.'

Paul left the sofa and joined her on the floor in front of the cage. He knelt and put his face close to the bars. 'Here, Mickey. Who's a clever boy, then?'

'He's not a bloody parrot.'

'No, but he's supposed to be supermouse, isn't he?'

'He's had his memory enhanced somehow. At least that's what I think the journal was telling us.'

'Should've called him "Brain."'

'Huh?'

'Sorry, too many years of Saturday morning children's cartoons.'

'Whatever. Your cultural references leave a lot to be desired, you know.'

'He doesn't strike me as that smart, really.'

'And you can tell that just by looking at him, can you?' Kathy found it impossible to keep the note of sarcasm out of her voice.

'He's got his back legs in his food dish.'

A little time later they were curled around wine-glasses, watching the late news. Neither of them had ever gone out of their way to watch the news before, and neither of them could now say exactly what it was they were watching out for. There were no stories of missing scientists, nor any of armies of hyper-intelligent mice gathering at the very borders of civilisation. Nothing whatsoever, in fact, to fuel their unspoken anxieties further.

'How much more of the journal is there?' Kathy asked, her words lazy, almost slurred.

'We're better than halfway, by the look of it.'

Paul stretched a leg out and pushed one of the piles with his toe. 'You want me to read some more tonight?'

Kathy thought it over, and shook her head. 'I wouldn't be able to concentrate anyway, it's too late for thinking.'

Too late for thinking. Paul kept his smirk to himself. According to Ian's journal, that was exactly the opposite of what they were trying to achieve. But Kathy was right – there's a time for thinking and there's a time to wrap all that up and let instinct take over. Paul's own instinct, however, was about the last thing he wanted or needed to be led by tonight. Instinct alone would only lead him into an amount of trouble he was nowhere near ready for.

'You're looking thoughtful,' she interrupted his meandering daydreams, 'despite what I said.'

'Nah. Just a little tired, that's all. Thinking of my bed,' he added with a slow, comfortable smile.

'That's always been your trouble.'

'How so?'

'Too much thinking of bed.'

'I fear I must protest my innocence this time. I'm only thinking of sleep, and how much I miss it.'

'Of course you are.'

Kathy was feeling more relaxed now. Her worries about Ian were resting in the back of her mind, ready to be stirred up, yet deep enough for her to feel protected from them. She lifted the bottle of wine from the table and shared the last drops between them, allowing Paul the more generous measure, which he accepted despite his hand-waving "enough" gestures.

Comfortable in each other's silence, they spent the next hour that way, curled into the sofa, wrapped around their wine-glasses, the television muttering quietly and throwing out its cold blue glow over the carpet. Kathy tucked her legs up underneath her, and the sole of her foot brushed against Paul's thigh. At her touch Paul felt an electricity flow through him. She drew her foot back, slightly embarrassed.

'S'okay,' he murmured, placing his hand on her foot for the briefest moment, and lifting it onto his thigh. He felt her relax instantly, and kicked himself mentally. It was all very well playing the friend-in-need role, and that was the charade he would have to sustain, but it failed to blot out his own tremulous feelings. He felt like a sham. He was a sham. But at least she couldn't see that. At least, not yet.

So he sat back into the sofa, trying to relax, trying to pretend her hot little foot wasn't resting on his thigh, and trying to pretend it was simply the sort of thing two close friends would, and should, treat as perfectly natural behaviour. He felt anything but natural, trying to make his wine last as long as possible, anything to delay the moment when he'd have to move. Amazing what her slightest touch could achieve. One tiny foot on the top of his leg and he felt he was being embraced. Between them was four foot of dead, empty air, and yet he had never felt closer to her than at that moment. He could have been sitting inside her.

Kathy *had* noticed his momentary discomfort, but put it down to Paul's natural aversion to closeness. She was silently glad when he took her foot back, placing it tenderly on his leg. Perhaps he was, somehow, slowly turning into a grown-up. Someone with the ability to feel at ease with his female friends as well as his male companions. She was glad of the closeness, and the touch. The touch of another person comforted her, made her feel not only safer, but stronger. That was something she realised Paul, nor possibly any man, would ever come to truly understand. That a woman could be strong alone, yet somehow infinitely stronger given something to protect. Sweet, really, how the men in her life were given over to believing they were the ones doing the protecting, whereas she was well aware the reverse was usually true.

The news had been replaced by one of the more banal American sitcoms, the actors whispering their lines out into an airspace ignored by their audience. Her glass was empty now, and she shuffled herself off the sofa.

'There's only one bathroom, so I get it first, by default, being the girl.'

'You get it by default, being the boss,' Paul acceded, lifting his glass to his lips to fetch out the remaining dregs.

She left him there, his gaze fixed in the air somewhere between the television and the sofa. He gave her a few minutes head-start, and then made his way upstairs. She was in the bathroom as he passed, the door standing open. He glanced in, and his glance turned into a stare. She had her hands over her face, rinsing off soap, her eyes squeezed shut. She was also naked, bar her knickers, and Paul's stare ran across her body quickly, lasciviously. His gaze lingered on the swell of her breasts where they hung over the sink, the profile of her body shone in the low light, mesmerising him.

Kathy seemed to become aware of him, or of somebody, watching her. She knifed the water from her face with the edges of her palms and turned to the door. Nobody there. Funny, she could have sworn… No, of course not. Not even Paul was that pervy.

That had been close. He'd seen her tense and then turn towards him, and thought for one horrible second he'd been caught. He'd side-stepped quickly, and once out of sight of the door had crept along the hall to his own room. Sleep was a long time coming for him that night.

Thirty

My own euphoria was far longer lived, it seemed to me, than the rest of the teams'. Now that the breakthrough had not only been made but measured in some depth, their thoughts had turned to planning the next stage of the operation. Mice were all very well, not to mention easy to obtain without arousing the slightest suspicion, but if the colonel and his team were to progress then the subjects needed to be far more advanced. They were talking of chimpanzees.

Apparently, Sylvester informed me early the next morning, we share something like ninety-eight per cent of our genetic make-up with chimpanzees, making them pretty much the ideal subject for advanced experimentation and study. He tends to wander along odd tangents at times, Sylvester, and he also informed me that we share about fifty per cent of our genetic structure with the humble banana. So you could argue, using his admirable logic, that a human is roughly equivalent to two bananas. A double-banana. Double-helix, double-banana. You can fill in your own jokes.

Sylvester is by no means the scientist of the team. As much as it fascinates him, the minute technical details leave him cold. The same is pretty much true of me. But I managed to glean a little more information from the colonel.

Put at its most basic level (in order for me to understand it, I assumed), the colonel has designed what he calls a "corrector protein", whose only function is to attach itself to its subject's DNA sequences, switching genes on and off, and ultimately enhancing the recipient host. The improvement of memory, according to him, is little more than the first sign. I rubbed my eyes, trying to erase the dollar-signs that had sprung up in them.

Thirty One

'Breakfast.' Kathy dropped a plate of bacon and eggs down in front of him.

'Excellent. You want me to keep reading?'

'Sure. Try not to spit all over the pages.'

Thirty Two

Over the following two weeks I returned to the farm more and more often, immersing myself into their lives as best I could. I helped them pack computers and machines I'd not yet been introduced to into boxes and crates. The majority of the laboratory though, bar a few too-large, and incredibly expensive gadgets, would be left as it was, for when we returned from Africa.

I could scarcely believe we'd progressed so far so soon. The colonel had hinted previously at a second-stage project in Africa, but I must admit I'd held out little conscious hope of actually getting there. The three of them had obviously gone over it in some depth however.

They'd picked on the Democratic Republic of Congo, formerly known as Zaire, as their ideal choice. High on the list of prerogatives was an alienated society, where paperwork could be easily surmounted by paper of the folding kind, preferably in US dollars, please and thank you. Formerly a warzone, the Congo was now living in that tentative stability that accompanies a ceasefire, and the outsider with the biggest wallet was going to make a lot of friends there. It was necessary to be as invisible as could be arranged, and the Congo was not a small place. And the subjects we required, chimps, were in reasonably abundant supply, with no paperwork attached. The country itself was in constant upheaval, and every foreign authority was even less interested in the affairs of the Congo's indigenous population than was its own government. The fuel that drove the country was money, and we had that in abundance.

A month to the day after M1's hoop jumping, Sylvester and Carl left in an old Landrover stuffed to bursting with all the equipment they could carry. They had four weeks head-start before the colonel and I would join them. We'd figured the most difficult stage would be the English customs, but even they are not exactly on high alert for equipment *leaving* the country.

Carl and Sylvester were going to drive all the way – I envied them. I couldn't begin to imagine how much fun that kind of trip would be. But it was going to be hard work for them also. They had a month to not only reach the Congo, but to find us a new base of operations. It wasn't all going to be plain-sailing. Had I not given them an open cheque-book, it would have proved an impossible task.

In those last four weeks I had a lot to wrap up at the office – finally making good on my promise to leave Kevan to his own devices. I took the two surviving mice, our little superhero M4 and the placebo M12, back up to London with me, with strict instructions from the colonel not to mix them up. He was all for putting the two of them down until I protested. M12 I intended to drop in at a pet shop but, as the colonel pointed out, the last thing we needed was for M4 to be allowed to breed, so I gave that one to Kathy for safekeeping. I think she liked him.

I packed, and joined Andrew on the farm for the last few days. There was little to do, and when I grew bored of watching my colleague incessantly scribbling away in the notebook he was never without, I'd wander the surrounding countryside, making the most of the Indian summer we'd been gifted. I'd walk in ever-increasing circles through the woodland surrounding the farm. I found it relaxing, and strangely comforting, being so far away from the city. And so quiet. I'd gotten so used to the perpetual background noise of the traffic that I'd forgotten it wasn't the norm at all. The murmuring of the countryside was far more, well, natural, I supposed. Gave me space to think.

Got a lot of it done, too, thinking. Or worrying, rather. I'm good at worrying. Worried about Africa, Kathy, the colonel and his team, my business, my investment, the future, everything. Worried perhaps about the consequences of the colonel's work, but I couldn't pin that one down. I've been known to worry about how much I worry.

Partway through all this worrying I spotted a pair of squirrels mating. That's not something you see in the city. The female was clinging to the broad trunk of a beech (or birch, or oak, like *I'd* know), and holding her tail daintily out of the way for her rodent spouse, who was far too engrossed in his duties to notice me. I watched them for a little while, feeling my worries remain exactly where they were, refusing to fade. No revelation here then, just two squirrels fucking in a tree. I felt better anyway.

On the day of our departure we locked the doors of the farm and padlocked the barn, then threw our bags into the back of my Lexus. The colonel didn't look back once – I don't think it's in his nature. I was alone in watching the farmhouse recede and dwindle in the mirror.

We got a direct flight to Cairo from Heathrow.

Once in the air, and having left behind the chill of an English autumn, I relaxed considerably. It's true that people in cities live in a faster lane. They walk fast, and talk too quickly – everything about them seems to be hyperactive. I should know – I'm one of them. But now I'd slowed down almost to a standstill, while travelling at 540mph and 28,000 feet. It felt like the start of a long-needed holiday, and I accepted the offered whisky-and-cokes, and daydreamed through the action movies, and finally drifted into a tinny, noisy kind of half-sleep. The flight took five hours. I can remember maybe only a minute or two of it.

The super-heated air at Cairo International Airport waited for exactly the time it took to open the 747's door, before rushing in to greet us with a sweaty embrace. Getting out of the airport and into the city proper took us next to no time at all, and the noise and insane clatter of moving humanity made even London seem somehow slow and stately by comparison. We located a little hotel with a river view – The Lux something-or-other – and checked in for a two day stay. We were slightly ahead of schedule, and when we'd found ourselves a pilot, we could take in a little of Cairo – at least that was *my* plan.

An hour after checking in I was showered, shaved, and ready to find a café or restaurant or bar somewhere. I was ready for my holiday. I banged on the colonel's door, and then walked straight in. He was sat at the desk beneath the window, oblivious to the amazing view it presented, and seemingly oblivious of me, as well. His laptop was open and glowing in front of him, and he was once again scratching away in his journal. I looked around the room. On the bed was his suitcase, unopened. His hand-luggage had been unzipped solely to retrieve his laptop, and then ignored. It was obvious he'd come straight in and set to work. He hadn't showered or shaved, and he was wearing the same clothes he'd travelled in. It was also obvious to me that I'd be dining alone tonight.

I tried, half-heartedly, to persuade him anyway. 'You not coming out?'

'I'll get room-service.' It was an acknowledgement, but only barely.

'Okay. I'll leave you to it.' I was uncomfortable now, and switching from foot to foot like a child. 'What about tomorrow?'

'Sure,' he said, actually looking in my direction, 'what about it?'

'We were going to find a pilot?'

'Yeah. Tomorrow is fine.' He swung back to his notes, and I left him to it.

He didn't leave his room for the entire stay – all one and a half days of it. Room-service catered for him, and I stayed out of his way for the majority of the time. I had other things to do. Chartering a plane was easy enough, though I had to pay a little extra for confidentiality, and then a little extra again when I revealed our destination. In its more turbulent moments, the Democratic Republic of Congo had been known to impound the occasional plane, and our pilot's insurance failed to cover that eventuality.

I saw next to nothing in Cairo itself, failing to tick off a single item on my 'must-see' list, and met no-one, save in passing, bar our pilot. His name was Michel, a softly-spoken, broad and filled-out Frenchman. He was probably somewhere in his mid-thirties, but he struck me as terribly young for a pilot. A quiet, reserved man, about whom I could learn very little, but for the fact his English was impeccable.

It was a seven-hour flight, a dog-leg south-east, suffered in comfort in Michel's six-seater Cessna, which was going to test the very limits of its range on this journey. I spent the time staring out of the window at the land passing below. I have no idea of the speed or altitude of the little aircraft, but it's safe to say it was both a lot slower and lower than the 747 we'd used for the first leg. I could see everything. At least that's what it felt like.

Toward the end of the flight, as we dropped

down towards Kinshasa, it was the colours that held me silent. The Congo River, Conrad's vast, uncoiled snake, a slate-blue amidst the deep greens and yellows and browns of the Republic's countryside. And then the dusty grey and brown lump at the bend in the river that was Kinshasa itself.

We said goodbye to Michel on the airstrip, and were met there by Carl and Sylvester, who treated us to coffee from a flask, and ham rolls. A regular picnic, right at the edge of the airstrip. Just before we left I caught sight of Michel's Cessna, taxiing around ready for take-off. I presumed he'd been refuelling while we ate, and I gave him a wave which went unreturned.

I had about a thousand questions each for Carl and Sylvester, mostly regarding their trip down, but it looked as though they'd have to wait. We climbed into the Landrover and Sylvester pointed her in the direction of Bandundu, about 180 miles of B-road to the north-east. The trip was noisy and uncomfortable, and conversation was impossible. By the time we finally rolled into Bandundu it was dusk, and we were ready for nothing but sleep, which Sylvester had sorted out on his way through, managing to book an entire floor of a three-storey guest-house on the outskirts of the town.

And Christ, the heat. Tired as I was, sleep was an age in coming. I laid on top of the sheets, naked and sweating and watching the fan lazily stirring the sticky air. Sleep must have caught me eventually, because I remember being awakened the next morning by Carl's gentle hammering on the door. Sylvester had slipped out early for supplies and we picked him up a couple of streets away, where he stood forlornly on the edge of the pavement, surrounded by boxes of tinned goods and other miscellany, and a small crowd of curious children, who he was trying to placate with a single packet of Polo mints.

Kundasa was a further 150 miles to the north, mostly cross-country, or as good as. The roads were little more than dirt-tracks, some of them a little less, truth be told. We drew a few curious gazes from people we passed, but then we didn't pass that many people, so their curiosity was understandable. When we got to Kundasa, a township so small I haven't yet found it on any map, we made a brief refuelling stop and then took off east for another sixty-mile slog through some treacherous back-roads, and jungle-draped nearly-roads. Then the jungle receded momentarily, and I had my first view of our new home for the next few months.

It seemed somehow incongruous – this brick and wood and tin monstrosity squatting unhappily against the edge of the jungle, as though it was trying to hold back the advance of the greenery,

Canute-like, seeking to justify its ugly existence. The wall around the encampment was eight feet high and crumbling in just about every place you cared to look. Inside this paltry defence were two large, single-storey structures I took to be barracks at first sight, until Carl later informed me it was little more than a military outpost and weapons cache – the sort of place that changed hands at every opportunity depending upon which uprising was the latest and most fashionable to follow. I'd tried to read a little of the history of the Republic before we'd left England, but I had neither the heart for it, nor the necessary strong stomach. It was a troubled place.

In the courtyard, about halfway between the buildings and the wall, stood one lone, miserable-looking tree. I couldn't see a single leaf on it.

'Home sweet home,' Sylvester said from the passenger seat, without a trace of irony.

Thirty Three

We settled into the place pretty quickly, considering. The largest of the two buildings contained a kitchen, bathroom and, for a reason I have never fathomed, seven bedrooms, two of which we converted into storage rooms, never finding a use, during our entire stay, for the last room. The second building, only marginally smaller, had previously been used for offices, and one very large common room, with a defunct pool-table pushed into one corner. The colonel and I had an office each, but Carl and Sylvester both declined the offer.

There was a further part to these facilities however, in which the team took a much greater interest. Below the floors of these "barracks", accessible through a wooden hatch, there lay an enormous, concrete-lined cellar which, to my untrained eyes, must have run the length of both buildings, and incorporated into its structure the foundations of both. This was the area that, over the course of the following month, the three of them would turn into a laboratory.

It's quite hard to explain the sense of redundancy I felt at first. I was the only one with exactly zero first-hand experience of engineering or science. I spent almost the whole of the first month effectively twiddling my thumbs, until my true role in the operations took shape. I had volunteered one morning to do the ration-run single-handed, as both Carl and Sylvester were needed in the lab. They were all busy as hell anyway, as Andrew had decided that we couldn't, for the sake of safety and privacy, transport his drug with us, but would have to start again, using his finalised formula.

So I made the trip to Kundasa alone, with a list of materials the team had prepared in fits and starts over the last week. We required mostly rations, but with a side-list of small hardware items – a roll of wire, screws, nails and lightbulbs, that kind of thing.

Most small towns, long before they either turn into cities or vanish entirely, grow up around a single major feature or industry, be it a railway or a river, a farm or a gold-mine. Kundasa seemed to have struck the earth in much the same manner as a meteorite however, completely at random. There was a little crossroads in its centre, where two roads of little or no account bisected before tracing their individual, weary paths into the surrounding jungle. After a half-dozen parallel roads on each side of this crossroads the town petered out self-consciously. There was a petrol-station positioned at one apex of the crossroads, and then the two main streets, which would comprise the lifeblood of the town, containing two general goods stores, one restaurant, a mechanic, and a pharmacy-cum-practitioners.

When I'd taken care of the list I'd been sent forth with, I stopped for a cold beer at a well-hidden bar, and spent a pleasant hour sitting there in the shade and watching next to nobody drift past the front door.

I must have missed her going in, and I've no idea how long she spent in there, but for the fact it must have been a briefer stay than mine. She wasn't there when I first walked in – I'd have remembered. But I glanced up in time to see her leave. And I felt as though I'd been kicked and caressed at the same moment. Her beauty both buffeted and bathed me. Her eyes caught mine, and held them for a legendary instant.

'Hey,' I managed.

'Hey,' she replied, and I'm certain she smiled, before she moved out of my vision.

I left a few coins on the table and was getting

up to leave when I felt a hand on my arm. The stranger ushered me back into a sitting position, plonked a fresh bottle of beer in front of me, and helped himself to a chair opposite.

'Sit. Sit. Stay a few minutes and let me enjoy some fine white company. It's rare enough I get any.'

I took his features in slowly. Definitely not the sort of man I'd have chosen to spend more than a minute or two in the company of, but apart from his racist remark that had my hackles up in an instant there was nothing about him that suggested malice or danger, so I decided to let him have the benefit of the doubt for the time being, and raised the bottle to my lips while he introduced himself.

'Jan de Voers. Spare-parts specialist. Always good to see a new face in Kundasa. A rare treat.' His fleshy face creaked open to reveal a voracious smile, and his porcine eyes creased at the edges. It was my turn to reciprocate, and I did so with a lie.

'Ian Ashbury. Tourist. Nice to meet you.'

'Tourist, huh?' He relaxed his grip on my hand, and I saw his glance take in the box of supplies on the chair next to me. Just the usual hardware no self-respecting tourist would be caught dead without. Transparent as my lie was, he let it go.

We swapped half-truths for a while, or shot

the breeze, as Carl would undoubtedly have described it. Jan was unexpectedly forthcoming, and I suspected he was secretly seeking to gain my trust. He was a fourth-generation Boer. His great-grandfather a land-owner of some importance. For three generations they'd farmed, and lived well enough on the fruit of their labours. Now the farm was owned by his older brother, and Jan was effectively the black sheep of the family – having left that insular environment to strike out on his own, to make his own mark on the world away from the comfortable embrace of a hundred years of family institution.

'Couldn't have picked a better time, mind you, what with the current state of affairs. Look at Zimbabwe. Wouldn't want to be a bloody white farmer in this day and age. No thank you very much.'

He fell quiet for a while, and we spent the silence watching what little world there was here go by.

'Met a couple of guys here about a week ago. Big black sod and some scrawny little white fella. Had the same luggage as you,' he waved a casual hand at my box of hardware.

I shrugged. I could feel my hackles rising once more.

'You're with them, aintcha? The little team up

at the old barracks? I'm just curious, don't mean any harm, you know?'

'Yeah,' I conceded, 'I'm with them.' I picked up my bottle again and finished it off, making overtures to leave.

'Hey. Stay, stay. I'm the soul of discretion. I don't wanna know what you guys are up to out there, I really don't. But I figure you could probably use a man of my talents on the outside, if you take my meaning.'

I relaxed again, just a little. I didn't trust Jan any further than I could have feasibly thrown him, but he had my interest now.

'For instance, you want your hardware at a decent price, you come and see me next time. Anything you need, short of a nuclear warhead, I'm the one can get it for you. No questions asked, naturally.' He grinned again, and I could see nothing malevolent in it this time.

He rose and went to the door of the bar. 'Hey, Stefan,' he shouted into the opening.

There was a reply I didn't catch, but less than a minute later Stefan, the palest barman in Africa, delivered another couple of bottles to our table.

'Let me,' I began, fishing in my pocket for change.

'Crap. This is all part of the sales pitch. I fill you up with beer, and then all the little items in my sample case start to look like bargains.' Another smile, accompanied by what I took to be a wink.

'You have a sample case?' I asked, and immediately regretted having done so.

He gave me a friendly, and half-withering, look. 'Drink your beer.'

He gave me time to think, at least. Much needed time. No, I didn't trust the man. There was just something about him, but then... But then there was one important aspect of the colonel's plans that needed the involvement of at an outsider, and that was the procurement of at least one live animal for his tests. I had no idea how the colonel planned to lay his hands on a chimpanzee, and I'm not sure he himself had given that much thought to the problem – a case of crossing that bridge when he came to it. Perhaps the solution was right here, after all. Perhaps Jan had landed in my lap for exactly that purpose. I took the risk anyway.

'There is one thing you might be able to help me with,' I started hesitantly.

Jan's face lit up and became deadly serious in the same moment. He'd hooked me, and now all he had to do was reel me in. In his best concerned-salesman's voice he asked me what I needed.

'A chimp. A live one.'

'Well, you don't fuck around, do you?'

I smiled at him for probably the first time. 'I

need your discretion too, naturally.'

'Naturally. Adult or infant? Male or female?'

'Adult. Doesn't matter which sex. I may need more than one at a later date.'

'Okay. Can do. Thousand dollars US.'

'Five hundred pounds Sterling.'

He paused for long enough to make me feel uncomfortable. I don't think he'd taken me for a haggler. 'All right,' he breathed finally. 'Take me a couple of days. I'll deliver.'

'You know where…'

'Yeah, I know where you are. Cash on delivery. Cash, mind you.'

'You're not going to ask me for a deposit?'

'I trust you as much as I need to. Tourist my arse.'

I smiled. It had been a lousy cover anyway. 'You can really do that? Get me the animal?'

'I've been here longer than I can remember now. Kundasa has always been neutral territory in the Congo – every war needs its Switzerland – and I've made enough friends, and money, from both sides to know that anything is possible. So yes, Mr. Ashbury, I can get you your monkey.'

To his credit, he didn't allow his curiosity to get the better of him. I was glad, as had he asked what I wanted with a chimpanzee I would have been obliged to walk away. I spent another half-hour in his company, talking generalities and enjoying the silence, which was only broken occasionally by the loud whirring from the cogs in Jan's brain going into overdrive.

I left Kundasa a couple of hours before sunset, not wishing to drive in the dark if I could possibly help it. I spent the return journey deep in thought. Perhaps I'd found my role in the team at last. Perhaps Jan would prove to be one of my better assets in the world outside our little compound. Perhaps I'd see that girl again. Perhaps perhaps.

Thirty Four

I kept my arrangements with Jan to myself. There was no point in letting the others know of my machinations until they had come to fruition, if they did. It was a big enough if, and should Jan let me down nobody would be any the wiser.

Besides, they were pleased enough that I'd managed to obtain everything on their list, and the work on the laboratory was only a week or two from completion. We were progressing so quickly, in fact, that the colonel allowed us a breather. Carl and Sylvester and myself took off for Kundasa, and lost ourselves there for the day, eating and drinking our fill, and successfully pushing the project to the backs of our minds for a brief while. The colonel himself didn't bother joining us. His idea of a day off involved sitting in front of his computer, or working on his journal. Each to his own, I reasoned, and couldn't bring myself to talk him into taking any free time of his own – it would have been futile at any rate.

The following day Jan came through on our deal. He rolled up late-morning in a flat-bed, which was red and rusting and dusted by the road, and carried an enormous cage on its back, containing an angry-looking primate. Jan rode in the cab alone, but in the back of the truck were three Congolese men, dressed variously in jeans, combat-trousers, and T-shirts. When the truck pulled to a stop, the three of them jumped down and began work on the tethers securing the chimp's cage. They were fast, methodical, and entirely silent for the duration.

I took Jan into my office, as something told me he'd rather have our transaction carried out in confidence. He flipped quickly and carefully through the wad of notes I presented him with, and then I went to fetch the colonel. I'd missed him, though. He was already outside, witnessing the arrival of our new guest. He clapped me on the shoulder as I joined him in the courtyard.

'You've excelled yourself.'

I remained silent. My false modesty speaking volumes.

'Go get the others. I think they'd like to see this.' The look he gave me was one of almost paternal pride, and I swelled slightly, despite myself. 'They're in the lab,' he finished.

It had become the "Lab" now, no longer the cellar. I shouted down into the open hatchway, 'Sly. Carl. Come see what I've got for you.'

Okay, that was my back-slapping moment. I'd carved out my own niche in the team now, and no longer felt so much like a fifth wheel. When the animal was unloaded, Jan shook hands all round, stopping only to offer the colonel a flowery introduction, before leaving us with our new charge.

I strode around the cage for a while, still preening slightly, I'm embarrassed to admit, before it dawned on me that the thing was far too large to get through the cellar hatch.

'How are we going to get it downstairs?'

'We'll build another cage in the lab, make that our first priority,' the colonel answered, 'and then drug him and carry him down.'

'Drug him?'

'Sure. I'm not going to open the damn cage while he's awake and kicking. Brute that size could kill you in a heartbeat.'

'He's a her, by the way,' Carl pitched in.

'What about feeding her?' I asked. It hadn't crossed my mind to wonder how Carl could sex the beast from a distance, just as it hadn't crossed my mind to pre-order a dozen tins of Chimp-chow from Jan.

'That's pretty straightforward,' Sylvester answered me this time. 'They're omnivorous, same as us. Eat pretty much anything.'

'Really? I thought bananas, you know, and fruit.'

'You don't watch a lot of David Attenborough, do you?'

'Not really my thing, natural history.'

'Shame. He did a feature on chimps a while back. Not your PG Tips specimens either. Wild, and very bloody vicious. Showed them hunting in packs; hunting other, smaller monkeys, you know, and then ripping them to pieces. You wouldn't want to get in a cage with one, believe me.'

My respect for Jan had grown out of all proportion. 'How do you think he trapped her?'

Sylvester thought about it. 'The cage itself is probably rigged. Throw something tempting inside, and the door crashes down when the chimp's inside.'

'Surely any animal could have triggered it, though?'

'True enough, I suppose. I'm not an expert. Why don't you ask Jan the next time you see him? We'll leave it as a mystery for now.'

Moving the animal into the lab was nowhere near as problematic as I had anticipated. The colonel produced a tranquilliser gun and we heaved the unconscious animal through the hatch and into her new dwelling. It came to me much later that Andrew had been expecting to have to hunt the chimp himself, hence the gun. I hoped I hadn't spoiled his fun.

We had a small accident though, or rather Sylvester did. We were heaving the chimp into her cage when Sylvester either slipped or tripped. The chimp was unharmed, as Carl was supporting the main bulk of her, and she dropped lightly onto the matting of her new home. Sylvester went down quite a bit harder however, and managed to gash his arm on the padlock-catch. Andrew threw a towel around his arm and we helped him up to the kitchen, where Carl cleaned out the wound and applied paper stitches before wrapping the whole ensemble in bandage. We gave him painkillers and put him to bed. The next day I drove Sylvester into Kundasa to get his injury checked, and to sort him out a tetanus shot if that proved necessary.

The little pharmacy-cum-practitioners was devoid of patients when we arrived. It was also devoid of staff, and I hammered merrily away on the brass counter-top bell to no avail. I gave up, and Sylvester and I sat down to wait halfway along a row of plastic school-chairs lined up against one grey-beige wall. A handful of drowsy flies toured about the room, and I imagined them dogfighting, their tiny black bodies swooping around in miniature Red Baron manoeuvres. There were no magazines, and Sylvester himself was proving to be poor company, understandably.

The heat in the waiting-room was stifling, not something I was accustomed to in November, and I felt myself getting drowsy. Sylvester had fallen asleep already and I must have nodded off soon after because the next thing I remember was being shaken gently by the shoulder and looking up into those incredibly depthless black eyes I'd seen only once before and would never again forget.

Her name was Elise, and judging by the white uniform, in wonderfully stark contrast against her deep chocolate skin, she must have been the nurse. I was partly right, it turned out. We had a brief, hushed conversation, in deference to my sleeping charge. I quickly explained the circumstances which had brought us here and, in answer to my questions, she explained that she was not only the nurse for this practice, but also its qualified pharmacist. Her father, Henry, who was the doctor, was away until later in the week, and she looked after his patients between visits. We woke Sylvester slowly, and Elise inspected the work Carl had done.

'Very good. Very professional.'

'I'll pass the praise on.'

'Not your work, then?'

'Not likely. I'm more the squeamish type.' We chatted around in aimless small-talk while she re-dressed Sylvester's wound.

'Do you need a tetanus?' she asked him.

'Don't think so. Pretty sure I'm up to date.'

We left with painkillers and a short course of antibiotics, just to be on the safe side.

I could easily have slept through Christmas, for all the impact it had on our solitary little group, and I would have missed New Year entirely had it not been for Carl, who had been reserving a bottle of Scotch for the occasion.

Yes, I'd found my niche, all right, but it was hardly a taxing one. Once or twice a week I'd drive into Kundasa to stock up on whatever foods or hardware we needed, and each trip I'd feel both isolated and somehow free. Free from the boredom of being a non-contributor. And I'd meet up with Elise.

I'd like to say our meetings started innocently enough, but since when has any liaison with the opposite sex begun innocently? Yes, truthfully, I was in lust with her. She was all the things that Kathy was not. And yet every time we met Kathy was the one thing at the forefront of my mind. With every flirtatious line that I foisted upon Elise, I would find myself wondering how Kathy would react to the same line. I think Elise could sense my obsession with Kathy better than I could most of the time. As a result our relationship turned aside into an easy friendship, and I was more than happy with that.

We injected Cecily on January the twenty-third. Sylvester had decided to call her Cecily, after a maiden aunt, so he claimed, and it stuck.

I wasn't worried when she appeared to drop into a coma, as Andrew had assured me it was half-expected, judging from their experience of M4. Slightly more surprising was the fact that her sleep was so long, a little over an hour and a half. She was awake again for no more than a few short minutes before they moved in and began their first round of tests. I left them to it.

The following couple of weeks centred around Cecily. Carl and Sylvester spent the majority of their time below ground, but the colonel retreated to his office once more, lost in calculation.

Thirty Five

Paul straightened up in his seat, placing his hands in the small of his back, and throwing back his shoulders. He rolled his neck and was rewarded with a satisfying click. He'd been speaking for two hours without a break, and he was parched. He walked past Kathy without a word and filled a glass from the tap in the kitchen.

Ian's revelations about Elise had hit her fairly hard, he guessed, and he couldn't blame her. Why he'd sent her his journal unedited would remain a mystery until he arrived. He'd have had to have been in one hell of a hurry to do such a thing, or in some kind of trouble Paul couldn't even begin to guess at.

He picked up the remaining handful of paper and, without daring to look Kathy in the eye, went into the living-room. She didn't join him for some time, and when she finally emerged from the kitchen her face was shining, as though she had splashed water over tears. Paul turned to stare out of the window once more, into the late-morning sunshine.

'You know where he's going with this, don't you?'

'Isn't it obvious?' Paul replied without turning.

'Yes, I think it is.'

A little more silence, and then, 'finish it.'

He took a swallow of water, and then plucked up the remaining pages for the last time.

Thirty Six

Cecily became Sylvester's focal point for the succeeding weeks. Five days after her injection Carl found him sitting in the cage with her; cross-legged and silent, the two of them staring placidly at one another. Carl had come to fetch me to witness this madness, but he left the colonel undisturbed.

I stood at the bottom of the steps, keeping one foot on the last rung in a subconscious effort to leave myself an easy exit, should it prove necessary. I peered around the comforting bulk of Carl's shoulder.

'What the fuck is he doing?' I asked in a hissed whisper.

'Sly?' Carl called out in a soft voice.

In return Sylvester gave us a friendly little wave and said, none too loudly, 'I think she's ready to come out now.'

'Whaddya mean, come out? I'm damned if I'm letting her loose in here. Have you any idea of the damage…'

Sylvester waved him down quickly. 'She was just a little confused and scared at first, Carl. She knows she's among friends now.'

'How long you bin in there?'

In all honesty, I could have listened to that clipped, lazy drawl of Carl's forever, or at least until it lured me into sleep. There was something about that amazingly deep voice that reminded me of a lullaby, even in times of stress and possible danger.

'Since about five this morning.'

It was gone eight now.

'What are you trying to prove, zactly?'

'Just that she's safe, Carl. Safe, and ready to come out of her cage now.'

'You want me to get the tranq gun, just in case?'

'No, Carl. I think she knows what guns are. What they do.'

Carl just stood and stared at the two of them for what seemed to be a very long time. I did a lot of staring of my own. Carl's gaze appeared to be saying "How can you know this? How can you trust a feeling like this?" But then he lurched unsteadily forward, all the way up to the cage. He looked at Cecily for an uncomfortable eternity, and she returned his gaze with only the mildest look of enquiry, before he finally made his decision and swung the door of the cage wide.

The two occupants of the cage remained exactly where they were for the best part of a minute, though it felt like an hour, before Sylvester dropped himself out onto the floor and then held a hand out for Cecily, which she demurely took, levering herself out from her confines with all the grace of a Victorian schoolma'am.

Cecily settled herself down next to Sylvester, gripping his hand gently as the two of them approached us across the floor of the lab. She went up to Carl first, who had retreated to my side almost as soon as he had opened the cage door. She reached up and took his hand, smacking her lips as she did so in a travesty of an air-kissed greeting. At that moment she seemed as threatening as a cucumber sandwich with the crusts removed. Carl remained both silent and astounded, obviously not conversant in the traditional chimpanzee greeting, and then Cecily's attention centred on me.

I took the hand she offered, not so much as in a greeting, but a more primitive reaction, as though the handholding, the contact itself, would tell us all we needed to know about each other. She may have had a point. In that first grip of Cecily's warm, leathery palm I suddenly understood Sylvester's madness. There was not an iota of malice in the changed creature before me. The creature we had helped to change, I realised. Her understanding of the situation she found herself in would always remain alien to me, but her intentions, for the time being at least, were crystal-clear. There was no danger here, and I felt somehow foolish to have imagined there ever had been.

'Andrew should see this.' I spoke to both of them, perhaps all three of them, without letting go of Cecily's hand.

'He's moved on already.' Sylvester's voice was full of understanding and yet, somehow, underscored with resentment. I knew Carl caught that unspoken accusation as clearly as I had.

Even so, unthinkingly, I thought to go and fetch Colonel Andrew Marten, as though I somehow knew better than he did the things he'd want to be witness to. I thought better of it in practically no time at all.

And I was right to.

Within two weeks, Cecily had grasped the fundamentals of draughts, and was competing on a fairly-level playing field with both Sylvester and Carl. I think perhaps Andrew had expected this leap, somehow, as he showed barely the slightest interest in Cecily's progress. He didn't show his face outside of his own office for nearly a fortnight, as much as the rest of us would have liked to have seen him revel in what was rightly his own triumph. Whatever devils drove the colonel in those weeks were beyond the grasp of the rest of us. He was not simply possessed, but in possession of something we could neither define nor ignore. We'd see his face, and his face only, from time to time, ghostly white against the window of his office, staring out at us, before disappearing below the frame in front of his monitor once more.

The experiments were over. What did we have left to prove, after all? That Cecily was a smart chimpanzee we were never in any doubt. That she was now the smartest non-human on the planet only she could have told us. The change from instinct to reason had been for her a sudden thing, a drug-induced experience, but for the rest of us there had remained the tests, and what conclusions we could draw. Cecily herself needed no proof. She knew exactly what she had become.

With Cecily, and the potential of Cecily, I had finally become comfortable with what we were doing. In order to become comfortable with anything, you have to understand it. And I thought that I finally, truly understood what it was we were trying to achieve.

And then, on the fourteenth of February, Saint

Valentine's Day, and Mecca for all the happily foolish lovers of the world, that understanding came undone.

Thirty Seven

On the morning of the fourteenth, Andrew Marten rose before daybreak and spent a few hours alone in the lab, disturbed only by the watchful eyes and occasional grunts of Cecily. I discovered him there, asleep, his head on the bench in front of him. I shook him gently, and when I got no response I tended to Cecily's breakfast. A couple of minutes later I heard him stir, and I asked him if he was ready for his own breakfast. At first he seemed not to recognise me, but then his gaze cleared as he came fully awake.

'Be right up,' he said, dismissing me.

I left him to it. On more than one occasion I'd been a bear in the morning, and when you'd spent months cooped up with less than a handful of companions, you quickly learned to let the little things slide. I disappeared up the stairs, but not before taking one last glance behind me, and noting the colonel tidying his bench quickly, and pocketing a phial I'd been unaware of at first. I brushed this thought aside, and headed up to the kitchen.

'Colonel, you feelin' okay?' Carl asked midway through breakfast.

Andrew answered with a tiny shrug.

'I only ask 'cause you look like shit.'

That, at least, raised a smile from Andrew. Carl was right, though, the colonel did look bloody awful – early stages of flu type awful. He was perspiring too hard for the cool of the morning, and an occasional shiver would pass through him. He was definitely sickening for something.

'Can I get you anything? Nurofen? Paracetamol?' I'd never have made a G.P., but we had a beautifully stocked medicine cabinet that hadn't been touched since Sylvester's accident, and it seemed a shame to see all those drugs go to waste.

'No, no.' Andrew waved our concerns aside. 'I'm going to hit the sack for a couple of hours.' He placed his hands on the table and pushed himself upright, scraping his chair on the wooden floor as he did so. 'It wouldn't be a bad idea if we all took the day off. I for one could use a break, and I suspect most of you could.'

Carl fidgeted, looking about to object but

then apparently thinking better of it. We watched the colonel traipse off to his bunk and then we just sat there for an hour or more, drowning in coffee and small-talk. By the time we'd covered every non-work-related topic we could think of, and were all heartily sick of caffeine, Cecily decided to join us. She was carrying a chequerboard, and she thumped it down on the table in front of Carl.

He gave us a weary look. 'Well, I guess that's my morning taken care of. What about you guys?'

I looked at Sylvester. 'Fancy a trip into town?'

He returned my gaze with one of his own, but there was something else there, some unknown trouble bubbling just below the surface. 'I've got a better idea. Meet me out front. Give me five minutes.'

Sylvester hurried out of the room and I watched carefully as Carl helped Cecily set up the black and white counters on the board in front of him. Carl had been teaching her the rudiments of the game and, although she had not yet won a game, she had also never made the same mistake more than once, and had grasped the difficult concept of sacrifice in order to aid progress. She looked intent on revenge, to my anthropologically amateur eye.

I lurked outside the door of the barracks, wondering what Sylvester had in mind and ended up not having to wait too long to find out.

'Give me a hand here, Ian, would you?' Sylvester called out from in.

I helped him lug an enormous cooler into the Landrover, and then climbed into the passenger seat. Sylvester got behind the wheel, started us up, and then took off at a speed I would never be comfortable with.

'So where are we headed?'

'You're gonna love it,' he grinned broadly at me. 'A fishing trip. Lake Mai-Ndombe is about an hour from here. We can hire a boat for next to nothing, throw a couple of lines in and kill some time, maybe even a fish or two.'

'I didn't notice any fishing rods,' I pointed out, helpfully, in my opinion.

'Grab my rucksack off the back seat there. In the front pocket you'll find a couple of lines.'

I found them. Each one consisted of two eight-inch pieces of flat wood joined together by two wooden dowels, around which the translucent-green line was coiled. The contraptions looked like capital aitches, but with two crossbars as opposed to the usual one.

'These?' I waggled them dubiously.

'Those. I used them as a kid, fishing for crabs off a New England dock.'

I studied the wooden aitches warily. Sylvester

made a hand-to-mouth gesture that mimed drinking and added, 'Who cares anyway? If the fish ignore us we can just ignore them right back.'

We got to the southernmost shore of Lake Mai-Ndombe around ten. The early morning mist had been burnt from the surface of the water, and the serene emptiness in front of us was hauntingly beautiful. There were animal sounds coming from all around the lake's edge, mostly birds and small mammals. Now and then you could hear the howl of a primate, but these were rare.

Sylvester trooped off to a likely-looking huddle of shacks. I was still taken by surprise that any essence of mankind could make itself at home here, a lifetime from civilisation, where at first glance everything, though beautiful, seemed so very inhospitable, too wild to be welcoming. I spent the age while he was gone unloading our mostly liquid picnic, which occupied far too little time, and I found myself restless for his return.

Return he did though, with a young black man, bare-chested and clad only in dark blue cords, who introduced himself as Yassouf. Sylvester fetched a six-pack of still-cool lager from our cooler, and handed them over. Along with a few low-denomination notes, this apparently sealed the deal.

We had the option of an outboard motor, but Sylvester preferred to power us out to the middle of the lake under his own steam, and we sculled along in near-silence, the plop and swoosh of the oars the only thing to break it. I'd been expecting a canoe, perhaps even a dug-out, but our little rowing-boat wouldn't have looked out of place at Oxford. I trailed my fingers in the water, and daydreamed of Ratty and Mole, until the thought of larger animals, and biting fish, sprung to my mind.

'No hippos or crocodiles in here, I hope?' I asked Sylvester, cleverly disguising, to my mind, my trepidation with a healthy dose of humour. I even managed a smile.

'Don't think so. It's a popular lake for the local fishermen, though that's not ruling out very much, to be fair.'

'You get freshwater crocs all over Africa, don't you?'

'True.'

'What about piranha?'

'Will you fuckin' relax,' he barked at me. 'No piranha is gonna chew through a wooden boat.'

'Sharks?'

That made Sylvester laugh, at least. 'We're gonna need a bigger boat,' he added in his best Roy Scheider.

It was nearing the start of the rainy season, though we hadn't seen a drop so far. The sun pushed aside the last high wisps of cloud and set about its burning task. By midday or one o'clock, we would not be able to stand the heat out here, not this exposed. For the time being, though, a balmy warmth engulfed us both.

Sylvester drew in the oars, and then set about tying and baiting our hooks with bread. He dropped a line over each side and tied them off loosely. I settled back in my seat, pulling my hat down just a little, to avoid the glare off the water which was just beginning to sparkle. I waited for Sylvester to speak. I had a feeling this trip wasn't solely a fish-bothering exercise. The man had something on his mind. He offered a can of beer to me.

'Little early for me,' I waved lazily. Not that early, I thought, but I wanted to stay sharp a while longer yet.

Sylvester took the can back, opened it, and handed it back to me. I took it from him and watched as he opened another one and gulped at its contents. He finished drinking, put the can between his feet and, wiping his mouth with the back of one hand, leaned forward to me, serious concern on his face.

'Drink a little.'

The look in his eyes troubled me, but I did as he asked and sipped from the can.

'You're going to need it.'

I drank a little more, now both concerned and curious. The cool beer was wonderfully refreshing though, that I had to admit. 'What's on your mind, Sly?'

He took another large gulp and sat back, lost momentarily in thought. 'A question of ethics, I suppose.' Another pause. 'About exactly what we think we're doing here.'

I relaxed a little. If Sylvester wanted to argue over the relevant philosophies of our work ethics, that was fine by me. I had not one doubt that I could persuade him that all was well at the mill and have us back on track for a spot of relaxation in no time. Sylvester was suffering from the willies at the last minute, that was all. I smiled.

'It just seems so wrong to me now. What we've done, I mean…'

'There's nothing wrong with progress,' I cut him short. 'Think about it for a second.' I held up my hand for silence when I saw he was about to open his mouth again. I was going to have my say now whether he liked it or not. 'We've done so much more than we started out to do. The memory retention of both our subjects is astounding – they never forget a thing. Applied correctly, Alzheimer's will be a thing of the past. Not only that, but what about its other uses. Apply M4 to a working animal. Say a dog, or even a horse or a camel or an elephant.'

'But what about...'

'Wait a second. I'm not finished. Let's just take the dog as an example, okay? A working dog, with its intelligence and memory-capacity increased a thousand-fold. Any dog, from a Yorkshire Terrier to a Great Dane, could be trained for police-work, or drug-sniffing at Customs, or shepherding. How about Guide dogs? You know how much it costs to raise and train one good Guide dog? Well, now it could be done in less than a month, maybe even a week. And for sheep-dogs? What if you simply raised the intelligence of the sheep? They could be trained to come to you at a whistle. Maybe they'd even stand in line waiting to be sheared, if they could be made to understand that it was good for them. Maybe you'd only need the dog to round them up when it came to slaughtering time. I've been thinking about it a lot. You know, we could change the face of the world in so many better ways simply by increasing the intelligence of domestic animals. Their behaviour could even be modified to suit whatever new environment we choose for them. I'm no scientist, but if the M4 drug works on a genetic level, then the raised intelligence factor could prove to be hereditary. Think about it.' I was grinning inanely by now, well pleased with myself and unable, or unwilling, to disguise it.

Sylvester turned his dark eyes up to me. 'I have thought about it, that's the trouble.' He finished his beer, dropped the empty can to the floor of the boat, and immediately opened another.

'Are you in some kind of a hurry to get drunk?' I asked him. He was not cheered in the least by my optimistic visions of the future and that only served to irritate me. We were quiet for a long while before he broke the silence once more.

'Another?'

'I've hardly started this one.' Another pause. I watched, my irritation growing, as he started on his third beer. I felt a selfish annoyance as it looked like our quiet days' fishing was going to be spoiled by a drunken depressive, albeit one I considered a close friend by now. I considered joining him in his drunken crusade, as it's never fun spending the day playing catch-up, but it looked as though I'd been nominated for the drive home anyway, so that was plan B out the window.

'I never took you for much of a drinker, Sly.' I offered this cautiously, but my concern must have been all too apparent.

His eyes settled on me, his face dark and brooding beneath his peaked cap. And then, with what looked to me like a shrug of resignation, his expression changed completely. A grin replaced his frown, and he slumped on his wooden plank of a seat, looking for all the world as though he were about to burst out laughing. His face was a mask of mixed insanities.

'This is the whole bloody point, Ian.' He spoke slowly, wagging a weaving finger at me with his drinking hand. 'I get the unnerving feeling this is going to be the last chance I get.' And this time it was his turn to raise his hand to ward off my protests. 'My turn. No offence, Ian, but I find your Utopian fantasising just that bit too good to be true. You've overlooked one bloody big factor.' He took a last swig at his beer, and then placed the can on the deck next to its empty fellows. He leaned forward again and clasped his hands tightly together between his knees, as though he were trying to wring an argument from his knuckles. 'Let's start with the mouse. Take one mouse, add M4 and stir, and you have supermouse. Now, supposing we increased that animal's intelligence a hundred-fold. A rough guess – maybe he's even getting smarter by the day. Do you think the same would apply to a dog? You'd get a dog with, say, one hundred times the intelligence of other dogs? It won't happen. And the proof it won't happen is Cecily. Cecily is not one hundred times smarter than your average chimp. She is, let's say, a thousand times smarter. It's exponential. You see where the ratio is leading?'

I stared at him blankly, unable to fathom his reasons for trying to turn our triumph into defeat. 'What's so wrong with making animals more intelligent?' was all I could think of asking. A weak non-argument, and I hated that.

'Nothing at all, Ian. Except maybe they'd get so smart they wouldn't want us to eat them any more. But that's not my argument here. The point is, the M4 capacity for increasing intelligence is directly proportionate to the subjects' original intellectual capabilities. What happens when we apply M4 to its intended market? What happens when M4 is used on a human being? You won't get a human one hundred or one thousand times brighter than the average. How about a million times? Or a billion? Or a billion billion? That's what bloody worries me.'

'It hadn't occurred to me quite the same way, I must admit. But do you think that's so wrong?'

'What would you do with that kind of power? What would the smartest person in the world do?'

'Me personally? Jesus, Sly…'

'Theoretical at the moment, I know. Let's look at it this way. Intelligence, or super-intelligence, is just another form of power, and much like money, everything depends on who's got the most. The saying that money is the root of all evil is pure bullshit, a popular misquote, we both know that.

Money itself is innocent. It's the owner of that money who is responsible for his actions. It's going to be the same with a super-intelligence. In theory, M4 is potentially the greatest gift that could be bestowed on any one man. It would give him, provided it did not kill him, the power to choose the correct and most appropriate solution to any problem he could possibly conceive. The theory is beautiful. In practice, however, things could be drastically different depending on the original character of the man or woman in question. For instance, suppose a megalomaniac along the lines of Adolf Hitler had been dosed with M4. All the solutions to his problems would have been crystal clear to him. Incapable of making a mistake, he would have been able to predict every possible eventuality and therefore allow for every outcome to every action he made. In short, if he had been a super-intelligence in his own time I would be addressing you in German right now. Are you starting to get this?'

'You're saying we have to be extremely selective in our choice of subjects.'

'No. No no no. In my opinion it's too late already. Look, who are we to judge the person more deserving of M4 above any other man? If I could make that kind of decision it would prove only that I myself am the most deserving case. Of all the people on the face of the planet you couldn't, not in a million lifetimes, pick out the single most suitable choice. But, supposing you injected somebody at random? Within a month you'd have a person who never makes a mistake. He's now the only one capable of making the original decision, which leaves you chasing your tail. Chicken or egg?'

'I get the idea, but I can't agree with your pessimism. Surely a super-intelligence, knowing the right choices, would always pick them, for the benefit of mankind?'

'Even if the right choice meant his own demise?'

'Well,' I struggled. 'I don't know.' I was flailing around for a thread of argument, and finding none.

'The point I'm trying to make, Ian, is that we are not ruled by intelligence alone. We are the cleverest creatures on this planet, the absolute masters of our environment, and yet that doesn't stop us waging war on each other, or doing our best within our jobs to tread on as many toes as possible in order to reach the top rung of our respective ladders. Man is the most fiercely competitive animal there has ever been, and the most ruthless. We are not governed by intelligence but by our emotions, be they love, hate, anger, pity, or any number of other conflicting states of mind. That is what really needs to be controlled. It's all about power in the wrong hands. If M4 could be administered to someone who is guaranteed to use it for good and for the benefit of man and his environs, then it should be used. Only then would it work. But such a thing, to toy with the genetics of emotions, such intangible stuff is, in my opinion, impossible.'

He fell silent once more and, as I had no words to offer, I joined him. I no longer considered Sylvester paranoid; there was certainly an element of truth in what he'd said, but it would take me a little time to get my thoughts in some sort of order.

I got a bite a few minutes later, and while I hesitated, quietly fascinated by the gently jerking line, Sylvester responded by pulling out a pocket-knife and severing it. The clear filament vanished quickly beneath the water. Sylvester then reached out and cut his own line. He kicked at the pile of empty beer cans, and gave me an odd, child-like frown and a shrug of his shoulders. Our fishing trip was over. I wasn't tired of Sylvester's company, far from it, but I will confess that I needed some time alone, preferably starting right now. I grabbed up the oars, and began a slow stroke back to the shore.

'There's one other thing that's been nagging at me,' Sylvester said, and I could have sworn there was a little slur in his words now. I answered him with raised eyebrows, no words.

'What does the colonel need with a virologist?'

'You mean Carl?'

'Of course I mean Carl.'

Good point.

Thirty Eight

Kathy waited patiently for Paul to take a sip of wine; to do whatever it was he needed to do to whet his palate before continuing. She was sitting on the lintel of the window, watching the air outside turn dark, clutching her own wine. Paul had been talking steadily for over an hour now, and if he needed a breather that was fine by her. When a minute or two had passed however, she could no longer contain her patience.

'Well?' she finally demanded, turning from the window.

'Well what?'

'What's next?'

Paul raised both hands defensively, feeling unconsciously embarrassed, as though he were somehow responsible. 'That's it,' he said.

'What do you mean, that's it?'

'Last page. There isn't any more.' He regarded her helplessly as she strode to the little table and fumbled at the pile of papers.

'That can't be it. There must be more.'

'Check the original attachment.'

Kathy gave him a querying look.

'I'm only saying that your Aunt may have missed out a chunk at the end, or run out of paper or something.'

'You think that's likely?' Kathy retorted more sharply than she'd intended. Nevertheless, she set up her laptop and checked the original message anyway.

When Paul came back from the bathroom, where he'd managed to uncramp himself sufficiently from his sofa-moulded body, he found her contrite and close to tears.

'There wasn't any more,' she snuffled into his shoulder as he held her as close as he dared.

'Shh…' He put a hand on her hair, and made little comforting noises.

'I am so, so scared Paul, and I've no idea why.'

He held her by the shoulders, and her face tilted up to regard him, her eyes glistening. 'Me too, kid. It's okay to be worried.'

They sat through the news, not expecting and not finding any pertinent revelations. Paul opened a second bottle of wine and they sprawled in front of the evening film, both of them seeing the images flash in front of them and yet not seeing the film at all. Kathy's sporadic tears dampened Paul's shoulder occasionally, and his presence served to comfort her. It had to, as he had no words for her that may have helped.

It was gone midnight when they finally retired to their separate rooms. Paul had an interminable wait outside the bathroom while Kathy tried to brush her teeth through her tears. When he finally laid his head on his pillow he had no doubt that sleep could not be far behind. He was exhausted. Mentally and emotionally drained from the day. He'd never regarded himself as a strong man, and to be strong for the two of them now was, in his opinion, beyond him. He had enjoyed life as a shallow, selfish man, and was well aware of his shortcomings, yet they began to bother him now. He really *did* care for Kathy, more than he would ever have admitted to himself, or to anyone else for that matter, and he knew he'd have to dig deeper within himself in order to take care of her.

Perhaps only temporarily, though. Ian was supposedly on his way back, and when he arrived he'd make everything all right. Ian had that knack, Paul believed, of making any situation all right. A word here, a gesture there. Some little action on

Ian's part was almost always enough to settle an argument, or stop a fight. Ian had a certain unnamed power over his surroundings, or so Paul had always believed. He was the big brother that every boy wanted for their own. There was no such thing as an Ian-proof situation. No job too large. Thinking of Ian brought a roomful of memories back to him. They'd been in some scrapes together, nothing life-threatening, but one or two certainly not good for their immediate health.

Come on. Sleep. Sleep!

It wasn't any use. The more he longed for that unconscious embrace, the more elusive it became. In order to achieve sleep you had to ignore it, and he was reminded of the Douglas Adams theory of flight – fall, aim for the ground, and miss.

Kathy was faring no better. Her mind was racing, whirling. There'd be no peace for her tonight. Worry turned to fear, and her fear kept her away from sleep, from the nightmares she knew would be waiting for her.

She slipped into Paul's bed shortly after midnight. Sensing he was still awake, she placed two fingertips to his lips to quieten him as she spoke.

'Don't get any ideas. I'm just scared, and I want your company, nothing else.' She took her fingers away, and when her fingertips brushed against his body she was instantly embarrassed, and not a little ashamed.

'I'll, er… I'll get some shorts,' he said softly.

'Sorry, I forgot.' She burrowed down into the pillow, head turned from him to spare his blushes. And found herself confronted with the sight of his naked form in the full-length mirror that stood next to the door. Caught between the devil and the deep blue sea, Kathy pretended not to watch.

And then his warm indentation returned to the bed beside her. He lifted one arm so that she could rest her head on his chest, and they held each other in silent turmoil for a long time, neither believing sleep would claim them until, hearing Kathy's slowed, deepened breathing, Paul followed her down into blackness.

Thirty Nine

Henry White stomped indelicately up the two flights of stairs to Elise's modest apartment. He was unsure as to whether he was more angry with her than worried about her. He could remember every occasion she'd skipped work through illness, and each time it was something relatively serious. Elise was no faker; not a lazy atom in her body. But she'd managed to get a message to him on every previous occasion, no matter how serious her illness. Worry replaced his quickly-fading anger as he approached her door.

'Elise?' He rapped his knuckles on the door and waited.

'Elise?' Louder this time.

'Elise?' He hammered on the door, and the first neighbours poked their heads out. Henry grinned foolishly at them, and returned his attention to the door. He gripped the handle and turned, the door swinging easily in. He stepped into the gap.

'Elise?' Quietly, tenderly.

He surveyed the room. No sign of her. She couldn't have gone out, surely? If she'd been planning a trip, he would have been the first she'd let know. If she wasn't at work, she had to be here. There was no reason he could imagine for her being elsewhere without his knowledge.

He took a second step into the room and saw the overturned lamp. His stomach performed a slow nose-dive, and then turned itself upside-down. He stepped closer to the back of the sofa.

And blood was the first he saw of her. Not some blood. Not a little blood. A pool, a lake of blood, spread out around her. He took in the uncomfortable sprawl of her body, and the ruin of her face and head. He noted the pistol gripped in her lifeless fingers, and then his strength left him completely.

Henry sank to his knees, his face pressed into the back of the sofa, while his fingers gripped the top. Great sobs shook him, and he let out a barely human cry, a strangled scream. Sorrow and anger, grief and rage battled within him. His fingertips turned white where the claws of his hands threatened to rip through the furniture he was holding. A foul blackness crept through him; a need to take vengeance on a world that could destroy so easily something so very precious and beautiful.

He let go of the sofa and collapsed to the floor with a heavy thump, drawing his knees to him, fists bunched into his chest, regressing to a foetal frustration, and oblivious to anything save pain.

The neighbours, overcoming their natural reticence at the sound of that anguished howl, crowded into the room, two of the women swooping on Henry like birds, and making dove-like coos of sympathy. Other neighbours arrived, and one of them, with a stronger stomach than most, managed to fetch a blanket from the bedroom to cover the travesty that had once been Elise.

In the doorway, John and Yasmine N'Gobo watched the scene passively. They watched the slow tragedy unfold before them, and eventually stepped in to lend a hand where they could. The neighbours, with the help of John, manhandled Henry off the floor and onto a chair in the kitchen, where he was pinned by heavily helpful hands. A boy was sent running for the policeman. Two of the women busied themselves around kettle and sink. Yasmine joined her husband in the kitchen, and there was no-one left in that other room now. Yasmine looked well. Too well, really, and one or two of the other women couldn't help but steal an admiring glance at her. She must have been hiding a cold though, for in the next instant she let out a violent sneeze.

Forty

Penny swung her feet out of bed with a little extra enthusiasm that morning. She'd been captivated by Ian's recorded escapades, and frankly couldn't wait for the next instalment. She got herself washed and dressed far more hurriedly than was usual, but laying out the cats food was a job she simply couldn't make any quicker.

Finally, with a mug of coffee in her hand, she sat herself back down in front of the glowing screen of her computer. She scrolled down through the document, picking up her place again easily enough. Ian had arrived in Africa, and they'd just taken delivery of a chimp. Whatever next? Penny sipped gingerly at her scalding coffee and paged slowly through the text, enjoying a book no-one else had read, which was a secret thrill of sorts.

A couple of hours later Penny was nursing her

second mug of coffee, and staring out at the flat grey skies from her window. That greyness was reflected in her eyes and in her heart. She knew trouble when she saw it, or read it, and this was definitely trouble. What kind of trouble however, was pretty much anyone's guess.

And now her patience, long by anyone's standard, was beginning to give out. A slow anger stoked a fire inside her that would only grow unless she tended to the cause of it. Kathy should have stuck with her photographer. Any bloody fool could see he was crazy about her. Why, oh why, had she ditched him for that bloody financier, that bloody half-man, that bloody Ian. That's bloody enough, she told herself. No use getting angry at what you can't change. But that wasn't to say she couldn't put a stop to this nonsense now. Right now.

A quick phone call to Emma, who'd look after her cats while she'd be gone. Pack a small bag – enough for a few days at the most. Hold the papers, check the 2CV for oil and water. Okay, ready.

Without a last glance behind her, Penny kangarooed toward Wales, with an heroic rescue of her favourite niece uppermost in her mind.

Forty One

Somewhere halfway between dreams and waking, Kathy placed a kiss on the neck of her human pillow, before receding to the shadows again, her arms tightening just minutely against him.

Nowhere near sleep, but in shocked wakefulness, Paul registered the kiss with an illegal thrilling. If she awoke now, perhaps he'd feign sleep. Perhaps not. He knew somehow that that kiss had not been meant for him, that it had been meant for her dream-companion, presumably Ian. But his body had not got the same idea. His body had registered the feather-light touch of her lips with pure instinct, and he could feel himself hardening despite his frantic thoughts to the contrary. He stared hard at the ceiling. No, not hard. Don't think hard. It was impossible, though.

Whichever way he consciously guided his thoughts, his instincts led him back to the unenviable position he now found himself in. This was his best friend's girl. Swallow the irony.

And then her arm was moving over him, her hand tracing a line down his body, to his thigh, where it came to rest.

She doesn't know it's me.

Her body snuggled closer in against his. Her lips parted and she placed a lazy kiss on his torso.

She doesn't know it's me.

She drew one leg up, her knee crossing his, coming to rest at the lowest part of his thigh. Her hand moved slightly, coming to rest against the by-now unmistakable bulge of his erection.

She can't possibly know it's me.

A tiny hum and sigh of appreciation escaped her lips on her discovery of his aroused state.

What the fuck am I going to do?

Her tongue flicked out and gave him the gentlest caress, searching for his nipple.

She's going to wake up. Open her eyes and realise it's not Ian she's holding onto.

Her hand was on his erection now. Moving languidly up and down the length of his shaft.

This can't be happening. How can she not know? They hadn't drunk that much wine last night, had they?

Now her fingers had slipped inside his shorts, releasing him, and her grip on him tightened as he himself became even firmer.

Perhaps she does realise it's me. That would make it even worse.

She eased her hips over his, raising her head to his chest, covering it with tiny kisses. He could feel the wetness of her beneath her nightshirt.

Looking at the top of her head now. Praying she'd look up at him and realise her mistake. Praying she wouldn't.

Then she eased herself slowly onto him, her slickness guiding him warmly home. And now she did raise her head, her eyes squeezed tightly shut.

He gave up on concentration, allowing his senses to take over for the time being. It couldn't last, let's face it.

She didn't open her eyes once, not for the duration of their lovemaking. For all the turmoil his mind may have been in, his body knew exactly what it was doing, and where it wanted to be. She climaxed a little before he did, and he gave himself a mental pat on the back, unable or unwilling to let go that last inane vanity. She collapsed across him, her hair spilling across his chest, her arms around his neck.

He felt himself wither slowly inside her, and then the terror set in. She'd look up, and discover his deception. She'd kill him for this betrayal of her trust. He'd been such a fool. How could he have let it go this far? She'd never forgive him for this. But, surely, it wasn't entirely his fault. She'd instigated their lovemaking, not him. She'd taken it, quite literally, into her own hands. And now this was the result. This fear. This terror. She was going to open her eyes and…

She opened her eyes, and looked into his, at first puzzled by his expression – he looked like a rabbit caught in a spotlight – before her gaze softened and a new smile played about her lips.

'Good morning, Paul,' she chuckled softly.

PART THREE

THE GHOST

Forty Two

'You can stop beating yourself up, Paul. Really.' Her tone was meant to be reassuring, but to his ears it sounded like condescension.

He didn't have a ready reply. He felt like he may never have a reply for her, no matter how long he worked at one. He washed up the breakfast debris in continuing silence, unaware of a single thing he could have said or done to turn back the clock and undo their treachery. That was the right word for it, certainly. Treachery. How could he have let himself betray his own best friend, and with the woman he now understood they both loved?

She was behind him now, her hands on his shoulders, and her touch had frozen him into a statue. 'Thanks, Paul.' She whispered the words and kissed his ear.

He turned on her. 'For the fuck?' He had no

idea whether he was angry or ashamed or both. 'For comforting you in your hour of need?' His voice rose an octave, and he turned back to the sink. 'What the fuck were we thinking?'

'It's not like that.' Kathy's voice was lowered, and from its distance Paul could tell she had returned to the table.

He grabbed a towel, and began to dry his hands. Turning to face her, his back resting against the sink and his hands making kneading motions within the twists of towel, he looked like an angry young god. 'You're the girlfriend of my best friend, Kathy. You do the math.'

And now Kathy really did not know which way to turn. 'Paul, it was only…'

'Only sex, yeah, I know. Thanks.'

'I was going to say companionship, or comfort.'

'That doesn't really help though, does it?'

'I suppose not.'

'What were… Oh, Jesus.' He flung the towel down in exasperation.

'This is really not fair, Paul.' Her voice was scolding and, at the same time, hurt.

And he'd never really had the strength for a proper fight, had he? His shoulders drooped wearily and he turned to face her once more. 'No. Of course it's not.' His eyes were fixed firmly on the space between his feet, and he couldn't bring himself to meet her gaze. The silence stretched out between them, becoming something they both could have touched.

'I still love you, you know?' And there they were, all his cards face up on the table for her to pick over and destroy at her whim.

'Yeah, I know.'

Forty Three

The sound of gravel being thrown against the windows and walls of the cottage announced Ian's arrival to them both. Few words had passed between Paul and Kathy since breakfast, and they had maintained an uncomfortable silence since his declaration of love. They'd spent the hours after breakfast busying themselves in separate rooms; Paul inventing tasks in the kitchen, where he felt safest, most neutral, and Kathy going through much the same motions in the living-room.

Her emotions, perhaps understandably, were in some turmoil. A strange mixture of fear, worry and desire had driven her into Paul's arms that morning and now, in the cold aftermath of their illicit union, she was having trouble reconciling her actions with her feelings. To be in love with two men at the same time was not exactly an ideal situation to find herself in. And she did love them both very much indeed. They were so different from one another, truly chalk and cheese: the one exciting yet unreliable, the other the very opposite. But to choose between the two of them would be impossible. Her head and her heart were at war with each other. It might come down to both of them, or neither of them. Either way, she was hung.

And now, hopefully, the answers were here. Ian stepped out of the hired Peugeot hatchback and strode all of the four paces to the cottage door. Even as he raised his fist to bang on the woodwork, Kathy pulled the door wide and practically fell into his arms, smothering his face with tiny welcoming kisses. He held her back at arms length for a moment, simply in order to study her face, as if putting his memory of her back in order. He pulled her close once more.

'I've missed you so much,' he whispered into her hair.

She felt herself close to tears now, and this time she took a step back, just staring at him as though it had been years, rather than a few short months, since she had cast eyes on him. He reached out to wipe a tear from the side of her nose.

'You scared the crap out of me, Ian.' She hung her head.

'I am so, so sorry,' he murmured.

She raised her head to him and sniffed back more tears. 'Come inside. Paul's here too, by the way.'

Ian raised his eyes questioningly.

'I had to call someone,' she explained.

'I'm glad it was Paul. I missed him, too.'

'Come on. In.' She tugged him across the threshold.

Paul had been waiting quietly for the greeting to be over. He suddenly felt like an unwanted guest here, the proverbial fifth wheel. When Kathy and Ian finally tumbled through the front door he left his sanctuary to make his presence known, and was suddenly very pleased he had, all notions of pariah-status leaving him instantly.

Ian's face had lit up on first sight of Paul, and he quickly closed the distance between them, hugging Paul close to him and exchanging pats on the back. They pulled apart, yet still clung to one another's elbows.

'Thanks, mate,' Ian breathed, and Paul read the unspoken in his friend's eyes. Thanks for being here. Thanks for taking care of Kathy, and thanks for giving me a fellow man to unload my troubles on.

Paul remained poker-faced and deadly serious, despite his inner turmoil. 'Good to have you back safe.' On the word 'safe' he clapped Ian on the shoulders, and then dropped his hands, stepping back in order to appraise his friend more completely. 'You must be hungry. Thirsty at the least?'

'Both,' Ian laughed. 'Dirty, too.'

'You get yourself in the shower,' Kathy advised, moving up behind him to give his sides a squeeze, 'and we'll sort something out for you.'

Ian turned to her and kissed her as hard as his obvious fatigue would allow, while Paul disappeared back into the kitchen, those dormant feelings rising once more to the surface.

He heard the water running upstairs a few minutes later, and then Kathy was at his elbow, silent with him for a while as he bent into the fridge to seek out the makings of a meal. Words failed to come to either of them, and in total silence Paul prepared a simple fry-up – Ian's favourite in days past – while Kathy uncorked a bottle of red and stood it to breathe for the shortest, most asthmatic, time while she fetched three glasses.

Ian joined them, lured down by the smell of hot food, in the living-room. He had thrown on an enormous white towelling bathrobe, bought at the time solely for its gargantuan luxury, and he had to roll up both sleeves in order to make sense of the cutlery. He ate in silence, as Paul and Kathy, perched respectively on the arm of the sofa and the low table, studied him intently.

'The condemned man's last meal.' He tried to make light of the situation and was rewarded with only nervous laughter from his companions. 'Seriously though, will the pair of you *please* piss off to the kitchen while I finish this. It's not that I don't appreciate the effort; I do, but I need just a tiny moment alone to prepare what I have to tell you.' The lie came easily enough to his lips. He'd had a five-and-a-half hour flight and a four hour drive to prepare for this very moment, and he'd spent the time doing little else. But it was both unnerving and infuriating having the two of them watching his every move, perched like vultures awaiting the scraps and tidbits he'd throw them later. Perhaps he *had* been alone too long, away from his idea of civilisation, for although he could understand their behaviour well enough, he couldn't bring himself to tolerate it.

'Shout if you need anything,' was Paul's last passing remark as he and Kathy removed themselves to the kitchen, and Ian instantly condemned himself as the worst kind of intolerant bastard. Still, give a guy a moment, you know?

Paul and Kathy fared no better in their kitchen exile. Both felt guilty of the pressure they were exerting on Ian, yet somehow they both knew the pressure wouldn't have been there in the first place but for Ian's damnable diary, and the fact that he was the one primarily responsible for their mutual anxiety. No words passed between them, but they were both aware of a rising anger toward each other, spurred on by both fear of what they might learn and fear of what Ian could learn. Anger which could, and given the present situation, probably would, boil over quickly into resentment and hostility. They passed the time glaring at everything but each other.

The chink of cutlery, and the sound of Ian's noisy slurping at the wine in front of him signalled the end of his meal and broke their enchantment, and they joined him in the living-room once more. Paul cleaned away the remains of Ian's meal – not that there was much left in the way of remains – Ian had stopped just short of licking the plate clean, and returned to the arm of the sofa.

'You ready?' Ian asked, in a voice that he had meant to sound as casual as possible, and failed at.

Paul and Kathy regarded each other for the shortest time, and in the instant their eyes met more than a million questions passed between them. Not a single one, however, was answerable, and in unison they faced Ian and said simply, 'Yes.'

Ian, who had glanced briefly at the pile of papers his two closest friends had had to wade through in the last couple of days, as though unsure of where he had left off his story, waited for the quick refill of his wine glass from Paul, and then began his story. Or, rather, finished it.

Forty Four

As the designated driver, Ian spent most of the journey to Kundasa seeking out the deepest ruts and gullies he could find with the wheels of the Landrover. It was a petty revenge, he knew, but Sylvester had not left off the drinking once they'd left the lake behind. On the contrary, once in the passenger seat he'd attacked another beer with gusto. And now Ian spent his time trying to upend as much of the can's contents into Sylvester's lap as was possible. He succeeded spectacularly several times, much to his companion's annoyance. Over the two-hour drive however, Sylvester began to turn the damp ordeal into a game, and was thoroughly enjoying himself, as tin after tin vanished slowly either down his throat or over his trousers. By the time they reached the township Ian was hot, frustrated, and bordering on the very angry.

Sylvester, by comparison, was not only deliriously happy but also blind drunk.

They stepped down into the relative darkness and cool of Stefan's Bar. At least, Ian stepped, while Sylvester staggered, and then slipped down the last two steps, through some minor miracle managing to stay on his feet. The barman barely raised an eyebrow, having presumably seen it all before, and batted not an eyelid when Sylvester ordered a bottle of wine to wash down his stomach-load of beer. To Ian's mind it was surely too hot to drink wine, and he got himself a cold beer, intending to patiently watch Sylvester slide into oblivion on his own. As it turned out, he didn't have too long to wait.

Sylvester's company was rotten. The further down the bottle he progressed, the more crass he became, the worse his jokes got, and the more confused and annoyed he made Ian. After an hour, much to Ian's relief, Sylvester simply put his head on the table in front of him and gave up consciousness. When the barman made a typically sporadic foray into the bar proper in order to fetch glasses and clean ashtrays, he simply wiped the table around Sylvester's recumbent form and left him to it.

Ian took the opportunity to fetch from the Landrover his laptop, which had become his constant companion, and return with it to the table, where he wrote up his journal to the present moment. He had in mind the idea of selling it one day – it might make an interesting story once edited down properly. And edited it would have to be. He needed to erase any record of his flirtatious relationship with Elise: there was no way that would wash with Kathy. And one or two of his other foibles and weaknesses could be polished nicely to make them appear more like strengths. He was, truth be told, quite eager to get back to his Docklands flat and start writing the tale up.

A couple of hours passed slowly and pleasantly enough. He'd had two refills of cold, refreshing lager – more than he'd ever dream of consuming in his home town, but here in the middle of nowhere, where any enforcers of the drink-driving laws were far harder to find, he had few qualms. Sylvester had only moved and grunted in his self-inflicted stupor once or twice the whole time, and Ian lost himself in his work, barely noting the comings and goings of the bar's other patrons, and the slowly-lowering ceiling of smoke-clouds. Jan, his very own pet Boer and favourite procurer, showed up on the periphery of his vision, but although they acknowledged one another, Jan did not approach, nor Ian invite him to do so. The next time he looked up from the glowing screen, the fat man had vanished.

Sylvester did come round eventually, as the

day made way for evening, and seemed a little better off for the rest he'd had. At Ian's insistence he managed to cram down some food, but left the plate looking as though it had barely been touched.

On the drive back Sylvester's heavy eyelids were jolted wide time and again by Ian's love of ruts, though this time he was not purposely seeking them out. Quite the reverse, in fact. He'd forgiven Sylvester his drunken behaviour and had decided that, after all, he'd had exactly the sort of relaxing, do-nothing day that he'd set out to attain.

They arrived at the barracks a little before six, and Sylvester mumbled a brief apology, which Ian brushed aside, before stumbling off to an early bed.

Ian found Carl in the kitchen, the draughts game apparently long over, packed away. There was no sign of his simian opponent, either.

'How went the games?' Ian asked, with a hint of mock-Caesar.

'I'll be dreaming of chequered boards tonight. Coffee?'

'Um…' Ian nodded assent.

'She's made remarkable progress,' Carl said, as he filled the kettle. 'After a couple of hours she won her first game. Then the following game went my way, and that was the last time I won. I don't know how many games we played after that, but needless to say I was beaten comprehensively every time.

Her playing just got better and better. The games were taking less than ten minutes at one point.'

'So you quit. I can hardly blame you.'

'No, I didn't quit. Humble as it may sound, I don't mind in the least losing to an ape, especially one we're responsible for enhancing. My defeat is a sure sign of our success.'

'That's a healthy way of looking at it.'

'Actually, it was Cecily who quit. I don't think she found me much of a challenge in the end. Grew bored of me.'

They slurped at their coffees for a while, each absorbed in thought, while outside the sunset finally gave up to the black, and the night-noises took over from the sounds of the day.

'I'm going to try her out on chess tomorrow.'

Ian frowned, but there was a smile on his lips when he spoke. 'I can see her up against Kasparov a month from now.'

'A terrible prospect,' and Carl smiled too, 'but perfectly feasible, frighteningly enough.'

'Andrew must have been pleased with her.'

'I haven't seen him since this morning.' Carl toyed with his mug and brushed some imaginary crumbs from the table. 'He took off a little while after you.'

'I thought he was resting today?'

'What the man says and what the man does…'

Carl shrugged.

'Yeah, two different things.'

When Carl asked about his own day, Ian played it down for the most part, skirting Sylvester's embarrassing drunkenness, and their conversation meandered slowly around, finding no resting place. The colonel had still not shown his face, and around eleven they called it a day.

Ian awoke with a start. According to his bedside clock it was twenty-past five in the morning. It was also pitch-dark outside; the sun wouldn't show itself for a good hour yet. He was groggy but also, for some unfathomable reason, a little scared. That couldn't have been a gunshot, surely? But the more he thought about it, the more certain he became that that was exactly what he'd heard. The proof came only moments later, when he heard Sylvester screaming something unintelligible, hammering on his door, before his footsteps raced off down the hall. Ian got out of bed fast.

He yanked on the trousers he'd left at the end of the bed and threw open his door, almost colliding with Carl, who was coming down the hall like an express train. The big man wore only boxer-shorts, but to Ian's mind this only served to make him look even more intimidating than usual. He was pushed along in Carl's bow-wave.

'I heard a shot. I'm sure I heard a shot.' Ian was fighting to keep the panic out of his voice.

'We all heard it. Where did Sly go?'

The answer presented itself immediately. Ian nearly fell through the open hatch in the floor: would have done so in fact, had not Carl grabbed his shoulders at the last second, bringing him up short. They started down the steps, Carl trailing Ian closely. What greeted them was a sight beyond his immediate comprehension.

Sylvester stood near the foot of the stairs, holding the rifle levelly in front of him. At the opposite end of the room, next to the open door of Cecily's cage, stood the colonel, his hands in his pockets, looking as calm as could be, an advert straight out of Country Life. Ian and Carl stumbled to a stop a couple of feet from the bottom of the stairs, and now Ian began to take in other details from the peculiar scene.

Like the table behind Sylvester, from which the test-tubes and other pieces of glassware had been swept casually onto the floor. And the fact that the table-top seemed to be swimming in liquid, presumably from those same test-tubes, which were seeping over the edge and running down the sides and away onto the floor. And the body of Cecily, collapsed in a clumsy fashion at the feet of the colonel. The slowly spreading pool of blood beneath her had been clue enough for Sylvester.

'Fucker killed her,' he struggled the words out between sobs.

Both Carl and Ian appeared shell-shocked, neither able to believe what their eyes told them nor able to decide on a course of appropriate action. It was Sylvester who decided for all of them.

'Fucking killed her.' This time it was a scream, and as Sylvester swung the rifle up to his shoulder, it was Ian who moved first, and faster than he'd ever moved in his life.

He got an arm under the rifle in a sweeping motion, and the second shot of the morning exited through the ceiling of the basement laboratory, the floor of the barracks. The struggle was over in an instant, as Carl's reflexes had proved only marginally slower than Ian's. He literally swamped Sylvester in those enormous arms, bringing any offered resistance to a swift close. Ian took charge of the rifle, and stepped well back out of harm's way as Carl applied his heretofore unseen pacification techniques, which appeared to rely solely upon a superiority in weight. Graceful it wasn't.

Carl manhandled Sylvester to the steps, and then manhandled him some more up into the kitchen. Ian lowered the gun, glancing only briefly at the colonel, who seemed completely unfazed, even at ease. Ian was beginning to feel shaky. His nerves had gone completely, and he could feel his knees tremble. He thought he might be going into shock. His brief act of heroism could easily have been enough to get him killed, and he put his tenseness now solely down to that. There was something else, though, something he couldn't quite catch. The colonel had been cool enough, certainly, but that didn't explain the unnerving feeling he had concerning Carl. The big man had acted throughout with the prescience of someone who had seen it all coming. He had seemed surprised only by Sylvester's actions, and keen enough to prevent the smaller man from taking any kind of revenge on his old friend the colonel.

Ian was left alone with the colonel in the laboratory. The danger had passed for now but it was Ian, rather than the colonel, who had been at the business end of the rifle, who was the most relieved.

'Let's get upstairs and sort this all out,' Andrew said. It was a calm, dispassionate tone he'd adopted, and Ian felt himself taken once more under that easy direction.

They seated themselves around the table in the kitchen. Ian had set the kettle to boil, and arranged four mugs for them: coffee the better to wake them, and put their nerves in order. Carl was sat in between Sylvester and Andrew, the better to restrain the former if it should prove necessary.

'Ask him why he did it,' said Sylvester.

'Did what?' Ian asked from his post.

'Killed her,' came the reply.

There was silence from all of them for what seemed a longer while than it probably was. Ian brought the coffees to the table and received a couple of muttered thanks, but otherwise the silence was complete.

'Guys,' Sylvester began, 'we are making one huge mistake. That gun is the only thing stopping him from killing the rest of us and taking off, you know that.'

'Oh Christ, Sly,' Carl spoke up. 'He's going nowhere. As for killing us… Ah, that's crap. Firstly, I don't see a motive; secondly, there are three,' Carl even held out three fingers for Sylvester's benefit, 'of us. And lastly, without blowing my own trumpet too much, even on my own I think I'm not that defenceless.'

'Wait a minute, wait a minute.' Ian held up his hands for peace and took a deep breath. 'Andrew, you really did kill Cecily?'

'Yes.'

'Why?'

'Why don't you ask Carl how many games he lost today? You were going to teach her chess next,

Carl, if I'm not mistaken?'

Carl had no answer, and Ian had nothing but questions. The colonel continued with barely a pause. 'It's all been a very cute little experiment, I know, but did you ever really stop to think just how clever a chimp can get? As clever as you or I, perhaps? Okay, maybe she'll never be able to master the Queen's English, but that's down to her physical rather than mental limitations. Her vocal chords could hardly be expected to perform the same as ours. That's only a physical shortcoming however, and even that may eventually be overcome with the help of M4. For now, let's concentrate on her mental attributes. As with the mouse, Cecily never repeated a mistake, nor compounded on one already made. Her powers of logical reason were astounding – to the extent that, for a simple example, she had beaten Carl at draughts more than a dozen times in a row by the time they'd finished. And she would never have lost again, not to anyone. For her, it was a simple matter of deduction, of always making the correct choice. She was thinking like a computer – an unbeatable computer.' He paused, awaiting a reaction which never arrived.

For Ian's part, he still could not see a problem arising from smart animals, regardless of Sylvester's arguments the previous morning.

'Undeniably the most important, and most

overlooked, characteristic of M4 is its ability to alter the DNA of its host. Here's the simple explanation – once M4 is injected into a host, your chimpanzee for example, it's not just the host that is altered. M4 itself changes, and becomes a new strain – let's call it "Chimpanzee M4". It's part synthetic, thanks to us, and part natural Chimp. The new M4 will affect only Chimps; other species are immune, even other apes. You want to hear the frightening part? It's infectious, incredibly infectious.'

'Hold on,' Ian interrupted. 'How can it be infectious? We've created a drug surely, not a frigging virus. Why are you talking about it as though it was a virus?'

'That's Carl's job,' said Sylvester, 'isn't it, Carl?'

Ian recalled their conversation on the lake, and in particular Sylvester's concern regarding their resident virologist.

The colonel held up a hand as if to allay their fears with this single gesture. 'It's not exactly a virus, no. We needed certain characteristics of the virus – its ability to jump from host to host, and its adaptability, but it's not remotely dangerous. It might help to think of it as a Trojan horse – we've effectively hollowed out the destructive element and replaced it with our own RNA corrector package. We've even got a name for the technique. We call it ghosting. We end up with a good, helpful virus. A positive virus. Cecily has already infected us all but, since we are a different species, the virus has simply broken down into its component amino acids in our systems. This happens because Chimpanzee M4 cannot survive outside its own environment. Pure M4 is inactive until it combines itself with the host DNA itself.

'Look, if she had managed to meet another chimp the virus would have gotten away from us. That chimp goes back to his group, and that group gets into a fight with another. Chimps meet all across Africa. They breed, and the next generation is infected hereditarily. Chimps are captured and transported across the world – to zoos, wildlife parks, laboratories. What I am suggesting, gentlemen, is that in as little as twenty years mankind becomes the second-most intelligent creature on Earth. Now look me in the eye before you laugh. You might be thinking "didn't Charlton Heston already do this one?" You know as well as I do the potential of this drug.

'But that's not all. M4 *does* affect its host biologically. In another week, or month, or year, Cecily's vocal chords would have been altered to such a degree that language would have been no problem at all. M4 has improving qualities, but it can only work to improve the environment it originally finds itself in, physically and mentally.'

'You,' Sylvester broke his trance. 'You took the bloody stuff.'

'Oh Christ, of course. Stupid. Of course he's such a flaming expert on the effects,' Ian broke out of his own reverie. 'He knows.'

'Yes, I know,' the new, improved Andrew Marten remained unflustered and emotionless. 'But I'm still learning.'

Ian remembered finding the colonel unconscious at his workbench barely twenty-four hours previously. What he'd mistaken for fatigue had apparently been the first stages of M4. He suddenly felt very cold indeed.

The colonel put his hand in his shirt pocket and pulled out three corked phials. Placing them in the centre of the table he spoke to his companions softly. 'Join me,' his voice as innocuous as a friend proposing a toast.

'You've got to be bloody joking.' Sylvester lunged for the rifle and swung it up in front of him, in the same instant pulling the trigger which should have ended Marten's dangerous game. There was an empty, dry click.

'Guess I was lucky there,' said Marten in a tone that suggested luck had played little or no part in his deliverance.

'You forgot to reload, Sly,' Ian pointed out helpfully, before relieving his friend of the weapon.

Sylvester burst out laughing, and Ian stared at him as though he were mad.

Carl beamed at him and said, 'I think he's finally got it,' as though praising a reluctant pupil.

'Got what?' Ian was mystified by the apparent insanity surrounding him.

'I get it, I get it. I get the joke, Ian.' Sylvester slammed his hands down on the table and took a few seconds to catch his breath. He reached for one of the phials and flicked it deftly end over end, catching it in his other hand. It must have been obvious to him that Ian was terrified he might drop it, because he chose that moment to share the joke. 'Look at yourself, Ian. Stop gawping,' he giggled, and then became suddenly serious. 'Haven't you listened to a word he's been saying? It's infectious. In the last twenty-four hours M4 has become a human strain. It's half-human and it's bloody infectious. Come on, you clown, he's got us every which way. The only way to win is to follow.' With that he pulled the cork and swallowed the contents of the phial. Tears of the purest misery began to stream from the corners of his eyes. He glanced at Marten. 'How long before…' and then he slumped in his seat, dropping the phial, oblivious to the world.

‘What about you, Carl?’ Ian asked. ‘This is as much your baby as the colonel’s. Aren’t you eager to get started?’

‘This is the last part of the experiment, Ian. There’s a phial for each of us, but taking the drug directly will teach us nothing about the effectiveness of its viral component.’

‘And in English?’ Ian mocked.

‘I’ll see how long it takes to catch it.’

‘In theory,’ the colonel added, ‘you should both become more susceptible to infection the longer you remain in this room, and the more air is cycled through my, and now Sylvester’s, lungs. The virus will be carried in the moisture in the air. Of course, a good sneeze will dramatically improve its odds.’

It dawned on Ian at that moment that Sylvester had been wrong. He still had a choice. But time was most definitely not on his side.

‘I’m going to make more coffee,’ he said, and slid back his chair.

‘I understand your trepidation, Ian,’ Carl said. ‘I really do.’

‘Then you’ll understand I still have a choice,’ Ian snapped back, grabbing the rifle and working the bolt clumsily.

‘Easy now. We’re not the enemy.’

Ian backed away from the table, the rifle pointed unsteadily at the floor. He only stopped when his back met the worktop at the far end of the kitchen. To his right, through the open door, he could see the sunrise boiling slowly up over the horizon.

Sylvester came slowly round after about forty minutes. He looked blearily round him, trying to get his bearings. Understanding seemed to dawn in his eyes; he shivered violently, and squeezed his arms around his chest. Coughing, he turned to the colonel. 'Hurts more than I thought it would.'

'That'll pass, Sly,' Andrew said tenderly. 'You'll feel shaky and nauseous for a couple of hours, a bit like flu, but it'll all be worth it, you have my word on that.'

Ian followed the scene with a morbid fascination. He'd kept his distance, and his silence, all this time, listening to Carl interrogate the colonel about his experience so far. They were so bloody cold, so clinical, it filled him with fear, and made him want to get out of there right this instant. Something unknown had frozen him to the spot, however. He was torn between fear and an indefinable longing for the unknown adventure unfolding before him. 'And what's the downside?' he asked.

Sylvester swivelled round to look at Ian, his glance taking in the rifle in the other man's hands. 'You really haven't listened at all, have you?'

'Yeah Sly, I've listened. But you were wrong. Infectious it may be, but I'm still awake, and that means I'm uninfected. Take a look at Carl there. Why hasn't he passed out yet? He's my canary. I'm not infected yet, Sly, and until I know exactly what I'm getting into, I'm staying out here where I still have a choice.'

'Please yourself,' Sylvester said nonchalantly.

'Let me help to persuade you, Ian,' the colonel said, his tone seductive.

'I doubt you can convince me there's no downside. Everything has its price.'

'Then I'll tell you the price of M4,' Andrew said softly, and relaxed back into his chair, his fingers laced across his stomach, taking on the air of a loveable grandfather contemplating nothing more sinister than his favourite brand of pipe-tobacco. 'It's like sharing your mind with God. God as a scientist, an experimenter. The virus worked on my mind and my body at the same time, and when it fully understood the way I worked, it began to improve matters. From one minute to the next I didn't know whether I would be sick, or euphoric, healthy or unhappy. All of my emotions were run through, tested thoroughly, and cast aside, until only those beneficial to me were allowed to remain. Anger and hate are lost to me now; only reason remains, and that's more than made up for what I've lost.

'Once my state of mind was settled, I could feel the physical alterations begin. No difference can be discerned from the outside, but my body is now functioning in almost every degree to perfection. My strength and stamina have increased to the kind of level Olympic athletes can only dare to dream about. Nothing is wasted. All of my energies and functions are now distributed impossibly efficiently. And you wouldn't believe how fast I repair.'

'You've surrendered anger and hate, which I suppose is no bad thing, Andrew,' Ian's voice was unsteady. 'But what about the rest of your emotions. What about love?'

'What about it?' the colonel began flippantly, and then turned suddenly serious. 'Love is for teenagers, and we're adults. I don't mean just the four of us, but the whole human race. As a race, we're at the stage of adulthood now, and it's time to leave childhood things behind. Romantic ideals and simple religions are not the stuff of the future.'

'Not your future, certainly. Are you going to decide on the future of humanity just as arbitrarily?'

'Yes Ian, I believe I am. To bemoan the loss of the little things: the angers and passions of the individual, is to entirely miss the bigger picture, the whole point of what we're striving to achieve here.'

'You're going to turn the human race into something new; bypass evolution just like that?'

'Truthfully? I don't believe I'm bypassing evolution, but rather fulfilling it. I believe that this moment has always been inevitable. The events of the last few centuries have shown us that. Everything has been accelerating to this point for more than a millennium, and I think the human race is now more ready for a change for the good than it has ever been.'

'How can you change something for the good by taking away what drives us? Without our emotions, our passions, and our instincts we would never have come this far. Intellect didn't bring us here, our strength of will did.'

'Strength of will can only carry us so far, Ian, that's my point. We've reached a plateau, and our burgeoning technology threatens to overtake us unless we make a radical change to the core of the society we find ourselves in now. It's the simplest things, the fundamentals, that we have to change. We live in a fast, complicated world, and it's getting worse. We build speed-ramps to slow the traffic and keep our children safe, and the same ramps endanger the lives of ambulance passengers. What's needed is not more precautions, more useless mollycoddling. What's needed is an attitude shift. You can't leave this to God, it's far too important and far too late.'

'So you're putting yourself up for the job?'

'I'm putting everyone up for the job, and together we'll put it all right.'

'But what about…' Ian felt his mouth go dry, and fear flooded through him as he watched Carl keel slowly over in his chair. That was the last step in the experiment. M4 was contagious, and it was airborne. How long before he succumbed too? He suddenly knew he didn't want to find out. The place his colleagues had gone to ahead of him was an alien one, and he was sorely afraid of it.

The colonel's attention was distracted from him momentarily, as the older man tried to straighten Carl and keep him from crashing to the floor. Ian took the opportunity to escape outside into the fresh morning air. He half-walked, half-ran through the door, and found himself gulping in great draughts of clean air. He realised he must have been breathing as shallowly as possible inside the hut, in some kind of subconscious effort to preserve himself from catching the virus. A futile effort, as Carl's response had proven, and he had been extremely fortunate to avoid the same fate. He staggered into the middle of the yard, desperate to put some distance between himself and the new-found plague within the Nissen's walls. He was still deliberating his next move when the colonel appeared in the doorway.

He swung the rifle up once more. 'Don't come any closer, Andrew, please. Just don't come out, not yet.' He was fighting hard to keep the tears from his eyes, his voice sounding strangled.

'I won't force anything on you, Ian, you have my word.'

'Just stay where you are, that's enough for now.'

They were silent for a while, and the last of the mist began to vanish from the morning as the sun made its presence felt. Ian could feel himself sweating already, but that had nothing to do with heat.

'It's not too late for your father, you know.'

Ian's attention snapped back to the colonel, and he could feel his hackles rise.

'Alzheimer's claimed my father a long time ago, Ian, but it's not too late to change the outcome for yours.'

'That's pretty low, Andrew.'

'Even though it's nothing but the truth?'

Truth it may have been, but that didn't make Ian feel any better. If the colonel was right, could he throw away the last chance his father might have? On the other hand, what kind of miracle was

Andrew Marten really offering here? The chance to offer his father extended life at the expense of his real self, the human part of himself? To spend your twilight years as some kind of automaton, thinking yet unfeeling: what kind of a life would that be anyhow?

Sylvester poked his head out into the sunlight, slowly appraising the situation.

'How's Carl?' the colonel asked him.

'He's coming round now. Still out. Looks comfortable enough, though.'

'Sly,' Ian called out, 'do me a favour, would you?'

'What do you need?'

'The sat-phone.'

Sylvester turned to the colonel as if for approval, and Andrew simply nodded assent. The wiry man vanished inside, reappearing again a few minutes later with the bulky briefcase.

'Just leave it at the foot of the steps, and go back inside for a while. I'll shout when I'm done.' To Ian's surprise, the two of them complied without a word, and when he was satisfied they were deep enough into the relative dark of the hut he sprang forward, grabbed the precious device, and retreated to the shade of the acacia. He didn't feel safe here, and had no idea of the colonel's possible plans for him once Carl was awake and functioning properly once more. He had no doubt, however, that any plan would involve his joining their party on the far side of humanity. He couldn't make the call here – couldn't afford the distraction that might open an opportunity for them, so he heaved the briefcase into the driving seat of the nearest Landrover, the one without Carl's hammock tethered to it. It was the nearest thing he had to a plan. Ironic really, he thought, because I'd have no trouble coming up with a workable plan if I'd just gone ahead and swallowed the bloody drug.

He felt extremely weary. It wasn't simply the early start, or the fear slowly poisoning his system. But what else could it be? He shouldered the rifle while he was fiddling with the Landrover's door and loading the briefcase, but when the colonel reappeared at the hut's steps he swung it back in front of him, wielding it as a priest would a cross.

'You were supposed to wait for my shout,' Ian reminded him.

'You don't seriously expect us to obey your every whim, rifle or not, do you? How many bullets do you have, Ian? Have you even checked? Do you think that a single bullet might stop a man like me? It'd have to be a headshot, or straight through the heart perhaps; I might well survive anything else. I can't be certain, of course, but I'm quietly confident.'

'I don't want to kill anyone, Andrew.' Ian could hear his voice cracking. 'I just need to think for a bit.'

'Ah, I could help you there.'

'Very bloody funny.'

Sylvester and Carl both stepped down into the daylight, but stopped and seated themselves on the steps at a word from the colonel. They didn't look good, but Ian knew they'd both be as strong as the colonel in a matter of hours. He needed more time, and it was the one thing he no longer had.

Forty Five

They listened in utter disbelief as Ian finished his story. Hands in his pockets, standing and staring through the window at nothing and everything, he told them of his flight to Kundasa, and then Kinshasa, and finally home; leaving out, naturally enough, any mention of Elise. Kathy would have gleaned enough from his diary to raise her suspicions, and there was no point in reaffirming them now: 5,000 miles from the scene of the crime. His story over, he turned to them.

Kathy approached him deliberately, and took him into her embrace, uttering soothing noises in his ear, and they held each other in comfortable silence for a long time. Eventually, when she sensed Paul fidgeting in the background, she eased herself out of the clinch and asked, 'so what so we do now?'

'I wish I knew, I really do.' I don't know what

Marten's plans are yet, and I don't know of any way to either stop him or avoid the virus.'

'Can it be avoided, this virus?' Paul chimed in.

'Short of wearing a gas mask, I really don't see how.'

'I didn't realise quite how unnerving it is to see the future. There's no antidote for this thing?'

'That's not the way the colonel planned it. An antidote implies that we set out to create something harmful. We didn't. We wanted, or at least I thought we did, to create a cure. Why would there be an antidote?'

'Drastic bloody cure, if you ask me.'

'Yeah, I know.' Ian hung his head, feeling ashamed of his part in this whole thing. Had he opened his eyes to what was happening around him earlier, as Sylvester had, could he have stopped it in its tracks? Even now, he doubted it.

'You look shattered, mate.'

'I haven't slept for more than a day, and I don't know whether I could even now, or if I've got enough time.'

'You don't think they're coming after you, these people?' Kathy sounded horrified.

'No, no. Why would they? It's not like I'm an integral part of their plan, whatever that may be.'

'Maybe you should get some sleep, Ian. We can talk about this later, when you're rested.'

Ian left them to it, and trudged heavily up the stairs, feeling his tiredness more than ever now. His two closest friends, the sight of whom earlier had raised his spirits more than he could have dared hope, would now have a great deal to discuss, and he was only sorry that it had to be him to bear them such terrible news. He couldn't help but feel he'd trapped them both in this hideous predicament. A typically English sense of guilt – he suppressed a tiny laugh at the thought.

He pushed open the bedroom door, and stopped on the threshold, aware of something suddenly wrong with the scene that greeted him. It was no one particular thing about the bed, or the rest of the room, that gave it away. There is a feeling a room leaves that tells you instinctively the tale of its last hours. Two people had shared this bed, it was glaringly obvious. He didn't need to check the pillows or sheets for signs of two non-matching hairs or other clues, although that's exactly what he found himself now doing, fighting the urge to believe the evidence of his own eyes.

He lurched over to the side of the bed, holding back the urge to vomit. He could feel hot tears spring into his eyes, and a sudden giddiness made the room spin around him. He sat heavily on the edge of the bed, hung his head in his hands, and let the tears come. He felt comprehensively betrayed, by his own actions as well as those of whom he had trusted most in the world. The bitter irony of his own infidelity in Africa had come back to him with a vengeance.

He supposed he had no-one to really blame but himself. He'd left Kathy on her own and unguarded for too long, only to scare her half to death with his message and then his journal. That too, could hardly have helped. He'd not edited it as he'd previously planned, and she may well have read enough between the lines to have raised her own suspicions about his relationship with Elise. As for Paul, well, what could be asked of him? The man was as shallow as a puddle and as trustworthy as rust. Strangely enough, he couldn't bring himself to see this as Paul's fault – it was, in fact, no more than he'd have expected with any other girl. But not this one, surely? Paul and Kathy had a history that was all theirs, but he'd assumed it to be nothing more than a distant memory by now. Apparently, though, he'd been proven wrong. Some people claimed that men and women can never be just friends – that beneath the surface their latent sexuality will always lurk. He hated to see people like that proved right.

He looked around him, and realised he had no idea of how much time had passed while he'd sat there feeling sorry for himself. His sprinkling of miserable tears had dried on his face, and he wiped the salty residue away with the palms of his hands. He took a couple of deep breaths, holding back a choking sob, and letting out a suppressed "Aah" of anger and frustration.

He'd have to talk to them. Thrash it out, that was the adult solution. Oh Christ, this was going to be a crappy scene. Women's tears were one thing he had absolutely no idea how to handle, and he had no doubt whatsoever that there would be plenty of tears. If he wanted to salvage what was left of his relationship however, it was something he simply had to get through.

He could hear their voices, drifting up to him through the open door. He could hear the worry in the sounds they made. They were worried about their future, and worried about him. Well, that was fair enough – he'd given them plenty to worry about, hadn't he? Sleep could wait; he'd do his best not only to settle their fears for the future, but also to sort out their plans for the present, and discover exactly where everyone's priorities lay.

He made his way slowly downstairs, and into the living-room. Judging by their voices, the two of them were in the kitchen, either working on dinner or sitting around sipping coffee. He suddenly couldn't care less which. Kathy must have heard him come downstairs, as she appeared in the doorway, and then made her way over to him, a look of concern (or could it have been fear?) on her face. She stopped a couple of feet in front of him, looked briefly bewildered, and lowered her arms to her sides. His continuing silence and empty stare made her more uncomfortable still, and she fidgeted her hands into her pockets before turning away from him.

They stood in awkward silence for a few moments longer, and then Paul entered from the kitchen. The sight of the two of them stood there quietly told him as much as he needed to know. They had been found out, he was certain of that, and shame, and not a little fear, washed over him. Shame for his act of betrayal, and fear of the realisation that he could lose both his best friends, not to mention the woman he now knew he loved, in the space of the next few minutes.

'Ian,' he began, and approached his friend with a contrite, pleading look on his face, his hands outstretched.

The punch took him by marginally more surprise than it took Ian, who'd had no original intention to lash out, but whose instincts had overwhelmed his common-sense all of a sudden. His knuckles throbbed with the pain of contact, and somewhere deep inside his head he could hear screaming. Paul had gone down heavily on his rump, and was clutching his face with both hands. Ian could see blood, and plenty of it, pouring out through Paul's fingertips.

He stumbled past Kathy, who had stopped screaming now, and was regarding him with unadulterated horror. He tore his gaze from her and headed, shocked, for the front door, stepping over Paul's sprawling legs as he did so, but refusing to look down at him.

As soon as Ian had slammed the door behind him, Kathy managed to break her horrified trance and went to Paul's aid. Gently, she pulled his hands away from his face, overcoming his resistance bit by bit.

'I had that coming,' Paul sputtered out through clogs of blood and snot.

She put a hand under his chin and raised his face to hers. His eyes were streaming, and his tears mixed with the bloody river beneath his nose. At closer inspection it didn't appear to be broken, though it didn't make for a pretty sight all the same. The bleeding would stop – an icepack would help see to that – but he was likely to end up with a couple of good shiners and a very tender nose for a while yet. She left him to clutch his face for a minute, and retreated to the kitchen for a wet cloth and a bag of frozen peas.

Ian gunned his little French hire out of the

driveway and into the tiny B-roads without looking back. Fresh tears, to mirror those he'd inflicted, filled his eyes. Anger and pain and hate and sadness had flurried together at the moment of his attack, yet had abandoned him now, leaving him as cold and empty as he imagined the colonel must feel. The car shot through the tiny lanes, the hedges on each side towering over the vehicle, impeding any view to left or right and making doubly dangerous the slightest bend. Now and then a passing place increased the width of the road, though not by very much, and the majority of them he sped past without giving further thought to their purpose. He continued like this for half an hour or so, speeding his way generally east, the only thought in his mind being to put some great distance between himself and the ruins of his previous existence. He was extremely lucky. Rounding one tight bend onto a comparatively straight stretch, his view was suddenly filled with the sight of the oncoming car. Without thinking, he slammed on the brakes and watched in terror as the gap between himself and the slowing Citroen decreased. Traction came and went erratically beneath his wheels and time itself, as is its wont in times of extreme peril, slowed to a crawl. The light-blue of the Citroen's bonnet approached him slowly and stately, its driver apparently having a great deal more control than he. He pumped the brake-pedal frantically, trying to control the slide he found himself in, and closed his eyes, squeezing them tight, and bracing his arms against the steering-wheel.

The two cars met with the lightest kiss, bumper to bumper. Ian opened his eyes, relief flooding through him. He waved a frantic apology at the other driver, who could have been a man, perhaps a woman – it was hard to tell behind the sun-streaked windscreen, and backed up a little in order that they might both ease around each other. Less than a minute later, he was past and on his way once more, albeit at a far more sedate pace, his senses now fully concentrated on the road ahead.

Penny, however, was furious. That idiot Ian had very nearly killed them both. Oh yes, Ian, I recognised you immediately, even though you may pretend otherwise. And I'll be having words with you later, she promised herself. She set off once more in the direction of her beloved Edie's cottage, her mind on Kathy now, and the many lectures she had prepared in her head which she had passed the time with since her outset.

Fury passed into mild annoyance at the nature of the younger generation in general. Muttering under her breath as she cruised sedately along, she tutted, 'you should have married that nice young photographer chap.'

Forty Six

The stark grey façade of his office building filled Ian with genuine comfort. The same stone steps and impressive oak door, the same carpet in the corridor, and the same polished silver in the lift. The same scenery he had witnessed every weekday for over seven years; their familiarity bred in him not contempt, but rather a feeling of safety, of sanctuary.

He swung in the glass door to his offices, and Holly looked up at him and smiled broadly, exactly as it specified in her contract. She was genuinely pleased to see him though – he could hear it in her tone.

'Ian,' it was very nearly a squeal, 'you're back. Welcome back.' She lowered her voice to a conspiratorial whisper, 'I have *so* missed you.'

'Kevan not been looking after you, angel?' Ian

couldn't keep the smile from his lips. It felt so very good to be back in the real world. His little domain of normality.

'Oh, you know,' she offered a shrug, and then perked up. 'But what about you? What *have* you been up to all this time? And not so much as a postcard either,' she reprimanded him with a swift pout.

'I'll tell you all about it later. First, though, I need you to get on the phone for me, and sort me out some flights.'

'Back to Africa?'

'Uh-huh. Same route as last time.'

Holly watched him closely as he shed his coat, draping it over the too-plush leather sofa that dominated the entire back wall of the reception room. 'Hope she's worth it,' she muttered under her breath.

Ian had thought of little else on his journey. He'd been a fool to have left Elise to fend for herself against those odds. Turned out he'd been a fool, full stop. The loss of both his fiance and his best friend was still hot in his heart, but distance and time would heal those wounds eventually. He was lucky, he knew, that he had someplace to go. Without that option, he felt, he could very easily fall apart.

'Where's Kevan?'

His suddenness had caught Holly off her

guard, and he watched in amusement as she flustered briefly before regaining her composure.

'He went home early. Bit fluey,' and she even wrinkled her nose and gave a little sniff in sympathy.

'That'll please Anne no end.' He could imagine Kevan's little mousewife scurrying around after him being, for the duration of his illness at any rate, the absolute centre of his life. She would truly be in her element.

Still, he thought, it could have been a damn sight worse. He'd seen flu symptoms recently that had scared him far more than the thought of a few days shivering in bed.

'Ian.'

He could tell by the slightly miffed note in Holly's voice that this was the second or even third time she'd spoken.

'Sorry, Holly. Miles away. What did you say?'

'I said, "You've got a visitor".'

A tall figure emerged from the shadows of Ian's own office, and Ian felt his spine turn to ice, and his brain to fire. He staggered backwards against the sofa, but failed to sit. The demon, the enemy, the antichrist stepped out into full view.

'Holly,' Ian hissed, and then with a louder hiss, 'Holly. Get out. Get out now.'

'A little late for that, Ian.' The colonel's voice

had lost none of its butter-smoothness.

'But she's not...' She couldn't be, could she? She had been genuinely happy to see him, genuinely irritated with Kevan. Those were the traits of emotion, and if she still had her emotions...

As though reading his mind, Holly said, 'We don't *forget* anything, Ian. I can still *remember* emotion.'

'So all of that was...'

The colonel interrupted, 'an act, yes. Your secretary has some Hollywood potential, don't you think?'

Ian had no idea what to think. Thought itself had gone numb. Surely this was his greatest fear of what M4 had to offer – the perfectly clear memory of something you could never feel again. His horrified gaze flicked between the two of them, and a sick knot began to form in his stomach. 'What do you want here, Andrew?' Somehow he'd managed to speak, but his voice sounded as though it had come some distance.

'I miss having you on the team, Ian, believe it or not.'

'How about not.'

'Okay. How about I simply believe you should be involved in this. You were there from the beginning, after all.'

'Was I? Was I really there at the beginning?'

The colonel held out his arms, palms toward the ceiling. 'Well, certainly one of the beginnings. Does it make that much difference?'

'Not to me,' Ian spat out, 'and certainly not to you. You were a cold one even before M4, and I can't believe you came back here for me alone. There's another reason.'

'Of course there is. All right,' the colonel plunged his hands into his pockets and sat himself casually on the edge of Holly's desk. 'I won't bother lying to you, as you've probably guessed by now. It's your money, Ian. I was hoping to persuade you to finance our globetrotting for the coming year.'

Ian almost laughed. He could feel it bubble in his throat, but it died on his lips as he met the colonel's humourless gaze. 'You're serious, aren't you?' He was incredulous, 'someone as smart as you needs to come to me, the last person in the world who wants you anywhere near, and ask for money? All that fantastic new brain-power, and you can't work out how to make a crust? You're amazing, you really are.' And now Ian did laugh, a good bellyful. He flopped back into the sofa, still chortling.

'It's just a matter of expediency, Ian. Yes, any of us could work our way toward a fortune given enough time, but I am still hoping to persuade you to join us, and in doing so to unlock your own substantial resources for our cause.'

'Cause, now, is it?' Ian had stopped laughing and was once more wary of this man although, somehow, no longer afraid of him. 'Where are the other guys, by the way?'

'We left Carl in Africa. He said he wanted to travel around, see the country of his ancestors. It had been on his to-do list anyhow. Sly's gone to the Far East, to mooch around China and Japan for a few months.'

'To spread the word, you mean?'

'Sure. Once M4 is in the system, the global arteries of commercial flight, it'll spread like wildfire.'

'So its pretty much too late anyway.' Ian said this last to himself and slumped heavily where he sat, feeling every ounce of his failure weigh upon him.

'Far too late, yes.'

'You really don't know what you're missing, Ian,' Holly chipped in brightly.

'That I can live with, Holly. What I'm not so sure I can live with is missing what I already have.'

There was a long, uncomfortable silence between them, Ian's mind filling the time trying to imagine Carl and Sylvester going about their crusade. Would there be restaurants, train stations, cinemas and theatres full of suddenly sleeping people? Christ, the possibilities: Football matches, political rallies, army barracks, hospitals, schools, prisons, concerts and car-boot sales. Everywhere humanity congregated. He tried to imagine how many people he himself would come into casual contact with on an average day and quickly gave up the count as impossible to measure. Carl and Sylvester had already been on the loose for days, going out of their way to meet as many others as possible – a pair of modern-day Typhoid Marys.

'And what did you have planned for us?'

'Travelwise?' the colonel asked, and went straight on to answer his own question. 'I had in mind the States for myself – lot of old friends to catch up with for one thing and, being a native, I'll be able to travel around a lot more freely and quickly than any tourist. I thought you and Kathy might prefer Europe. The two of you could have an extensive, not to mention culture-soaked, honeymoon.'

'Slight change of plan on the Kathy front, Andrew.' He hadn't thought of her in, God, whole minutes, and the memory of her betrayal brought fresh pain.

The colonel could see the anguish in his friend's eyes and was genuinely sorry for him. He told himself this was the case, anyway, as he was having a hard time actually *feeling* sorry for him.

‘So what will you do now?’ The colonel managed to inject a warm note into his query.

‘I’d been thinking about going back to Africa, to Elise,’ and when Ian said it out loud he realised how right it felt. It would be so good to see her again, in the flesh. His mind swelled with the memory of that very flesh, warm and dry and pressed tightly against him. Her eyes, her smile, her laugh. A lifetime with Elise would be barely enough to discover all about her. Yes, that was what love was all about. Without love, why bother with life?

The colonel was unusually quiet, seemingly brooding on some dark matter. His continuing silence began to unnerve Ian, and eventually he had to ask, ‘What is it? What’s wrong?’

Forty Seven

Paul kicked and stomped his way through the six inches of mud left behind by the latest rains, and pulled his coat tighter about him to keep out the evening's chill. His nose felt a lot better than it had that morning, though it was still tender, and the cold air did nothing to numb its sensitivity. Quite the reverse, in fact: he could feel tiny needles of pain throughout the upper half of his face. The swelling in his eyes had subsided also, although the first dark indications of the shiners to come were already visible.

He must have covered less than two circuitous miles in the hour since he'd left the cottage, his pace slowed to almost nothing by the unfriendly, beautiful terrain. You had to hand it to country-folk, he thought, who would happily turn down the riches of the city for the far greater wealth of their natural surroundings. The country's great secret –

the riches of the heart. Oh, don't let me turn into a bad poet, not while I'm still young.

This walk was his excuse for leaving the girls to have their own time together, as all girls must, to discuss those things no male ear should ever need be privy to. It also served as a good excuse to get away from the unbelievably nosy Aunt Penny, who had scrutinised him hawk-like from the first moment she had stepped across the threshold. Her enquiries had seemed endless, and Paul's comfort zone had shrunk to the size of a polo mint. He'd had to get out before he'd snapped and said something he would've regretted. At the crest of the next hill the cottage came at last into view, and Paul sat himself down on the stones of a long-since ruined boundary dry-wall.

He soaked up the scene before him, his photographer's eye taking in the tiny details, mentally framing this tree and that fence. The broken, fraying rope where once a tyre may have swung, still hanging from its branch. The wooden wheelbarrow, surely an antique, leaning against the whitewashed wall of the cottage, beneath the kitchen window. Paul stayed that way for the best part of the next hour, watching the shadows lengthen, and the cottage change colour in the gathering twilight.

His rapture was dispelled by the twin beams of

a car's headlights picking their way through the lanes towards the cottage. At any rate, he assumed it was headed toward the cottage as there was precious little else to find up here. More visitors?, he wondered. Perhaps another friend of either Kathy's or her invasive Aunt. Or perhaps even Ian, come back to patch things up between them. That last wouldn't have surprised him. It would be exactly the type of thing Ian would do, which would only serve to add to the already enormous mountain of guilt Paul had shouldered as his own. He supposed he ought to go down and show his face, it was only polite after all. But no, if it was Ian returned to make amends, then he could wait and sweat it out for a while longer yet. When the car stopped and two men climbed out, one of them recognisably Ian, he was sorely tempted to go down there, and had even got to his feet to do exactly that, but something held him fast, something deep-rooted and primeval.

Penny had vanished upstairs at the first sight of the headlights in the distance and now, with the knock at the door, Kathy found herself trying to coax her Aunt back down the ladder from the attic, where she could hear Penny bustling around, going through boxes that hadn't seen the light of day in five years or more.

'What *are* you looking for up there?' Kathy asked, practically shouting up through the gap in the ceiling. Frustrated at receiving no reply, she left the foot of the ladder and returned downstairs to answer the door.

Paul saw the door swing open, and the two men enter quickly. Everything was obviously under control then, and his presence in front of Ian would probably only serve to turn an uncomfortable scene into an ugly one. Best to stay put for the time being, he decided.

Kathy's initial joy at Ian's return evaporated the instant she caught sight of his companion. Although the stranger confronting her was a handsome, tall man in obviously rude good health, with a smile that could have parted waves, there was an element about him that unnerved her. It was impossible to put her finger on it. He was simply wrong somehow. Although she had never met the man in the flesh, she knew instantly it was Ian's famous colonel.

As the two men entered the cottage, Kathy unconsciously backed off three or four paces, her eyes widening in alarm at the look on Ian's face. There was nothing there. Where there should have been at least a smile of welcome, or a frown of anger, there was nothing but a flat determination, a blank knowing that unsettled her deeply.

'Ian…' To Kathy the sound of her voice had reverted to that of a suddenly timid child.

Ian drew the syringe from his pocket. 'For you,' he said simply.

Kathy felt a strong hand on her shoulder, and she was pulled suddenly backward, only just managing to keep her feet, as Penny stepped in front of her and levelled the shotgun at Ian's midriff. The shotgun looked a formidable piece of work, and in Penny's confident grasp it seemed more than capable of doing the job for which it was intended. Penny herself had a lot less faith in the weapon, which had been nestled in oilcloth for the majority of its existence. Still, nobody else need know of her doubts, and she gave up a silent prayer to the gods of bluff.

Somebody up there must have been listening, she thought, judging by the look of bewilderment on Ian's face. He started to move backward out of the door, forcing the colonel to step back out of the cottage before him. Penny matched them step for step, the twin barrels of the enormous gun never more than a few inches away from Ian's chest.

Paul watched the peculiar exit of the stranger, followed by Ian, both stepping slowly backwards out of the cottage door. When the shotgun emerged, with an obviously irate Aunt Penny attached to the stock, he stood and took a couple of paces forward before bringing himself up short. Was he really needed down there? It certainly looked like Penny had everything under control. And if he went blundering down there now she may easily end up taking a pot-shot at him, if her nerves were anywhere near as frayed as his right now. No, give it a minute. If he shouted his arrival she might not shoot him by accident, but then would the distraction give her adversaries some chance to act? He squatted down on his haunches, lest she see him and be distracted anyway. It was nearly complete dark now. Three hundred yards lay between him and the pool of light around the front door of the cottage. He would wait and watch from the shadows.

The colonel stepped to one side as they exited the cottage, and the three of them formed a triangle on the gravel outside. It had been a deliberate move, and now Penny had not one but two targets to aim at. She wavered momentarily, swinging the shotgun towards the colonel and then, apparently catching herself, swinging it back toward Ian once more. Her hesitancy had been enough for the colonel, though. He knew a bluff when he saw one.

He took one step toward the old woman, and she swung the barrels his way with as much menace as she could muster.

'Colonel?' Ian was still very much undecided about this turn of events, and was looking to his partner for a little guidance on the matter. Confronting a shotgun by walking straight up its barrels was not part of any plan he deemed sensible, however.

The colonel held up a hand to silence Ian, and addressed Penny. 'Ma'am, my name is Andrew Marten. I feel we haven't...'

'I read your story, Mr. Marten. I don't need to know any more about you. I just need you to leave now.'

'Not possible, I'm afraid.'

'Don't patronise me, young man. You've got a perfectly good car there. You just get back in it and take yourself off now. And you can take him with you as well.'

In the doorway behind her, Kathy silently cheered her on, stopping short of clapping and waving her pom-poms.

'Miss...' the colonel began again.

'Go.' Penny jabbed the shotgun toward him like a spear.

And then Penny began to do the oddest thing. She lowered the stock of the shotgun, slowly raising the barrels in the air, bringing them through a slow arc until they came to rest under her chin. All the while the colonel stared at her in deep concentration and Kathy stared too, with growing horror. Penny stood absolutely rigid, her head pushed slightly back with the weight of the barrels beneath her chin. Her eyes were wide with fear and incomprehension. What was happening to her? She'd lost all control over her own actions. Don't let this happen. Don't let it end like this. She could feel her own finger begin to squeeze gently on the trigger. Please don't.

Her finger let go of the trigger, and she felt the pressure at her neck vanish as the barrels of the gun seemed to lower themselves of their own accord. She continued to lower the weapon until the barrels were pointed at the ground. Slowly, she raised her eyes to the colonel. He gave her a warm, friendly smile, and she felt her heart turn to ice.

Paul witnessed the scene with a horrified fascination. He had absolutely no idea what exactly had transpired between the three of them, and his fear mingled with confusion as he watched the colonel's ghastly display of power. He saw Kathy skip quickly inside, obviously afraid for her life, swiftly followed by the other three.

He picked himself up, brushing mud

absentmindedly from his knees, and made his way down the hill, picking his way quickly and carefully and, more importantly, quietly, through the grass and low shrubs towards the windows of the cottage.

As Penny turned to enter the cottage, she caught Kathy's look and their eyes locked momentarily. That moment was all Kathy needed to understand the battle of wills that had passed between her Aunt and the colonel, and how thoroughly the old woman had been beaten into submission. Her own heart sank, and her mind began to race, seeking an escape route from this oncoming nightmare.

Both the colonel and Ian were wielding syringes now, and as Kathy retreated from them so her Aunt advanced, until she stopped short in front of the colonel who, rather than use the needle on the old woman himself, offered it out to her in his open palm.

Kathy let out a horrified screech, 'Penny, no.' But her Aunt simply took the offered gift and, with little more than a smile of resignation toward Kathy, plunged the needle into her upper arm and shot the plunger home.

Kathy fled. One glimpse of the monstrous sight of Penny's willing surrender had been enough to turn her remaining fear into adrenaline, and she bolted across the room toward the stairs. She nearly made it, too. Something heavy landed across her back and she crashed to the floor. She struggled crazily, kicking and screaming herself around until she was on her back, the figure of Ian looming large above her. She could see the hypodermic in his fist, and she squeezed her eyes shut tight and kicked and pummelled until the last of her strength left her.

She felt the needle in her thigh, its sharp invasion akin to rape. She felt violated, abused. And in her last waking seconds another bitter thought came to the fore. Where the fuck was Paul when you really needed him?

He simply hadn't known what to do. It was honestly, really, as simple as that. He had meant to intervene, he really had. Meant to storm in there wielding… Well, wielding what? Shotguns were obviously no bloody use whatsoever, and what else did he have? A good heavy rock perhaps? A nice pointy stick and maybe some mud to throw? What use could he be against all of that… that stuff? That whatever-the-hell-it-was the colonel did.

And now it was too late. Far, far too late. Sorrow and fear brought hot tears to his eyes, and he suppressed a small sob, afraid of being heard. With his hands pressed to the window, he lowered his face from the scene inside and smothered his tears in his collar. He stayed that way for uncountable minutes, and then raised his face to peer in through the glass once more.

To see the colonel and Ian regarding him with curiosity. How long had they been aware of his presence? Did they have another needle perhaps, prepared especially for him? Were they even interested in taking him too?

His feet answered for him. Paul pushed himself away from the window, and ran faster than he'd ever run in his life.

Forty Eight

Kathy's vision was blurry at first, but it cleared quickly as she blinked the tears from her eyes. She felt weak and groggy, and feverish too, as though she was coming down with something like flu. She remembered Ian attacking her, but then nothing else, and she had woken to find herself propped comfortably on the sofa.

'How long have I been asleep?' she asked, a tiny slur in her words.

'Not long.' It was Ian. 'Just over half an hour, that's all.'

She raised her head to look at him, the man she had once loved. She hated him at this moment. Hated the fact that he had forced himself on her against her will. Even now, so soon, she could feel the anger leeching from her. Soon she'd feel nothing for him, one way or the other, but she *could* hold onto the memory of what he'd done. She would be able to remember, she hoped, the way she felt now.

Her mind was reeling and she felt dizzy and sick. Memories of events she'd long believed forgotten were thrust to the forefront of her thoughts, and then receded just as quickly, re-filed for easy access. When she tried to lie on her side her body suddenly spasmed and she began to shudder violently.

'It'll be over soon, Kathy, don't worry. You'll feel a whole lot better soon.'

She ignored him, squeezing her eyes shut and turning her face into the cushions. Her mind was filled with tiny sparks, constantly whirling, and her body felt like it was covered with white-hot pinpricks, intermittently disrupted by the sheets of ice-water that sluiced across her skin.

After an hour of this, she felt ready to tackle a glass of water, and after a further hour she managed to force down some food: bread and butter and cold-cuts straight from the fridge. It was past midnight by the time the last of her symptoms left her. Ian had been with her throughout, not eating, but occasionally sipping at his water.

'Where's Penny?'

'In bed upstairs. Andrew's with her.' There was a darker note in his voice which elicited an enquiring glance from Kathy.

'She didn't have quite such an easy time of it as you. Possibly her age. Andrew gave her something to help her sleep. It's okay, by the morning she'll be a new woman, if you'll excuse the pun.'

'What about Paul? What did you do with him?'

'He ran off into the night. Would you like me to go get him?'

'You know where he's gone?'

'No idea.'

'Then don't waste your time.'

'Oh, we could find him easily enough.'

'How, exactly?'

'Perhaps I'd better let Andrew explain that one.

Kathy started, and turned on the sofa to where the colonel stood directly behind her. 'Jesus, you made me jump. Do you have to sneak up on people like that?'

'If you'd been concentrating, I wouldn't have taken you by surprise,' the colonel said soothingly.

'What's that supposed to mean?'

'Try it,' the colonel said as he moved around to the front of the sofa. He squatted down in front of her, his hands clasped between his knees, his eyes drawing hers almost hypnotically. 'Close your eyes and visualise your Aunt. Picture her quite clearly.

Got her?'

Kathy nodded. She had imagined her Aunt in an everyday pose, sitting and chatting, the picture quite sharp. Then this image began to dissolve, and was replaced with another, the two overlapping at first. The second image was that of her Aunt sound asleep in the upstairs bedroom, where Kathy assumed she was now. The picture seemed far too clear to be simply her imagination. 'What am I seeing here?' Her troubled eyes skipped from Andrew to Ian and then back again.

'You won't really believe it 'til you go look for yourself.' Ian sounded almost smug, as though he had just pulled off the most marvellous magic trick. 'Go on, go upstairs and have a look.'

Kathy did exactly that. Standing in the doorway of the bedroom she was presented with an impossible scene. It was an exact replica of what she had seen not two minutes previously, in the privacy of her own head. Every detail was perfect, exactly as she had visualised it, from the turned-down coverlet to the wrinkles in the pillow around her Aunt's head.

Back downstairs, she confronted Andrew with something approaching wonder. 'What the hell just happened?'

'Beats the crap out of GPS, doesn't it?' Ian smiled at her.

'Empathy, Kathy,' the colonel began to explain. 'If you know someone well enough, you'll be able to place them instantly, at any time, anywhere in the world.' He raised his hands in a half-shrug. 'I don't profess to know exactly how it works, but you've gotta admit it's a pretty neat trick.'

'That's how you could have found Paul, isn't it?'

'Of course,' Ian said.

Kathy tried again. She pictured Paul in her mind's eye. Images flashed through her mind, including the image of her poised above him while they made love. She dismissed this last as inappropriate and unhelpful, and settled on a simple vision of him in his own apartment, dressed in jeans and T-shirt and surrounded by his pictures. Slowly the image faded and was replaced by another. In this one Paul's face was a mask of pain, his eyes wide and filled with fear. Kathy mentally drew back, and the effect was like a movie camera panning out. She could make out details of his surroundings now, and there was something else. A feeling of direction, somehow. Even without recognising his surroundings, somehow she knew which direction he'd taken, and where she could find him now.

'He's in trouble,' she snapped out of her

scrying, 'I've gotta go get him.'

'We'll come with you,' Ian offered immediately.

'No. Definitely not. Besides, you can keep an eye on things from here, can't you?'

'There is that.'

She grabbed a coat from the back of the door and slid quickly into it. Throwing open the door, she stepped out into the cold black of the night, where the colonel caught up with her.

'Take this.' He placed the syringe into her hand. 'Whether he likes it or not, he may well need it.'

She found him in under an hour, which was extremely good going over this territory, regardless of her built-in tracking system. He looked a sorry state. One leg was folded ridiculously beneath him, and he lay in the lee of an enormous boulder, on his back in the damp grass. She bent to him, and snapped her fingers right in front of his face. There was no response. She held the palm of her hand to the front of his face and felt a reassuring draught of warm breath.

She busied herself making him comfortable as Paul swam in and out of consciousness. He finally came to, by which time he was confronted with a roaring fire. He tried to shift around, and ran his hand down his side to his leg, where he could feel straps and a length of wood. His rescuer had indeed been busy. He shuffled around again, trying to sit, but the sudden sharp pain from his leg threatened to send him back down into blackness.

'Stay still, you idiot.'

'Kathy. God, am I glad to see you. How did you get out of there? How did you get away?'

'I didn't.'

'Oh.' And then, 'Oh, Jesus.'

'Don't worry, Paul. I remember what it's like to be afraid, and I won't force anything on you that you don't want.'

Their eyes met, and Kathy's smile brought out one of his own.

'Mind you, you don't know what you're missing. I've got some very neat tricks.'

'I'll bet. How did you find me?'

'I'll show you later. More to the point, how did you get all the way up here, and why? The broken leg's a nice touch, too. You don't do things by halves, do you?'

'Long story. Didn't think it'd be quite that easy to get so lost and fucked up.'

'Listen Paul, this is important. I've got a needle full of M4 for you. If you use it you've got a very good chance of repairing that leg and getting down out of these hills.'

'I've got a pretty good chance of that anyway, haven't I?'

'No, frankly.' She sounded like a matron, and the effect was beginning to scare Paul. 'You've got all the signs of exposure, and that will lead to pneumonia and possibly death. But I've got the cure to end all cures.'

'I'll pass, thank you very much.'

'You'd rather die?'

'I'd rather take my chances.'

'Mind if I ask why?'

'Oh, come on Kathy. Is the old Kath still in there anywhere? It's me. It's Paul, the original shallow man.'

'I never called you shallow.'

'You didn't need to. I know what you thought of me and, hey, you were right. But without my passions, and my lust, what the hell am I? I couldn't take another photograph again as long as I lived, and I couldn't live any kind of life photographing fucking furniture for a living.'

'Yeah, I know you couldn't.' She changed tack. 'I brought you some food. It's not much, but you're going to need your strength.'

She watched him eat. They chatted around a few subjects while Paul fought to retain his consciousness, but eventually he gave up the fight and drifted away from her. Kathy fussed over his unconscious form for a while, adjusting his head to what she believed would be a more comfortable position, and draping her coat over him. She had no use for it, which only slightly surprised her. She had no problem with the harsh cold, and besides, she was close to the fire.

Satisfied that Paul was as comfortable as she could make him, Kathy left his side and sought out a convenient rock for herself while she waited. The sky began to lighten slowly, and Kathy spent the time mulling over her recent past. All the things she'd lost and all the things she'd gained.

She glanced back at Paul, and it crossed her mind to give him the shot regardless. She turned the thought over and over in her mind in synchronicity with the hypodermic in her hands. And she spent the time watching the sun come up. It was going to be a bright, sunny day at last, which she might once have called beautiful.

THE END

Acknowledgements

A thousand thank-yous to the following wonderful people, without whom none of this would have been possible:

First and foremost, to my family, for their unending support.

To Robin Stubbs and Ronnie Lamont, for hauling my fat from the fire in more desperate times.

To Russell Evans & Cathi Elliott-Clarke, for feeding me properly, and also for Cathi's excellent eye for errororors.

To the league of readers, spellcheckers and critics whose input has been invaluable: Steph Hayes, Tricia Wright, Maureen Dunn, Garth Kimber, Ian Hunter, Peter & Pam Beazeley, Carol Sterne, Pete & Debbie Morgan, Janne Koponen.

To Steve Johnston, for the secret door.

To Matt Platts, for webbery.

To Chris Smith and all the staff at Halstans for their help and expertise.

To the Iron and Boot refugees, for their interest and enthusiasm.

And, most importantly, to Kathy Soulsby, for the inspiration and the nagging card.

About the author

Clive Wright lives in Buckinghamshire, a greenish pasture of Middle-England. His not quite spectacular career has spanned posts as a lifeguard, petrol-pump attendant and, when times were particularly tough, part-time window cleaner, barman, and Landrover-driver.

Cold Ghost is his first novel.

The author is currently working on a second novel, and is seeking representation.

For further information see: www.clivewright.com